Bryce Th

THOMAS HAMILTO

CW01660427

First published in Great Britain 2023
Thomas Hamilton

A CIP catalogue record of this book is
available from The British Library

ISBN: 978-1-970696-24-4 (Paperback)

Printed and bound by
Amazon

FIRST EDITION

BRYCE THOMAS

IN THE DEAD OF DAY

CHAPTER ONE

Two police cars with flashing blue lights warned drivers to keep to the far side of the country road. The woodland had been taped off and nobody was being allowed to go near the crime scene where the body lay.

By the time Detective Inspector Baintree arrived, it was eleven a.m. One uniformed police officer stood on the road side outside the circle of blue and white tape and, through the wide belt of trees that bordered the road, Baintree could see three more officers in white coveralls making a search down near the river that raged fiercely past a footpath at the other side of the wooded area. He flashed his identity card at the policeman on the roadside and he let him through with a lift of the hand that was more a cursory wave than brief salute.

Doctor Brown was already there knelt on a plastic bag that he was using as a mat beside the body. Brown was a normal, practicing GP who was regularly called out by the police as the medical examiner where people had died in suspicious circumstances in the remote areas of this part of Wales. Today, his trip had been over sixty miles along narrow country roads but Baintree had travelled even further. Both he and Doctor Brown had met in this course of work many times over the past five years.

A quick glance around was enough for Baintree to surmise that the body had been dragged up from the path into a patch of long grass that formed a small clearing in the tree belt. 'Hello, Mark,' he said as he made his way through the trees towards the doctor. 'Anything for me?'

Brown turned his head to see his old friend. 'Quite a lot really,' he stated. 'Definitely murder. Single knife wound from behind. Expertly done if you ask me.'

'I am asking you. Nobody else is going to tell me.'

'Quite.' He turned, pushed himself up off his knees and picked up his temporary mat.

'Is that it then?'

'Not quite,' Brown replied as he turned back to face Baintree. 'Killed between nine and midnight, I reckon.'

Baintree nodded and thought for a moment. 'Anything else?'

'Got an ID if that's any use.'

Baintree sighed, shook his head at his friend and held out his hand. The doctor put his hand in the pocket of his coverall and pulled out a plastic bag containing a wallet, a wristwatch, a dog-tag medallion on a gold chain and a quantity of coins. As Baintree put on a pair of rubber gloves to inspect the contents, Brown explained, 'Not a robbery and no attempt to make it look like one. His money's still in his wallet and the gold Omega watch was still on his wrist. No ID in the wallet but the name John Prosser is on the medallion. It's a tag stating his name, a hospital number and that he has a pacemaker. It also lists some of the drugs he's on for a heart condition.

'That's useful,' Baintree commented and then asked, 'No driving licence?'

Brown shook his head and smiled. 'No, but the dog-tag seems to fit with his implant. Wish they were all as easy as that.'

'If it's really his tag. Shouldn't be hard to check out though,' Baintree stated. 'Thanks Mark,' he said as he turned to go over to the nearest police officer. He wound his way past several scrub oak trees. 'Who's in charge here?' he asked as he approached the photographer.

'Sergeant Tattler, Sir.' He pointed to one of the other policemen.

'Who found the body?'

'A man and his dog, Sir,' the constable replied. 'Apparently he walks along the pathway by the river every morning. We're about three quarters of a mile from the village.'

Baintree nodded and watched for a couple of minutes as the other two police officers finished their search of the crime scene. 'All done here,' the nearest of the two stated, and led the other policeman back towards Brown. 'I'm Constable Tattler,' he said as he got nearer. 'You know who it is, do you?' he asked, implying that he already knew the identity of the victim.

'If you can enlighten me, constable, please feel free to elaborate.'

'Yes Sir. I knew this man from a few years ago. He's not a local man. He came from London but he was connected with a crime that took place near here. I've done a quick search on the files and apparently he's just got out of prison. The name's Prosser, John Prosser, Sir. Served his full term from what I can discover. No time off for good behaviour.'

'None at all?'

'No Sir,'

Baintree scowled and thought for a moment. 'So if he wasn't a local man,' he asked eventually, 'what was he doing back in this area?'

'I don't know that Sir. But I do remember that there was a detective from London involved with the case.'

Baintree nodded. 'And how many years ago was it when our Mr. Prosser was sent down?'

'Eight, Sir.'

CHAPTER TWO

Up ahead the thick stone walls of the farm yard danced mockingly in the simmering heat. The taxi cruised slowly along the narrow country road and, on Rebecca's instruction, the driver negotiated the gap between two neglected, rusty old milk churns that had once stood proudly, polished and new beside the gate posts. He followed the uneven and pot-holed farm lane for another hundred and fifty yards towards the house, moved slowly into the yard and pulled his car to a halt alongside an old, rust-spotted Escort. Rebecca opened the taxi door and stepped out. She handed the driver some money, closed the door behind her and then waited while the taxi drew out of the yard. Only when the sound of the engine had faded away in the distance did she turn towards the old car. The Escort was the last thing to be taken away from Cil Cwm Farm.

She unlocked the car door, opened it wide then leaned inside and wound down the windows to let out the suffocating heat of the sun. Just Like that awful and unforgettable day eight years ago, it was a hot, stifling, dead of day afternoon, no clouds, no breeze and a blistering sun. Even the birds that normally twittered to their mates and to their nestlings had taken a siesta. While she stood and waited for the inside of her car to cool down, she took one last look at the deserted, old, stone-built house. It would not be empty much longer, she thought, and then scanned across the rolling fields that dipped down to the dark green woodland. The song of a single skylark broke the silence as she looked at the becalmed and waveless sea of long grass that was going to seed and should have been cut by now. That, too, was waiting for the new occupants to arrive. Finally, as if drawn by some irresistible force, her gaze settled upon the faded white doors of the stone-built garage across the opposite side of the concrete yard. The building had remained locked ever since the undertakers had taken the body of her father away to the mortuary eight years ago. Only recently had it been re-opened for potential purchasers to view it and for the auctioneers to make sure that any tools and equipment had been taken out for the farm sale. Now, the last time she would ever be there, she felt compelled to take another look inside. She took out a small bundle of keys from the back pocket of her faded jeans, unlocked the door, pulled it open and stared inside until her eyes became accustomed to the gloomy interior.

Slowly, she glanced over the dusty mortar of the stone walls and the oily planks of the inspection pit, but eventually and inevitably her eyes were drawn to the heavy oak beam. She could see him hanging there now, the rope cutting into his neck, the deep scars on his skin where he had clawed at the rope in a last effort to undo what he had started, his purple tongue hanging out, and eyes struck with the fear of realization that there was no turning back the clock, not even to regain the brief moment it took, in a muscular spasm, to kick away the high stool from which he had plunged to his death. Her eyes narrowed as a knot of revulsion and hatred formed in her stomach. She would never forgive him for what he had done.

Breathlessly, she turned on her heel and ran outside, slamming the door closed behind her. She leaned back on it to hold it firmly shut until her pounding heart slowed and her composure returned. Then, without turning around, she twisted the key in the lock, withdrew it and strode over to the car. She thrust herself heavily inside, slammed the door and started the engine. It fired almost immediately but she gunned it mercilessly before letting the clutch out and speeding away. She didn't once look back.

'Well, that's it,' she muttered to herself with a tone of finality. The move was made. It was a relief. Since the death of her father, her mother had become frail and ill in health. For those eight years since the day she and Rebecca had found him hanged by the neck, Dorothy Hampstead and her daughter Rebecca had struggled to make ends meet. But now the fight was over. It had ended with the sale of the farm.

CHAPTER THREE

Compared with the place they had left, Pendle Court Farm seemed like another world with its vast green fields of wheat and blankets of oil seed rape rolling over an undulating landscape, dissected by lines of dark green hedges. A glistening, silver ribbon of water meandered along the plane below the long farm road that led through a wooden gate and up to a huge double-fronted farm house. A vast border of mature beech trees encompassed the gardens and lawns that spread out around the house. In the distance, to the west and the left of the farmhouse, through the gaps in the trees, could be seen the tops of the modern steel-framed farm buildings, and over to the right, but not so clearly visible, were the older, brick-built stables where Rebecca had spent much of her summer holidays when she had stayed and played at Pendle Court as a child in years gone by.

She loved the farm and, as she drove towards her new home, Rebecca reflected on how she came to be there once more. For several years Mrs. Hampstead had persuaded Rebecca to continue her education at school despite the fact that, because of her frail health, she could not run the farm on her own. Rebecca had offered to leave school and get a job locally to support them both but, until her daughter was old enough to drive, her mother would hear none of it. 'Once you are old enough to get a proper job with a proper career then I shall sell up,' her mother had stated, 'but until then your education comes first.' Rebecca was approaching her nineteenth birthday. During the last year Dorothy had scraped together enough money to get her daughter through her driving test and to buy for her and tax and insure a cheap car. With the car came independence. Rebecca could leave school now and go to wherever she wanted to get a decent job with decent career prospects. No longer was Dorothy's daughter going to be obliged to stay and help her mother.

Of course, Rebecca never saw it that way. She loved her mother and she loved the country life, but she knew her mother was right. The time had come for her to leave the nest, spread her wings and see what job prospects existed elsewhere.

Her uncle Andrew had seen it too. For years now he had watched from a distance and noticed how his sister, Dorothy, was struggling both physically and financially. He also fondly remembered Rebecca's visits to Pendle Court Farm when she was a child and, despite his niece no longer visiting for summer holidays, Dorothy had kept him informed about Rebecca's progress. And so it was Uncle Andrew who suggested a solution to Dorothy's problem. He asked her if she would like to retire and move to live at Pendle Court. Plainly, Dorothy's farm was never going to be able to satisfy any ambitions to which Rebecca might aspire even if she had any, and considering that all the good job prospects offered to her meant moving some considerable way from her mother and the hill farm, Andrew offered Rebecca the opportunity to live and work on his farm.

Rebecca smiled at how things had worked out. If she was going to leave her home then it had to be to go where her heart called her to follow. Once it had been established that her mother would sell up their hill farm in Wales and move to Pendle Court, Rebecca had taken very little persuading to accompany her.

'I've been meaning to have a word with you, Becki,' Andrew said one morning during breakfast as if it had been the first chance he had had to speak to her since she had arrived. Five whole weeks had passed since the move and Rebecca had settled in, not just as Andrew's only niece, but as one of the farm workers. Her heart was in farming and she was loving it. Unlike working on her mother's hill farm, and despite working even longer hours, farming here seemed to have a whole different meaning to that of toiling simply to survive. Since moving to Pendle Court, not once had the idea of job-hunting crossed her mind. And as Rebecca buried herself in the work on the farm, her mother, Dorothy, had gradually begun to relax. The dark shadow of her husband's death may not have faded, but her financial worries had finally come to an end. Rebecca had noticed that over the past weeks her mother had regained some of the vigour and energy she'd had before those dreadful events eight years ago; and seeing her mother's health returning, along with absorbing herself in the daily work of the big farm far away from Cil Cwm, Rebecca's recollection of what had happened when she was ten years old had been pushed far, far away into a distant memory.

Andrew's dark blue eyes gazed into Rebecca's as he waited for a response.

'What about?'

'I was wondering if you'd be interested in taking over this farm,' he said almost too casually.

'Pardon?' Rebecca didn't think she had heard right.

'Are you interested in taking over this farm,' he repeated in just the same informal tone as he concentrated on cutting a slice of toast.

Rebecca stared at her uncle, wondering if it was a life dedicated to farming that had eventually turned him mad. 'I thought you'd invited mum to stay here to solve *her* problems,' she said, frowning, 'and that I was just collateral damage.'

'Oh, Becky!' Dorothy exclaimed. She sat silently listening to the conversation, but couldn't help releasing the outburst. Andrew had told her what his intentions were the night before and she was intent on keeping out of any discussions. What Rebecca did, had to be what Rebecca wanted.

Rebecca smiled at her mother. 'You know I'm right, mum,' she said.

Andrew laughed. 'Well you are old enough to start forming your own ideas about where you live and what you want to do, and it's true, you had nowhere to live once your mother sold up and moved here, but I had hoped that you would move here too. And since you moved here, I've seen how much you love working on the farm. From the very first day you arrived you have not once treated it as just a job. You put far more into it than that, and not once have you looked for work elsewhere. So I thought you might want to look at working here as a job opportunity.'

'But...but most of the farm is rented isn't it?'

'True'. He lifted his eyes to her face and smiled confidently. 'But that doesn't mean I can't pass it on to you.'

Rebecca took a bite of her toast and ate for a moment while she collected her thoughts. 'You mean you want me to take over the tenancy? What has old Lord Myler got to say about that?'

Andrew frowned. 'He can't say much. He died six months ago.'

'Oh, I hadn't heard,' Rebecca said apologetically, and then, 'Won't the estates have to be sold?'

Andrew nodded. 'I was offered the chance to buy this farm,' he stated with a slight shrug of his shoulders.

'And?'

'And I couldn't afford it. I'd have had to borrow more than a million pounds; hardly sound economics. Remember, I'm sixty three and about ready to start taking things a bit easier. And besides, I don't have any children to leave my work to. I've already got four hundred and fifty acres of my own land that I've bought in bits and pieces over the years. Small farms mostly, but they're spread out around the edges of this farm.' He paused and watched Rebecca for some response, but she continued to look at him, knowing that he would tell her more. 'Since your Aunt Connie died,' he continued, 'there hasn't seemed much point in carrying on getting any more land.' He paused again and looked at Rebecca who was now sitting with her elbows on the table and her chin resting in her cupped hands. 'Until, that is, I got around to thinking about your coming here and getting some of the benefit of my work. You are my only heir.'

Rebecca was silent for several minutes while she thought over what he had just said. 'You're serious about my coming in with you then?' she said eventually. 'Is that the reason you asked us to come and stay?'

'Yes,' Andrew replied plainly, and then added, 'Partly. There doesn't have to be just one reason for doing anything. He waited for Rebecca to carry on talking but she remained silent, contemplating the proposal. She stood up and plunged her hands deep inside the pockets of her jeans, walked over to the window and gazed across the yard. It was some time before she turned back to face him.

'Well then,' she said very seriously, 'we'd better discuss what I'm going to be paid! It's bound to be an improvement on a farm worker's wages.'

Andrew grinned when he saw that Rebecca was fighting in vane to suppress a smile. 'Great! Then we'll settle on a starting salary of say, what, twenty thousand a year?'

Rebecca stared at her uncle, her eyes wide, her mouth slightly open. 'Er, yes, that sounds about what I had in mind,' she blushed, 'Give or take a few thousand!'

'And ten percent of the net profits, shall we say?'

Rebecca was speechless but succeeded in stopping her bottom jaw dropping any further.

Andrew's grin widened even more. 'Of course, you'll have free lodging, and if you want to move out there will always be a farm cottage available,' he said as if trying and persuade a reluctant applicant.

'Move out? But I've just moved in!'

'Well you may get married or something. We wouldn't want that to cause any problems with our business arrangements would we?'

'I'll be here for quite a while then,' she replied seriously and then frowned. Eventually, after a minute's thought, she spoke. 'And?'

'And?' Andrew said raising his eyebrows.

Her face was serious as she sauntered towards the table and sat down facing him. 'And how do I go about earning the right to take over this farm of yours?'

'Oh! That *and*.' Without another word, he pushed his chair back, got up and went out of the kitchen only to return a minute or so later with a blue folder in his hand. He placed it on the table in front of his niece.

'What's this?'

'That is a load of papers for you to study. Read them, go to a solicitor for advice on them if you wish to discuss the Agricultural Holdings Act and what the new legislation holds in store, and then we both sign them.'

Rebecca picked up the folder and opened it.

'There's an agreement by me to transfer the leasehold to you when I'm sixty five,' Andrew explained as he sat down. 'There are conditions of course. You'll have to show you can run the farm as well as I can so that we can persuade the new landlord to agree to transfer before or on my death.'

Rebecca looked up from the folder. 'I don't want you to die,' she said profoundly. 'You aren't ill or anything are you?'

Andrew laughed. 'No, I promise you, this is just business. As far as I know I'm as healthy as I've ever been. I hope to live a long time yet, but having said that, I would hope you will outlive me!'

Rebecca reddened. 'It all seems a bit macabre,' she said sadly.

'Rubbish!' said Andrew as he reached for the last of the toast. 'It's a fact of life. If you realize that, then we'll be well on the way to sorting out your problem and mine.'

'What problems are those?' asked Rebecca, puzzled.

'Well,' he said wiping a smudge of marmalade off his finger, 'I'm heirless and you are jobless.'

'Jobless? I thought I had a job here!'

'Not if you turn me down,' Andrew said with a grin.

Rebecca closed the folder, stood up and kissed her uncle on the cheek. 'Then neither of us has a problem any more, Uncle,' she said and smiled softly. She poured herself a bowl full of cereals. Andrew seemed in no hurry to go and he sat and watched her. He could tell she was still thinking about their conversation. He waited patiently until she was ready to speak. 'If you turned down the offer to buy the farm,' she said with a serious frown, 'who's bought the Myler estate?'

'Some trust fund,' Andrew said, raising his eyebrows as acknowledgement that he knew little more than he was telling her.

'Oh, it's not been bought by a person then?'

'Well there'll be people behind it, of course. I've written off to them to sort things out. The papers you've got in the folder include an agreement in principle by them for you to continue the tenancy, provided that you satisfy the conditions set down; like the suitability test and so forth. We'll tie that up as soon as we can.'

'I see,' Rebecca said, still mulling everything over in her mind. 'It appears that you've been planning this since before we even moved in.'

'Long before,' Andrew replied frankly.

Within a month, the landlord, *Spears Trusts*, had agreed the transfer of the lease on condition that the farm showed no detrimental deterioration and, that within a year, Rebecca showed at least her ability to run the farm as well as her uncle Andrew.

Rebecca wasted no time in getting down to knowing every little detail there was to know about the farm. Andrew was an early riser, but he was never up before Rebecca. She would be sorting out the office work an hour before he arrived for breakfast. The six full time farm workers took to her straight away. They admired her enthusiasm, her energy, and the way she treated them as equals. She asked them rather than commanded them to undertake tasks, often joining in with them and doing her full share. In return, they helped her learn her job of running the farm by teaching her their skills. Moreover, in the presence of a young and beautiful woman, they worked to impress her.

The youngest farm worker, Garry Dealer, was twenty eight, the oldest, Earnest Henshaw, was as old as Uncle Andrew. All the workers were married and lived on the farm in tied cottages. Their wives, young and old, kept a close eye on their men, who, for some reason, seemed to dress a little smarter, shave a little closer, swore less and generally became more affable. Of course it could have been because their wives were being just a little more attentive.

CHAPTER FOUR

Rebecca heard the approaching vehicle long before it came into sight. She turned and waited for it to appear, and a few seconds later, a shining new Range Rover cruised through the gateway, drew up beside her and braked to a halt. An electric window buzzed as it descended into the door frame and Andrew leaned out of the opening. 'Well?' he asked, a broad grin cracking his face from ear to ear, 'what do you think of it?'

Rebecca went to the open door. 'It looks all right, Uncle,' she said, and nodded her approval. 'But what's wrong with your other one?'

'Too old,' Andrew stated in a tone that sounded like a reprimand. She *must* have noticed that the previous vehicle had needed replacing!

'Too old! It was only eighteen months ago that you bought it new! I do the accounts. Remember?'

'That's what I mean, I've got to keep on top of this car job, you know, or else I'll get up one morning and find I've got an old banger like that thing of yours.'

'Old banger!' she spluttered.

'Well, there are not a lot of them about now days.' Then he added, lightly, 'Not in one piece at any rate.' He continued in a more serious tone, 'It's about time you went out and got a new car for yourself.'

'I wouldn't get much use out of it,' Rebecca shrugged. 'I don't go very far. I've driven further around the farm off road in the Jeep than I've been on the roads in the Escort.'

'Then it's about time you did get out a bit,' Andrew scolded. I'm not saying that I don't commend your enthusiasm, but you really ought to take a break sometime. You've not had a day off since you came here, and you work from first thing in the morning till you go to bed at night. Hardly a recipe for happiness, you know.'

'But I am happy, Uncle. Don't you see?'

'Oh I'm aware of that more than anybody, my child, and it has made me happier than I could possibly have dreamed, to have you here to step into my shoes. You're everything and more that I expected. But you know what they say…'

'Yes,' Rebecca interrupted, 'but my name isn't Jack.'

'God forbid,' Andrew grinned, continuing his light hearted banter. 'But I'm going to insist that you start taking some time off.'

Rebecca kissed him on the cheek. 'Right then,' she said softly and squeezed his arm. 'I'll go into town this afternoon and spend a bit of the money I've been earning lately. There's nothing like being told you're dispensable!'

Andrew laughed. 'Good heavens, I actually think you mean it!' He pushed the vehicle door wide open and stepped out beside his niece.

'I do,' said Rebecca as if determined to carry out a threat.

'Then since I can't persuade you to get a new car,' Andrew said, putting his arm around her shoulder, 'then you'll have to take a spin in the Range Rover and see how it fits. Perhaps then you'll change your mind and get something a bit more befitting your position.'

'I will when I've got the use for it, Uncle, I promise.' They linked arms and walked towards the house. 'It's nice to drive a new car, but I just don't have the time or the inclination for one as yet.' She thought for a moment as they walked. 'In the meantime,' she said after some deliberation, 'I'll take you up on your offer. How's that?'

Andrew beamed at her.

After an early lunch, Rebecca bathed, and changed into some light cotton clothes more in suiting with the hot afternoon. It was the first time she had worn a skirt since she started work at the farm. Jeans were by far the more practical attire for climbing on tractors and around grain silos, but it felt good to be feminine again. With a splash of perfume under her ears and a cooling breeze around her ankles she set off to town. 'See you later,' she shouted and waved as she climbed into Andrew's new Range Rover. She adjusted the seat, fastened her seat belt, checked the controls, and turned the engine over. Yes, she decided as she opened the windows, there was a thrill in driving a brand new car. She sat and listened to the engine whispering back at her for a moment or two and then, tossing her head back to remove a fallen wisp of hair from her face, she cruised away from the house.

It felt good; comfortable, powerful and fast, as she drove along the winding farm lane. For the first time in months she was relaxed and carefree, her mind on the afternoon ahead and the things she had decided to buy.

At the same time, a horse and its rider meandered off the main road and up the lane towards Pendle Court. In the calm and gentle, sprawling, countryside, it was a quiet and peaceful sunny afternoon, ideal for thinking and riding.

In the Dead of Day

The warm and gentle breeze through the open window lifted Rebecca's hair in its jet stream. It was refreshing and stimulating as she let her mind wander ahead of her to the shopping mall and all of its contents.

The horse lifted its head, pricked up its ears and dilated its nostrils to scent the air. 'What's the matter boy?' the rider whispered. But if the horse could have answered him, it was already too late.

Without a moment of warning, as it rounded a curve in the lane, the Range Rover loomed down upon the horse and rider. Rebecca had no time to think. It was all over in a split second. By reflex she had swerved the vehicle and missed the horse's side and the rider's leg by the thickness of his leather boot. With brakes full on, the Range Rover headed off the lane, crossed a small ditch and hit solidly against an ancient, stag-headed oak tree which retaliated with a shower of old dead branches. The horse reared into the air, its rider fighting to stay mounted at the same time as trying to bring the crazed creature under control. 'Whoah! Steady boy, steady!' he shouted, grabbing a hold of its mane with his left hand to release some of the pressure of the bit on its mouth as his other hand kept him in the saddle by hanging onto the reins.. 'Whoah there!'

Time seemed eternal as the mount came under control, stamping and fidgeting on the concrete road. Eventually, soothed by the voice of its master, but still blowing hard through its dilated nostrils, the horse was calmed enough to stand still. The rider patted it on the neck and then glanced towards the crippled Range Rover, whose driver, shaken and unnerved, was struggling out of the seat, hampered at first by the inflated air bag, then by the safety belt and then, again, by a door that would only open six or seven inches because of the pressure of the crumpled wing against it.

Rebecca, banging her knee as she struggled free, pushed herself from vehicle and limped angrily towards the man and the horse.

'Can't you control that animal?' she demanded as it shied away from her menacing figure.

'Steady Hassan my boy,' the man said in a calming voice and at the same time, patting it gently on the neck. 'I'll let you know in a minute,' he replied as his mount fidgeted. Eventually, when the horse was calmed again, he dismounted and, stroking it gently on the nose, he stood looking at Rebecca's pale angry face. But despite the shock and anger he saw written on it and the tousled hair around it, he seemed strangely taken captive by what he saw; the dark blue eyes burning into his, the firm square jaw flexing indignantly at the trouble he had brought upon her.

Once again the horse lifted its head skittishly as Rebecca stepped closer.

'Steady boy!' the man said calmly, and then, turning his head to look into the horse's eyes, he added, 'Damned stupid creatures, really.'

Rebecca's body stiffened. 'I think that has much to do with the competence of the rider,' she stung. 'Horses are one of the most intelligent creatures on this earth.'

'I was talking to the horse!' the stranger replied cuttingly. 'About damned stupid women!'

Rebecca's pale face flushed red with anger. The horse flinched again and took a step backwards as it sensed the hostility. 'You're holding him on too tight a rein,' she snapped angrily, 'He'll never calm down with an idiot like you hanging onto his mouth.'

The man's eyes looked like flints. 'It would help,' he said slowly, 'if some idiots didn't drive like they'd just robbed a bank! You damned near killed the both of us.'

Rebecca's knee began to throb and tremble uncontrollably. To prevent the man noticing, she transferred her weight onto her other leg, put her hands on her hips as casually as she could and fired another salvo. 'Oh, that's just fine! Blame me! Well, if people who can't ride kept themselves and their horses off other people's lanes, there would be less chance of them causing serious accidents. Look what *you've* done,' she shouted and waved her hand at the crumpled vehicle.

The stranger laughed, enhancing the whiteness of his teeth against a sun-tanned face. 'Yes, it is a bit of a mess. Still, it shouldn't cost much to knock the old bus back into shape. Then you'll be able to try and kill somebody else.' He turned to lead his animal back the way he had come.

'Old bus!' Rebecca screamed. 'Damn you, it was brand new! And now you've smashed it. It's all your fault.'

The stranger's face suddenly hardened as he turned back to face Rebecca. 'It had nothing to do with your driving too fast then?' he asked, still keeping his cool.

'Too right it didn't! You shouldn't have been on the lane in the first place.'

'Not even if I'd been in a car?' the man asked, his voice now beginning to carry a note of anger. 'If Hassan hadn't been a horse,' he went on, 'and if he hadn't been able jump to one side, you'd have killed me for sure.'

'I...'

'Who's to say I wasn't coming to see the farmer?' he cut in before she could speak.

'Oh, you were coming to see my uncle, were you?'

'No, as it happens I wasn't. But that isn't the point. Every visitor has a right to travel safely to the door of the person he is visiting.'

'You just said you weren't visiting,' Rebecca argued. 'So you were trespassing.'

'I might have been visiting, I might have been trespassing, but the point is, you still have no right to go around running people down with that oversized go-cart just because you don't have the brains to realize that somebody might be coming the other way.'

Rebecca stared at him, speechless. She had never found it so hard to win an argument in her life, and this time she needed to. Her knee was dented, her ego was dented, and even more, her uncle Andrew's brand new Range Rover was dented to the point of being completely smashed. And to add insult to all that, the tall, dark haired stranger looked at her in a way that made her wish she'd kept her denims on! Why, today of all days had she to be feminine! Her breasts heaved against the cotton dress as she took a deep breath. Exasperated, she fired her final volley. 'You suffer from verbal diarrhea, do you know that? Or is it that your brains have rubbed too hard on the saddle?' she sniped and turned back to the Range Rover before she lost any more points. The stranger just stood and grinned.

She squeezed back into the driving seat, started the engine, selected four-wheel-drive and located reverse gear. She began to reverse onto the lane then stopped abruptly when she realized that not only was the wing of the Range Rover binding against the front wheel, but there was a definite sound of a cooling fan ripping against a buckled radiator. 'Do you need a hand?' the man shouted over the sound of the grating engine.

'No thank you,' Rebecca shouted back. 'You've done quite enough for one day.'

'Send me the bill when you get the old crock mended,' he shouted as he turned away.

'If I knew who you were, you could rely on it,' she shouted after him as he turned once again and began to lead the horse away.

'Simon Park,' he shouted back against a sudden silence as she stopped the engine.

'Is that supposed to mean something?'

'I live at Thatch Cottage.' He threw her another glance over his shoulder, smiled, and began to walk the horse slowly away the way they had come. Then, having second thoughts, he turned the horse, put his foot in the stirrup and mounted it with the grace and ease of a seasoned rider. He held out his hand. 'Jump up and I'll give you a ride back to the farm,' he called, seeing Rebecca limping.

Rebecca just glared back at him but Simon Park just grinned again, pulled lightly on the reins and walked his horse away down the lane. Watching after him until he had vanished down the winding road, she thought how much she detested the man: an intense dislike of his arrogant and confident manner. She hated the way he looked at her, a kind of knowing look that made her feel weak and feeble and at a disadvantage, and she hated him for his summary dismissal of the whole catastrophe. Her heart pounded against the inside of her breast with frustrated anger and hurt pride.

Eventually, she turned to her immediate task. The Range Rover had no tool to prize the crumpled wing away from the jammed wheel. After a half hearted search, Rebecca threw her arms in the air, sighed and tried to slam the door, which by this time was harder to close than it had been to open. How she wished she had never got up that day. She wished she had never set off in the new Range Rover, and more than anything, she wished she hadn't to go back and explain to Uncle Andrew what had really happened. 'What a rotten awful day,' she groaned as a lump of anger and frustration fermented inside her. She would feel foolish and awkward explaining it to her uncle, the one person she admired the most, the one person she didn't want to let down. 'That Simon Park has a lot to answer for,' she mumbled as, looking down the empty lane, she fought to control sobs of despair. She smothered them by biting her bottom lip. A few deep breaths made the feeling pass and then, standing erect and with a painful limp, she strode out for home.

CHAPTER FIVE

'I've smashed your new Range Rover, Uncle,' she said as he and her mother stood in the doorway and watched the hot and dishevelled young woman limp up through the gate.

'Oh you haven't!' Dorothy exclaimed and put her hands over her mouth.

Andrew stepped down the front steps to the yard and walked towards his niece. He put his arm around Rebecca's shoulders. 'What happened?' he asked anxiously as he led her to the door.

'I was driving too fast around the bend in our lane and had to swerve to miss a man on a horse,' she replied in a matter of fact tone.

'Not the proverbial dog, then?' he chuckled.

'Nope, definitely a horse.'

'Are you all right, child?' he asked as they walked side by side into the lounge.

'Yes, Uncle, I'm fine.' She gave him a weak smile. 'Could do with a sticky plaster on my ego though.' She shrugged as Andrew let go of her and she flopped into an easy chair.

'Are you sure now? You haven't hurt yourself have you?'

'I'm fine, honest,' she insisted.

'A strong pot of tea is what's needed,' Dorothy stated and turned to go and solve the problem.

'I'm really sorry about all this,' said Rebecca, rubbing her leg.

'Oh you needn't be. It's only paint and metal. So long as you're all right, that's all that matters. But just remember, I can replace a car but I can't replace you. You're supposed to be going to out-live me, remember?' He put his hand on her shoulder to reassure her.

Rebecca took hold of his hand and squeezed it affectionately. 'I'll be careful in future, Uncle, I promise.'

'Right, well we'll take a tractor and sort the Range Rover out later. Now, what about the horse and its rider?'

'Oh,' Rebecca said with a slight grimace. 'I'm afraid I shouted at him and told him it was his fault for being in the way.'

The noise subsided as Andrew brought his raucous laughter under control. Rebecca had expected rebuke but instead he laughed, a chuckle to begin with, but as it infected his niece, fermenting bubbles of laughter inside her too, his laughter burst out of him like the froth out of a champagne bottle. 'Well you know what they say,' he said, wiping a tear of mirth from his eye, 'attack is the best means of defence.'

'Huh. Well I feel pretty bad about it now, but at the time... well, all I could think about was what I'd done to your new Range Rover. I was angry with myself really. It just came out at him.'

'Anybody we know?' he asked, wiping another tear from the corner of his eye. He pulled up a side chair and sat beside her.

'It turned out to be the man who's staying at Thatch Cottage.'

'Oh him! I've never met him. He seems to keep himself to himself down there. I heard he'd bought the place from the Estate. What's he like?'

Rebecca reddened. 'Oh, you know,' she said, and without elaborating, pushed herself up from the easy chair and went through to the bathroom to bathe her knee.

Andrew smiled after her.

'So you've met the man at the cottage,' Andrew said later as they all drank their tea.

'If you can call *that* meeting,' replied Rebecca. 'You say you've never met him?'

'He seems to be a very private person. I've passed him a couple of times on the road and he waved the last time our eyes contacted. But you know how it is. Unless you've got something to say then you keep on with what you are doing and as I'm usually on a tractor then my mind is on my own business.'

'Isn't he a farmer then?'

'Goodness no! As far as I can gather, he bought the cottage with a couple of paddocks at either side of it.'

'A holiday cottage is it?' asked Dorothy.

'Don't think so. He's supposed to be living there. Spends all his time travelling and writing books.'

'What sort of books?' asked Rebecca.

'Novels I think.'

'Well I've never heard of him.'

'Neither had I until he moved in.'

CHAPTER SIX

Two weeks later, Andrew received an envelope addressed to him. It contained a short, hand written letter and a cheque. He read it:

Thatch cottage,

I took the liberty of asking at the local garage. Please find enclosed a cheque to cover cost of repairs to your vehicle.

Sincerely, Simon.

'Huh. *'Simon,'* is it?' Rebecca said angrily when she saw the letter. 'Well I don't need him to pay for my repairs. I'll settle that bill when it arrives,' she said in a finite tone.

Andrew didn't argue. 'So why are you angry?' he asked. 'The man only wants to make amends.'

'He's so damned arrogant and sure of himself. I've seen him riding about on that horse of his as if he owned the place.' She thought back a week or so to the time she had driven past him in her Escort on the country road. He had waved to her and she had forced a faint smile from her burning face. She looked straight ahead, drove slowly by the horse and then, once safely past it, she sped off under the leafy beeches that lined Pendlebury Road.

Good to see you looking where you're going, he had shouted to her through the open window. *Still, there won't be much damage if you crash that one!* She flushed pink again as she reflected on his words.

'Yes, well he hasn't done us any harm has he?' Andrew broke into her thoughts.

'Well I'll not have him trying to make a fool of me.' She took the cheque out of Andrew's hand and glanced at it as she prepared to tear it in half. 'Phew, is that what it cost!' she gasped and then checked her surprise. She tore it in two, picked up a new envelope and put it inside. 'I'll post it back to him,' she stated flatly.

Rebecca drove the Range Rover into the yard at Thatch Cottage. She had intended dropping the envelope in the post with the rest of the farm mail, but at the last minute something made her put that one letter back on the dashboard.

It was the first time she had seen Thatch Cottage close up and she sat and looked at it for some time before getting out of the Range Rover and walking up the path to the door. The cottage looked as if it had been re-thatched and completely renovated on the outside. The walls were constructed from pink brick as high as the tops of the windows and half timbered from there up to the thatch of the roof. The brilliant white mortar between the thick, irregular dark oak timbers made their strength even more impressive. The garden had been landscaped with a small lawn with several young trees around its border. A pergola adorned with pink and white roses passed over the crazy pathway that ran around the side of the cottage, and scented jasmine grew up beside the white small-framed window panes, giving the place a look of contained isolation.

She looked for a letter box in the door and then by the front gate, but there wasn't one to be seen. She groaned as she began to regret not posting the envelope. If Simon Park was in, he would, no doubt have seen her drive into the yard, in fact, he would probably be watching her and laughing even now, but it was too late to turn back, she had to brave it out. She knocked on the door and stood back to take another look at the place while she waited for a reply.

The setting sun was throwing long shadows across the lawn. It was a truly tranquil place. She was beginning to relax a little now and was glad she had changed out of her working clothes, though just why, she couldn't think. After what seemed like ages she heard the latch being unfastened and she turned to face the door. Simon's tall figure filled the gap where the door had been a moment earlier. 'Oh, hello!' he said with a look of surprise and pleasure.

Rebecca didn't glean much pleasure from the thought that he was pleased. 'I've returned your cheque,' she announced and handed him the envelope.

Simon studied her for several seconds while the last rays of sunshine caught her hair. 'Well,' he said eventually, blinking his eyes away from what they beheld and focussing on the envelope. 'I'm glad to see you can admit it when you are at fault.' He lifted his hand and took the envelope from Rebecca's palm.

There was something strangely electric in his touch as the tips of his fingers brushed against hers. She reddened, and breathless and flustered by the pounding inside her chest, she retorted. 'If you'd been where you belonged, it wouldn't have happened in the first place.'

'Then why are you returning the cheque?' he asked with a self assured grin.

Rebecca felt her heart thumping faster. Every time she saw him he made her angry. His whole presence put her on guard and off balance. His dark brown, smouldering eyes flicked over her, soaking up what they saw but Rebecca held her own gaze firmly on his face. Her whole body could sense the rest of him without looking any further.

'Because I didn't want you to think I take money from strange men,' she said as dispassionately as she could.

'Strange men or strangers?' he asked with his inimitable smile.

'I haven't made my mind up yet.'

Simon chuckled and stepped back into the hallway. 'Then come in and let's get to know each other better.' His eyes settled on hers. Instantly she felt her resolve melting and looked down at the floor.

'I doubt if we've anything to talk about.' Her voice was brittle as she fought to settle her turmoil of emotions.

'Then don't talk,' he said seriously and stepped to one side to let her pass.

Rebecca stood her ground. *Come into my parlour*, she thought. Well I'm no fly. 'I suppose that since we're neighbours, and you did try to make amends for what you did, then I ought to at least try to be neighbourly.'

Simon still smiled broadly and Rebecca thought she detected him shaking his head ever so slightly. She wondered if he had missed the point - a barbed one at that!

'I make a pretty mean Soda Stream,' he chuckled. 'Do you fancy one? I've got eight flavours to choose from.'

Rebecca felt she should say no. She didn't feel at ease with this man. He was unleashing feelings within her that she had never realized existed. His confident manner was totally unsettling and he seemed to have little difficulty in keeping her at a disadvantage. His dark eyes burned into hers. 'Vanilla will do fine for me, thanks,' she said lightly after an internal struggle that he was bound to have noticed. She stepped past him and quickly diverted her mind to the task of examining the interior of the cottage. The walls of the entrance hall were painted in pastel shades of yellow, cream and blue, and on each wall hung two small watercolours in gilt frames. The polished mahogany parquet floor gave a warm look to the place and its dark rich colour contrasted with the four plain pine board doors. The door on the left was open and inside a small room she could see a leather topped desk and a small gate legged table centred on a blue rug. On the desk were stacks of books and papers that surrounded a laptop computer.

Simon lifted the latch on the pine-board door on the right and gave the door a nudge. It swung open to reveal a modern kitchen of about equal size to the other room. 'Go through,' he said politely and waved her on.

'Thank you.' Rebecca stepped past him and sauntered over to the window that looked out upon the paddock at the back of the cottage. A small and well repaired stable stood at the opposite end of the pasture, its bottom half-door closed, the top one open.

'That's where I keep Hassan,' Simon explained. 'He's an Arab, you know.'

'Yes, I can tell an Arab from a thoroughbred,' Rebecca said cuttingly.

'He's quite a spirited chap, really.' Simon opened a pine cupboard door and took out a couple of glasses.

'That explains a lot,' Rebecca replied almost sincerely. 'It'll get easier for you with experience,' she confided.

'Oh, you know about riding, then? I thought you might, but wasn't sure. I hadn't seen any horses up at Pendle Court.'

'Only Tiny,' Rebecca said with a straight face. She watched as Simon filled two bottles with water.

'Tiny?'

'A Shetland pony. Retired now. Used to ride him when I was a child.'

'You're an experienced rider then!'

Rebecca ignored him. 'Got good stables up there though. I had thought of getting a horse but I don't really have the time to do any riding at the moment.'

'You can borrow Hassan if you ever get the chance,' Simon offered, handing her glass of clear liquid.

Rebecca considered for a moment before replying. 'No thanks. He's a fine looking horse, but I prefer my own mount thanks.' She sipped her drink gingerly.

'Sometimes I'm away for weeks,' Simon explained. 'Freddie Hines, the farmer next door, has a daughter who has said she'll look after him for me while I'm away.'

'Oh good. This is quite tasty,' Rebecca put in quickly and changed the subject. She wasn't interested in his horse. 'You're a writer, aren't you?'

'I try to be,' Simon replied as he brought his drink over to the small round table. 'How old are you?' he asked, bouncing the ball back firmly into Rebecca's court. The question was totally unexpected.

'How old are you?' she retorted quickly.

'I'm thirty two,' Simon revealed willingly and smiling at her across the table. 'Now will you answer my question?'

'You look older.' she replied evasively.

'Gee thanks!' There was a silence for a few seconds while Rebecca came to terms with his question.

'I'll be nineteen next Saturday,' she admitted eventually.

'You look older,' Simon said with a broad grin.

'Touché!'

'You're the young woman that's to take over from Andrew Hampstead, aren't you?'

'You're very well informed!'

'Oh, I keep my ear to the ground. There's not a lot else to do around here.'

'Besides work.'

'True.'

'And riding your horse,' she added.

Simon chuckled. 'And riding my horse,' he conceded.

'Do you work long hours?' asked Rebecca, suddenly feeling more at ease.

'Well I work when I like basically. But I work fairly long hours. I might get up late but I sometimes work until two or three o'clock in the morning. There are certain times of the day when I find it hard to think, and others when words just flow out.' Although Simon had looked calm and relaxed from the moment he had opened the door, Rebecca noticed that, he too, suddenly seemed more at ease 'What hours do you work?' he asked after taking another sip of his lemonade.

'Oh, just normal hours.'

'Being?'

'Well I don't clock on or off, but I have breakfast in time to start at seven in the morning. I have lunch around twelve, take short break around fourish and finish some time in the evening. Usually seven o'clockish. It all depends what work we are doing any particular day.'

'And those are your *normal* hours?' Simon asked, trying to keep a straight face.

'Most of them,' she said bluntly.

'Most of them? You mean there are more?' Now a smile had escaped up one side of his cheek. He took a sip of his drink to stop it spreading.

'Well there are days when we have to work through late into the night or even early in the morning. Harvesting before the weather breaks or helping a cow to calve, you know; things like that.'

Simon nodded. He looked genuinely interested in everything she was telling him. She recalled a time before she moved to Pendle Court, when she told a boyfriend what life on a farm was really like and he'd run a mile. *No drinking time*, or words to that effect, were what she heard as he disappeared into the sunset. She'd expected Simon to be the same.

'And the farm workers don't do all that?'

'Well, yes, of course they do, but sometimes it's all hands to the wheel, or whatever it is that people say.'

'All hands to the pump.'

'I knew it was something like that.' She smiled. Simon Park was knowledgeable as well as… well she didn't want to think about his good looks at the moment.

'Sounds more appropriate to farming than the original saying,' Simon explained. 'They'd say *all hands to the pump* on ships during storms. I expect *all hands to the wheel* would be far more appropriate if they had a horse-drawn wagon stuck in a field.'

Rebecca laughed at the thought of a farmer telling all his workers *all hands to the pump* when they were all staring at a heavily laden, bogged-down hay cart.

'And Anyway,' she said, getting back to the original subject. 'I love what I do so, whatever time of day or night I am working, it never seems like work.'

Simon smiled and nodded. He could tell from her face that she was absolutely serious. 'Then we are both very lucky people,' he said knowingly.

Suddenly, as he looked into her eyes, Rebecca sensed an affinity. It was nothing specific, nothing she could quantify. But there was something. The way he thought, the way he acted, made her feel she knew more about him. Yet she knew nothing except that, on meeting him, she had felt a sudden clash of emotions. 'Do you live alone?' she asked him. That should establish a few facts.

'I came to live here because I wanted peace and quiet,' he stated, impressing upon Rebecca's mind that two would have been a crowd.

'I see,' she said as if he had given a full explanation. 'Bit of a recluse then?'

Simon pretended not to hear. 'Your birthday? Have you arranged to go anywhere?'

That was sudden! 'Er, not really,' she replied vaguely.

'Not really? What does that mean?'

Rebecca thought for a moment. 'It means no,' she answered.

Simon chuckled. 'Then I'll come and pick you up and take you out to dinner. All right?'

'All right,' Rebecca said without thinking. She began to regret it as soon as the words were past her lips. 'But for now, I'll have to be going,' she followed on. It was too late for retractions now. 'I have work to do yet.' She finished off her lemonade and went to the door as she came to terms with her decision. 'What time?'

'Say seven?'

'Seven.' She suppressed a smile as she turned to face him and then turned to go out of the doorway.

He stepped outside behind her and walked alongside as he escorted her down to the parked Range Rover. 'Good to see the old bus is back in shape again,' Simon quipped as she opened the door and climbed in.

She let the smile escape from the corner of her lips then squeezed them together to hold it back. Simon could still see the smile in her eyes. 'See you,' she said to him with a wave of her hand. She swung the machine around and out of the driveway without looking back.

'So you've made friends with him after your little fracas?' Andrew said when Rebecca told him she had called at Thatch Cottage.

'Had to drop his cheque back in for him. I forgot to post it,' she lied.

Andrew smirked. 'Do you still intend paying for the repairs?'

'What choice do I have?' she replied with a shrug. She had said she would pay the bill, (granted, before she had seen it) but she wouldn't go back on her declaration of independence.

'Well, there is one thing I should have pointed out,' he answered after letting her think about it for a moment. 'The insurance company has agreed to pay out.'

Rebecca pursed her lips and put her hand on her hip. 'You might have told me,' she said, knowing in her heart that she was glad he hadn't.

In the Dead of Day

CHAPTER SEVEN

Usually the office door was left wide open to provide continual awareness of who was coming or going. But today, the sound of men's voices could be heard from behind a closed door. Rebecca decided that, for the first time since arriving at Pendle Court, Andrew must require privacy. She looked for her mother but Dorothy, too, was busy elsewhere so she made herself a quick snack, scribbled a note to tell her mother that she had made her own lunch, and then lost no time in getting back out on the farm.

Both Andrew and Dorothy were about when Rebecca returned to the house later in the day but there was a definite tension in the air. Andrew's mind wasn't really on the matters in hand. She spoke to him several times but only got perfunctory responses before he wandered off into another part of the house. Her mother, too, seemed distracted.

Two long days passed with hardly a word passing between them, despite Rebecca's efforts, but on Saturday morning Rebecca was relieved that the tension in the atmosphere had suddenly dissipated. At breakfast, her mother and her uncle were suddenly as cheery as ever. They both greeted her warmly with birthday wishes and her mother presented her with a tiny gold wrist watch wrapped elaborately in a small square package. 'Thanks mum,' she said affectionately after opening the gift. She kissed her mother on her cheek and placed the new watch on her wrist beside the man's wrist watch she always wore when working on the farm.

'Here,' Andrew said and handed over his gift. Uncle Andrew's present seemed even smaller. He handed her a brown envelope.

'What is it?' she asked as curiosity gained on her. She slipped her finger under the flap and opened it. 'A log book!'

'I thought it was about time you got yourself a decent car. It will save me having to use the Jeep when you've pinched the Range Rover.'

Rebecca glanced over the document. It had her name on it. She read out aloud. 'Private, Mercedes, A Class, white!' She stared at Andrew with an open mouth.

'Well don't I even get a kiss?' he teased.

Rebecca pulled herself together. 'Uncle Andrew! What are you thinking of? I...I...'

'You deserve it,' Andrew said with a dismissive wave of his hand. 'Anyway, I'll be able to borrow your car now! Come on, we had better go out and inspect it!'

The three of them went outside, and for a time, Rebecca clean forgot about her evening date with Simon Park. Andrew made it quite clear that she was to do no more work that day and to make sure of it he ordered her to drive her mother and himself to a restaurant in the country for a mid-day celebration.

But by mid afternoon Rebecca was thinking once again about the man she was going to see in the evening and, despite her determination not to let her feelings show, Dorothy and Andrew guessed that she was looking forward to going out with Simon Park more than she would ever admit.

It was five o'clock when the Mercedes cruised back up the farm road and pulled up in front of the house. Rebecca wasted no time in leaving the others as they got out of the car. She ran up the steps and into the house and, by the time the others had reached the front door, she was already in the shower. Gradually, she lowered the temperature of the water to cool and, after a few minutes, she began to relax after suffering the hot prickly heat of the day. Eventually, feeling totally refreshed, she emerged from the cubicle, dried herself on a thick, soft, white bath towel, dusted herself lightly with talc and then wrapped herself in a fresh cool bath robe. She never wore cosmetics while she was on the farm, but now she spent a considerable time putting on a minute amount of make-up, not too much to detract from her natural good looks, but enough to accomplish its task.

She spent more than a proportionate amount of time selecting her clothes. After much deliberation, she slipped on flowing cream and chocolate coloured, light cotton voile dress with a not too daring neck line that left room to fully display her one and only gold necklet. Then, finally, she dabbed some *Dior* on her wrists and behind her ear lobes before going down stairs. It was nearly seven o'clock.

Dorothy and Andrew were sitting having a light evening meal when Rebecca walked into the kitchen. She sat with them at the table with a cup of tea and sipped it slowly to pass the time. Every few minutes she glanced out of the window towards the wooden gate at the entrance to the farm.

'I'm looking forward to meeting this Simon Park,' Andrew announced, to break a long silence.

'Really?' Rebecca replied coolly. 'He's just an ordinary sort of chap.' She glanced at her new watch. 7.20 already!

'What time did you say you were supposed to be going out?' asked Dorothy.

'*Supposed* to be seven!' Rebecca said, shrugging her shoulders, fidgeting and pulling a face. She stood up and paced the floor a couple of times and then went to the door. 'I'm off to the office,' she announced and left the room.

As she entered the office, she glanced at her watch. 7.30. From the hall the grandfather clock chimed its confirmation. She looked at the computer and sighed. Her mind wasn't on work. Simon was half an hour late and it felt like ages. She turned on the computer and waited for it to boot but then, after a few minutes deciding what to do on it, closed it back down again. She thumbed through the papers on the desk for a while, not with any real motive, sighed again, and eventually threw them back down and went over to the window.

The clock outside the door chimed again. It was eight o'clock. Darkness was falling outside and yet there was still no sign of approaching headlights.

'Where is he?' she whispered to herself. She took several deep breaths and went back to the desk but it was impossible to concentrate. If it hadn't been my birthday, she thought, I wouldn't have given him a second thought. She squeezed her lips tightly together to suppress her annoyance. She had been stood up, and on her birthday at that. Not even a telephone call to say he couldn't come! Even if he had been out he could have used a mobile phone, but then she realized that he probably had the same unreliable signal that they received at and around Pendle Court. But being stood up hurt, and what made it really sting was that he had made a fool of her in front of Uncle Andrew. A crashed Range Rover wasn't enough. He had to humiliate her on her birthday. 'Well he won't do it again!' she muttered angrily. Her moment of self indulgence had passed and with an air of finality she marched up stairs, changed out of her dress, put on a thick polo-necked sweater and jeans and returned to the lounge.

'Not turned up love?' Dorothy said compassionately, already knowing the answer.

'He must have forgotten we had a date,' Rebecca said blandly. She sat down heavily in the armchair and picked up a newspaper. Then she added, 'Well it wasn't a date exactly.'

'He could at least have telephoned to say he wasn't coming,' Dorothy consoled as Rebecca flicked the paper into shape.

'The least he could do,' said Andrew, glancing at Rebecca hiding behind the newspaper. 'Why don't you ring him?'

'Why?' Rebecca asked, bringing her hands down abruptly.

'Well I thought...'

'I've lost all interest in going out with him or anybody else tonight. All I want to do is relax a little before I go to bed. I have a busy day tomorrow and it's nearly my bedtime anyway, all right?'

'You have a busy day every day Becki,' Dorothy submitted.

'Then all the better that I didn't waste my time going out with that...that person,' Rebecca replied and lifted the paper again.

CHAPTER EIGHT

Rebecca normally went to bed early, and it wasn't long before she was on her way to her room. But tonight she found it hard to get to sleep. Her mind was churning over, thinking about the excitement of her birthday, the lovely watch and the beautiful car from the two people she loved most in the world. Then there was the excitement of looking forward to meeting and going out with Simon. Or was it just the excitement of going out. She didn't go out half enough, she decided. But she'd felt there was more to it than that, something about the man that she couldn't explain exactly. It was that something that kept coming back into her mind time and time again as she pushed the disappointment of the evening to the furthest recesses of her mind. Did he hate her for what she had said? Was that why he had set out to deliberately spoil her birthday? He had seemed so genuine when he asked her to go out with him.

Every little noise seemed to break her out of her shallow stupor. She lifted her head from the pillow as she heard Uncle Andrew shut the outside door. Much later, an owl calling its boundaries, made her eyelids open wide, and for several minutes she stared at the blackness of the ceiling before dozing back off into a fitful sleep. The night dragged on as she tried in vain to get Simon out of her mind. Whichever way she lay, his face was still there in front of her, smiling sincerely. She closed her eyes tightly but the vision was even clearer. He can't have been sincere, she thought. At the very least he could have picked up the phone. At the back of her mind she could hear it ringing. Her hand picked up the receiver.

'Hello. Is that Rebecca?'

In the Dead of Day

'Simon! Where are you?'

'I got called away on an urgent story. My way of life doesn't fit in with keeping appointments. I'm terribly sorry. Forgive me.'

'Yes, of course I do.'

'Can we fix it for tomorrow?'

She smiled to herself and turned her head on the pillow once more as her mind churned through countless versions of what might have been said had he called her. As she stirred, she could still hear the telephone ringing faintly inside her head, lapsing momentarily into silence as she sank deeper into the sea of sleep. Then, again, she became aware of the ringing sound as her slumber reached the shallows. If only he had called, she thought again as she surfaced to consciousness. She sat up and looked out of the window. The light breeze outside was beginning to rustle the leaves on the trees, and the quiet lingering mist, turned silver grey by the bright moon, was beginning to drift and disperse.

With a deep sigh she shook her hair away from her face and lay back against her pillow. She picked up the clock from a small side table and studied the luminous dial. It was 5.00 a.m. She heard the clock downstairs chime out the hour, breaking the silence of the night, and then she heard something again, louder, clearer, not at the back of her mind. The telephone *was* ringing, no mistake about it. She thrust herself hastily out of bed and threw on her dressing gown as she ran out of her room. Sliding her hand on the polished mahogany banister to keep her balance in the semi light cast by the hall table lamp, she ran down the stairs as fast as she could.

She reached the hall table and picked up the receiver but, as she did so, the ringing stopped. She groaned and ran her fingers through her hair as the dialling tone purred loudly in her ear. 'He ought to know I'd have to get out of bed,' she said aloud, her voice booming around the silent house. She lowered her voice. 'Why couldn't he ring it a bit longer,' she whispered to the bulbous head of the newel post. She thought about ringing 1471 but knew she could never ring him first even if the number wasn't withheld. She curled her arm around the newel as she turned to go up the stairs again, but just as she was about to put her foot on the bottom of the staircase, the telephone rang again, startling her and making her miss the step. She lurched forward, catching her balance only by holding onto the post. She spun around and sprang at the telephone receiver. 'Hello,' she shouted desperately so as not to let him ring off, 'Hello...'

'Hello, is that Miss Rebecca?'

'Heh? Oh, yes, it's Earnest, isn't it?' She recognised his way of addressing her. Unlike all the other farm workers, he never used her surname. It was always *Miss Rebecca* to Earnest Henshaw. 'That's right Miss. I've bin trying to get through t'ya for quite a while,' he explained and continued without waiting for her to ask why. 'There's bin a fire at Sunnybridge Farm.'

Sunnybridge Farm was a farm that Andrew owned on the outskirts of Pendle Court.

'Oh my God! There's nobody hurt is there?'

'No Miss. It's empty y'know, or at least... but anyway, the police are there and they say they want t' see yer about it.'

'Is the fire out now?' asked Rebecca, her mind in turmoil.

'Yes Miss?'

She thought for a moment. 'All right, Earnest, I'll come out.'

'The police say they are coming over to see you.'

'I see. Well thanks for letting me know, Earnest.'

'Yes Miss Rebecca. I'm sorry I had t'get y'up s'early.'

'That's quite all right Earnest, don't worry.'

'Good night Miss.'

'Good night.' She replaced the receiver and stood and thought for a minute or so before going upstairs. She knocked lightly on Andrew's door.

'Yes,' he murmured. She could hear him stirring. 'Come in.'

'I've got something to tell you Uncle.' She didn't wait for him to ask what. 'Sunnybridge Farm cottage has been on fire,' she said as she peered around the edge of the door.

'What!' Andrew exclaimed and sat bolt upright.

'Earnest says the police will be calling.'

'Police? Oh, yes. I expect they will.' He rubbed his eyes with his finger tips. 'What's the damage?'

'Just the house he said. He didn't give any details.'

'But how? The place has been empty for ages.'

'I don't know.'

'I think we'd better go out and see what the damage is then,' Andrew decided. 'I'll be down in a minute. We'll have a quick look and then we'll know what we're talking about when the police call round.'

Sunnybridge farm was the furthest of all Andrew's farms from Pendle Court. It lay along the same road as Thatch Cottage, and some one and a quarter miles beyond. Daylight was already beginning to squeeze its way through the gap between the skyline of trees and the dark grey clouds as Andrew and Rebecca drove past Simon's home. Rebecca noticed that the curtains were drawn. A wisp of dark smoke wafted out of the chimney pot and was carried swiftly away in the light morning breeze. Obviously Simon Park was still in bed. Her stomach tightened at the thought of the way he had humiliated her, but it didn't hurt any more. Now that she knew him for what he was, she felt only anger.

Andrew noticed her watching the trail of smoke fluttering from the chimney. 'Looks like he's still in his bed,' he commented with a nod towards the cottage.

'That isn't surprising. It *is* still only six.' she said in Simon's defence and then wondered why she had said anything at all.

'I bet he sleeps later than us every morning.' Andrew said with a quiet chuckle.

'More than likely,' Rebecca confirmed. 'I wonder how an empty house caught fire?' she half asked to keep her mind on her own business. Simon Park's sleeping habits certainly weren't any of her affair and she had no intention of making them so.

Andrew noticed a tone of indifference in her voice and, realizing that they had higher priorities, began to think about the trip they were making.

'It's abnormal to shut yourself away in a country cottage like he does.' Rebecca had spoken but her uncle didn't hear her, or at least, he didn't answer. He negotiated the narrow road in silence as she watched the green hedgerows flash by. As they rounded a bend, the charred remains of a once thatched, single storey cottage appeared between two ancient oak trees that towered at either side of the entrance to the property. Now all that was left were four badly scorched walls with black square holes where the windows and doors once were. The ground around the remains was muddy and wet, churned up by the operations of the fire brigade during the night. The fire engines had gone and an unusual silence gripped the whole area as Andrew pulled to a halt at the gate and stopped the engine. A wafer-thin mist hung over the fields in the dipping river valley that lay beyond, the dark hedges protruding and disappearing like the backs of some arched sea monsters. Somewhere in the distance a starling broke the silence for a moment with its shrill tune, and then fell silent again as Rebecca and her uncle emerged from their vehicle. The stench of burnt thatch filled their nostrils. They could almost taste it.

'What a mess!' Rebecca gasped. 'It was so lovely here.' Shivering, she zipped up her jacket and pushed her hands deep into the pockets.

'Not much left I must admit,' Andrew commented caustically, and opened the front gate.

Rebecca walked down the moss-covered paving stones towards the gaping cottage doorway whilst Andrew stood back and looked on, his face grim, his lips pursed with an unfamiliar resignation, an expression which, had Rebecca turned and seen it, would have worried her. To Rebecca her uncle was nothing less than totally confident; totally in control.

But she didn't look back.

'Hold it!' an unfamiliar voice shouted from behind her. It wasn't Andrew's voice nor was it that of anyone she knew. She spun sharply on her heel. Sitting on a rustic garden bench behind the broad girth of one of the oak trees was a man in a dark grey overcoat. A thick red and yellow scarf was twined two or three times around his neck, its plain ends draped either side of his chest. He wore no hat on a head of short dark brown hair that was combed backwards, making his tiny ears protrude like pompons on a tea cosy. He stood up, hands still in his pockets.

'Pardon?' Rebecca said in a startled voice.

'You can't go in there.' His authoritative manner matched his fixing stare, a mesmerizing gaze from large brown eyes set back in deep shadowy sockets.

'Who says so?' Andrew demanded as he came into view from the gateway and stood between his startled niece and the stranger. The man's eyes shifted from Rebecca towards Andrew. His sullen face didn't move, nor the head that held it.

'I'm Detective Inspector Greythorpe,' he announced with an almost unnoticeable movement of his lips. A gloved hand emerged from his heavy grey overcoat pocket and wiped a droplet from the end of his porcine nose. 'And who might you be?'

'I'm Andrew Hampstead. This happens to be...'

'Your cottage,' Greythorpe interrupted. 'Yes, now you have said who you are, I know your business here.' His large eyes burned into Andrew's. 'Or do I?'

'How do you mean?' asked Andrew angrily, glaring at the man's dour face.

'Have you any identification, sir?'

'No, have you?'

The detective pulled his other gloved hand from his other coat pocket and held up his warrant card.

Andrew walked over to him and studied the photograph. 'Good likeness,' he said in a way that Rebecca thought was meant to offend. 'What can I do for you?'

'If you don't mind, you can keep off this site until our men have had time to examine it more closely and determine the actual cause of the fire.'

Rebecca frowned. 'You mean you don't know already?'

The large eyes fixed on her again, still no sense of life in the face. 'I should say we have a good idea, Miss... er...' He tilted his head interrogatively.

Rebecca didn't oblige by giving her name. 'You suspect arson, then?' she probed.

'I didn't say that Miss.'

'Then what is it you said you thought you knew?'

'We'll be able to tell for sure now that it's coming daylight.' He paused momentarily as Andrew moved towards the gaping hole that had once been the doorway. He considered the scene carefully before Greythorpe spoke again. 'Now don't go touching anything, sir,' he protested.

'You're quite right of course,' Andrew submitted. Don't Uniform usually do the standing Guard when something like this happens?' he enquired.

'Oh, they're on their way, don't worry,' the detective replied, his steely eyes following Andrew. But he gave no further explanation.

Andrew turned to his niece and put his arm around her shoulder. 'Come on Becki. We'd better leave them to get on with it then.'

Greythorpe watched them as they drove away. For the first time his face moved. He scowled, narrowed his eyes, and bit pensively on his upper lip. 'Hum,' he muttered quietly as he stared blankly at the empty road. He wiped another droplet from the end of his nose with the back of his glove, turned and walked back to his bench. He glanced at his wrist watch. 6.55. Another five minutes and his constable would arrive back with some plastic cups of soup and bacon sandwiches from the café next to the station. Another hour and the forensics team would be there. He pulled up his coat collar and plunged his hands deep into his pockets as a fresh breeze began to pick up and sway the branches of the ancient beech. He looked up at the gathering cumulus clouds in the sky. 'Looks like the weather is going to break,' he said aloud and sat down.

'Who'd want to burn down your farmhouse?' asked Rebecca as they drove away. Andrew didn't answer. Once again he was deep in thought. He was frowning as he gazed ahead, driving automatically, seeing everything but noticing nothing. He didn't notice Rebecca glance across in front of him towards Thatch Cottage as they rounded a bend in the road. He didn't notice that the curtains of the chocolate-box house were still drawn. Neither did he notice that Simon was not inside, but was walking his unsaddled horse around the paddock in front of the stable. Rebecca noticed. She watched Simon for a split second before he and his mount disappeared out of view, first behind the rose-draped pergola and then behind the rest of the cottage, as they moved past.

Going riding, no doubt, she thought, strangely annoyed. Obviously thinks a lot about that horse of his, if nothing else. If only he thought as much about... She stopped herself from thinking it. She felt hollow inside. She wasn't used to people forgetting she existed, not after they had met her. That wasn't at all usual. In fact Simon Park was downright unusual.

Andrew was silent for the entire journey. He pulled into the drive of Pendle Court, stopped the engine, got out and walked straight up the steps to the front door. He opened it, flung it back on its hinges and disappeared inside before Rebecca had even closed the door of the Range Rover. The policeman has definitely got to him, she thought. He hadn't shown it when he was there, but since driving away from Sunnybridge Farm, his silence had spoken volumes. She caught up with him in the kitchen. He was standing with his back to the kitchen door, leaning forward with his fists on the pine table, and saying something to her mother who was sitting facing him. Her face was ashen.

'Don't be silly,' Rebecca heard her mother say to him. Then, when she lifted her head and saw Rebecca, Dorothy's mood suddenly lightened. 'What a do!' she exclaimed, forcing a smile. 'Police an' all.'

CHAPTER NINE

At two hours past noon the telephone rang. Rebecca picked up the receiver. 'Pendle Court.'

'Rebecca! Is that you?' She froze. She knew the voice.

'Yes,' she said acidly.

'Simon here,' the distant voice announced. 'I…'

'Who?' she butted in. She heard a sigh at he other end of the line.

'Simon Park.'

'Is it farm business? If it is, then you'll have to speak to my uncle. It's my afternoon off.'

'Rebecca! I called to explain...'

'That's quite unnecessary. You don't have to ring to explain that you forgot an appointment. It was obvious by your absence.'

'No. I didn't forget.'

'And you thought you'd take time off from that damned horse of yours to tell me so. Well that's extremely good of you but you needn't have felt such an overwhelming concern.'

'I rang you so you'd know why I couldn't make it.'

'As I've said, it isn't necessary to explain.'

'Look.' The voice sounded angry. 'I bought you a present and everything. I couldn't come because...'

'It's quite all right Mr. Park,' Rebecca broke in. 'I really am not in the least bothered. Let's forget it shall we? I was rather too busy myself, anyway.'

'Look, damn it! Are you going to listen?'

'It suited me fine that you didn't turn up as it happens,' she ploughed on, oblivious to his protests. 'The fact that you hadn't the good manners to pick up a telephone and tell me you weren't coming, just put you in the same light as I had already seen you.'

There was another silence. An explanation would take too long. She would have shouted him down again before he got through the first sentence. 'I'm sorry,' he said in a soft voice. I couldn't come and I couldn't telephone straight away. I rang you to tell you I couldn't get away till now. It was Hassan...'

'Yes, I saw you out with him first thing this morning.'

'You don't understand. I wasn't *out* with him.'

'Liar!' She wanted to slam the receiver down, but there was still something inside her, suppressed by the anger he'd released, a feeling, not to win a verbal battle, not even to battle at all, just a feeling of wanting to talk it out.

She quashed it.

'Wait! Let me explain will you?' Simon shouted as the line went dead.

Rebecca ran to the stairs. She took them two at a time, ran across the landing and burst into her room, slamming the door behind her. She leaned against it, holding her breath and squeezing her eyelids tightly closed. With her heart pounding and the pulse in her temples drumming loudly in her ears, she began to crave for oxygen. Several gulps of air steadied her heart beat but did nothing to relieve the ache inside her. Surely, meeting a man, a complete and utter stranger, just twice, and then only once on friendly terms, couldn't, *shouldn't* affect her insides like this! With a sigh of frustration, she walked over to the bed and slumped heavily down upon it.

She cradled her head in her hands for several minutes until reason began to reign. Eventually, she sat upright and ran her fingers through her hair, pushing the fallen tresses back off her face. The whole silly episode was over now, and she had cast aside the disappointment and anger Simon Park had unleashed in her. He had made her think about him, when he obviously had no thoughts for her, but she wouldn't worry any more because he wasn't worth worrying about. She was much better off without letting a man like that get under her skin. He was out of her life for good.

CHAPTER TEN

Three men in Wellington boots and plastic overalls had the job of sifting through the ash inside the blackened stone walls of the cottage at Sunnybridge Farm. The cloud had closed in and a fine clothes-drenching drizzle had arrived on the fresh westerly breeze.

A combination of a thatched roof, brittle dry timbers and dry weather had ensured the disintegration of anything remotely flammable. It was a total burn-out. The fire had burned away the old, dry wooden floor that lay over a small coal cellar, collapsing the timbers inwards and leaving a well of intensely hot cinders, fanned to flames by a steady breeze through the iron-barred air vent in an outer wall that faced down a steep grassy slope. There was little left of the coal and logs that had been stored there except a steaming heap of black cinders and grey ash, turned to grimy silt by the water that had spilt into the bottom of the hole from the fire hoses.

'What can you tell me?' a voice asked from behind Sergeant Dolci.

He turned and faced Detective Inspector Greythorpe.

'That in that hole, believe it or not, was a coal cellar.' The sergeant said, proudly pointing in the direction of the pit where one of the forensics team called Stockwell painstakingly laboured. Stockwell, a young thin man with smudges on his forehead where he had wiped the perspiration and the trickling rain from his brow, was raking methodically through the sludge.

Greythorpe gave out a disgusted grunt. 'Of course it's a cellar!' he exclaimed and raised his arms in resignation. 'Loads of these old farmhouses have cellars. The bigger the house the bigger the cellar. The small houses had their cellar under the house. The large houses have part of the cellar under the adjacent yard to make it easier to load in coal.'

'Yes sir.' The ginger haired sergeant watched him walk back to his car and waited for him to assume the same reclining posture he had held for half of the afternoon since the rain had driven him from the rustic bench. Dolci looked at the lifeless face of the senior officer from Scotland Yard, the large brown sunken eyes that could look right through a man, and at the leather gloved hands placed palm down on the charcoal grey worsted knees of his suit. A sudden penetrating glance from Greythorpe made the sergeant turn away and look at Stockwell, who was standing in the hole where the cellar had been.

Stockwell looked up at the freckled face of his sergeant, smudged his brow again and whispered, 'What the hell is that chap doing here, a bloody Scotland Yard inspector on our patch, out here in the middle of nowhere, and he's bothered about what is at best a dubious case of arson?'

'Don't underestimate him,' Dolci replied sharply. 'He must be onto something or he wouldn't have been one of the first on the scene.'

Stockwell raked through the slime again, working towards the furthest internal wall. 'Perhaps this is what the old man is looking for.' He hooked out a piece of solid debris the size of a small horseshoe.

'What is it?' Dolci asked and bent forward to see down the pit.

Stockwell didn't answer immediately. He pulled out a plastic bag from beneath his overall and plopped the article into it.

'Not sure if I want to clean it and find out,' Stockwell replied with as grimace. 'You'd better get Greythorpe over here. See if he's interested in looking for himself. It looks like we're onto something in this corner.'

Earnest Henshaw was sitting at the kitchen table, sipping a mug of coffee, when Rebecca finally emerged from her room.

'Hello, Earnest,' she said, and smiled a welcoming smile.

'Hello, Miss Rebecca. Have you got over my early call?'

'Oh, don't bother about that. Did you get some sleep?'

Earnest smiled. 'I slept till dinner time. Mary said you hadn't called, so I just came round to tell Mr. Hampstead what went on there last night, Miss.'

'Where is he then?' Rebecca looked around.

'Mrs. Hampstead says he went out, Miss. She said he's bin out all day and so she told me I should wait and she'd fetch you instead, Miss.'

Rebecca pulled up a chair and then lifted the coffee pot from the tray to pour herself a drink. 'Right then, Earnest, what did happen, then?'

'Well, the first I knew of it, Miss, was when the fire engine came tearing past our cottage at one o'clock, sirens blasting and lights flashing. Made the wife almost have a heart attack it did, I can tell you. She nearly fell out of bed in her rush to get to the window.'

'Yes, I'm sure it was quite startling,' Rebecca said sympathetically. She suppressed a smile. Earnest's face seemed deadly serious and she didn't want to give him the impression that she found his wife or his description of her, comical.

Earnest smiled, however, and continued in his slow explanatory way. 'When I pushed past her and managed to look out of the window, I could see the fire at Sunnybridge as clear as anything. I gave your place a ring straight away but then, not getting any answer, I put on my togs and went on there to see what I could do.' He stopped and sipped his coffee. 'There weren't much I could do though and that's a fact.'

'You said the police were there.'

'That's right, Miss. They were already there when I got there. They were definitely convinced that somebody was living in the place, but I told them it'd bin empty ever since Mr. Hampstead bought it.'

'But they didn't believe you.'

'No Miss. The firemen said there were definite signs of somebody living there. Daft I call it. I mean, who'd know better than Mr. Hampstead?'

'I see.' Rebecca drank her coffee down and placed the empty mug on the table. 'Who reported the fire?'

'I think it were Mr. McCauley, Miss.'

'You mean McCauley the vet?'

'Yes Miss, at least, that's what I thought I heard one of the policemen say. He said for the uniformed man to get a statement from McCauley in the morning.'

'I see,' Rebecca said, pouring herself another coffee to give herself time to think. Eventually she asked, 'Did you see anybody in or around the farmhouse before the fire?'

'No Miss and I'm the nearest neighbour to Sunnybridge.'

'I know. That's what makes it sound so absurd. If anybody would have known it should have been you.'

'Oh. I'm sorry Miss,' Earnest said with self reproach.

She smiled at the elderly farm worker. 'That wasn't meant to be a reprimand.'

'Oh. Yes. Right y'are Miss.' He nodded that he understood.

She took his mug from his hand, poured him another coffee and handed it back to him.

'What I meant to say, Earnest, is that I can't understand what they were talking about. I'm as sure as you are that the place was empty.

'Not so sure I am sure now Miss.'

CHAPTER ELEVEN

Despite the fire, Monday morning brought another day of work. It was a long day on the farm and when Rebecca arrived home, she walked into the house expecting her mother to complain that she was late for dinner, but instead, Dorothy was eagerly waiting to tell her the latest news; not that Rebecca needed any telling. Her mother had painstakingly arranged a large bouquet of yellow roses in a large vase on the little semi-circular side table that stood in the hallway facing the front door.

At first, Rebecca stood and looked at the flowers; dozens of them. They are beautiful, she thought, but stopped short of going up to them and reading the tiny card that stood at the base of the vase.

Dorothy wiped her hands on the sides of her apron. 'My word!' she exclaimed excitedly. 'He certainly knows the way to a woman's heart!'

'Just who are we talking about here mother?'

'Why don't you read the card and see?'

Rebecca sighed, sauntered over to the table, picked up the card and read it.

Sorry!

Best wishes, Simon.

'Got a way with words, hasn't he?' her mother grinned.

'Just whose heart is he supposed to be on his way to?' Rebecca snapped. 'If you want them then it's all right with me. If you don't, then throw them out. I can buy my own flowers if I want some.'

'Huh! Well to me he doesn't seem like the sort of man to forget about you.'

'Well I've already forgotten about *him*.' She walked past her mother and into the kitchen. 'What's for dinner mum?' she asked, trying to change the subject.

'Perhaps there was a good reason for him not turning up on Saturday,' Dorothy suggested as she dogged her daughter's heels.

'Sure there is!' Rebecca stated. She went over to the cooker, lifted a lid and looked into one of the saucepans. 'He was too busy.'

'It wouldn't hurt to ring and thank him for the flowers, though,' Dorothy persisted.

'I agree mother! Give him a ring if you feel so grateful. He'll probably ask you out. Mind you, he won't turn up!'

'If that's the way you feel,' Dorothy said with a resigned sigh. 'But he'll probably keep sending you flowers until you answer him.'

'Gosh, dumplings!' exclaimed Rebecca, picking up a large spoon from beside the saucepan. 'I haven't had those for years.'

Dorothy sighed. She snatched the spoon out of Rebecca's hand, banged it down on the work top and then took a ladle off a hook above the hot-plate. 'Here,' she said crossly, 'give me room. Let me dish them out.'

By nine fifteen that evening, Rebecca had already retired to her room for the night. She had tried to get absorbed in a novel, but there had been too much background noise so she left her mother and Andrew watching the *Nine o'clock News* and went to bed. Yet, having sought the seclusion of her bedroom, her mind focused no better. She turned to the task of rearranging her ornaments on the small occasional table that she had positioned next to her bed. On it was an Imari trinket box, a Hummel goose girl, a ceramic paperweight owl and, her favourite, a small, heavy bronze sculpture of a Shetland pony. She picked each up in turn and felt all their contours with her finger tips. Then she placed them gently back in position, guarding her pillow. Finally, she slid beneath the sheets, turned out the small reading light and laid, hands behind her head, looking out of the window at the clouds passing in front of the silver crescent moon. She thought of all the things she loved most in the world, her mother, Uncle Andrew, the farm with its rolling fields of corn and green hedgerows. But then, suddenly, her mind came back to the thing she had been trying not to think about, the vase in the hallway, the vase full of beautiful yellow roses. She pictured them in her mind for several minutes until, suddenly, her thoughts were interrupted by the chime of the door bell. She didn't bother getting up; Uncle Andrew would see to it.

'Good evening, sir. Detective Inspector Greythorpe. You remember? Down at Sunnybridge Farm? Yesterday morning?' The detective stood at the door looking no better for the sleep he had caught the previous night. His eyes were deep bottomless, black holes.

'Good evening,' replied Andrew and stepped back from the door. 'I expect you've come to ask me to admit to burning down my own property,' he remarked dryly.

There was no sign of the comment registering on the detective's poker face. He might have not made the remark except for the reply through ventriloquist lips. 'Did you?'

'No, but I thought I'd get that question out of the way for you.'

'Very kind of you, sir, I'm sure. I'll try and remember how helpful you've been,' he replied in a droll voice.

'Go through and take a seat.' Andrew waved him to the light of the lounge doorway. He closed the front door and followed the policeman down the wide passage. As Greythorpe emerged into the room, his eyes moved around, examining everything there was to see. They flitted from one thing to another, hovering over each in turn before flicking away to the next, like a hornet hunting for food in a kitchen. Nothing special about the room he thought. Comfortable, rural, but certainly not the sort of opulent lounge he was looking for. Only Dorothy saw the minute inspection made by the policeman's eyes. She was sitting to the left of him, on the sofa facing the television and the doorway. The shiver that shook her body didn't go unnoticed by the expressionless little weasel of a man.

'Sergeant Greythorpe,' Andrew announced.

'Inspector,' the detective corrected. Dorothy looked past him, wondering who had spoken, and then settled her eyes back on his face. Instinctively, or perhaps through force of habit, the detective repeated his statement. 'Detective Inspector, Ma'am,' and then, 'Mr. Hampstead, here, denies burning down the cottage at Sunnybridge Farm.' There was no trace of inflexion in his voice. It unnerved Dorothy. She couldn't tell how serious the assertion was meant to be. Did he expect Andrew to admit to burning down his property for the insurance? Did he expect her to admit to the crime of protecting him? Did he expect any answer to such an outrageous comment?

'Well he would wouldn't he?' she said eventually, trying unsuccessfully to be as off hand as the occasion warranted. It didn't sound off hand when the words eventually emerged.

'He would?' It was definitely a question. She saw a slight rising of the right eyebrow above an otherwise frozen face. The voice had given nothing away.

'So would I if I hadn't set fire to it,' she added curtly. 'Innocent people usually deny doing things that other less informed people accuse them of doing,' she almost snapped but regulated it to come out as a firm reprimand.

'Quite,' said Greythorpe in a condescending tone. He turned to face Andrew who had stepped into the room and had positioned himself next to the inspector's right shoulder. 'You can substantiate your story can you?'

'I wasn't aware I'd told one,' he replied quite sincerely.

With a sigh, Greythorpe ploughed on. 'Let me put it this way. Can either of you prove you didn't do it?' He looked first at Dorothy who was trying to hide her agitation, and then back at Andrew.

'Can you prove we did?' Andrew countered firmly. 'As far as I know, in cases involving the police, the onus of proof is on the accuser.'

'Does the fact that we were here all night on Saturday, count for anything?' Dorothy put in quickly. She didn't want Andrew saying anything he might regret later.

'Only if you were together at one o'clock in the morning. I take it you were?'

'You take what you like young man,' Dorothy argued. 'But you don't take it that I have said anything I haven't. You seem to think we sat up all night talking or something. It's a farm here if you hadn't noticed. We go to bed early and we get up early, you know.'

'Yes, I know. I had the privilege of meeting your husband *very* early yesterday morning, at Sunnybridge Farm with your daughter.'

'My husband!' Dorothy said, aghast. 'You'd have a job on!'

'Oh?' Again the inspector's eyebrow dictated a question.

'We are brother and sister,' Andrew explained with a glance at Dorothy. 'The young lady you saw with me yesterday was my niece, *Dorothy's* daughter.'

'*My* daughter. And before you ask, I use my maiden name,' Dorothy stated.

'I see,' the inspector said vaguely.

'And therefore,' Dorothy continued, 'we are unlikely to be able to substantiate anybody's story once we had all gone to our beds.'

'I do beg your pardon,' Greythorpe said, not as if he meant any apology, but more to himself for presuming the couple were man and wife. He had always made it a rule not to presume anything and here he was breaking that rule before he had even got going.

'So what exactly is your problem, Sergeant?' Andrew asked, deliberately demoting him. The inspector let it pass.

'The problem is the body, sir.' His eyes searched deep into Andrew's soul as Andrew stared back into Greythorpe's own sunken eyes.

'What's wrong with your body?' asked Dorothy, naively.

'Nothing I can grow out of,' replied the detective. 'But the body I *was* referring to was the body, or the remains of a body, should I say, that we discovered in the cellar of the burned out cottage.' He watched Andrew's reaction. Andrew's face had set.

'A body? In Sunnybridge Farm?' Andrew's voice was even. He held the inspector's gaze. There was an uncomfortable silence while their eyes wrestled.

'That's right sir.'

Dorothy looked at them both. Her eyes were wide with shock and disbelief. Her face drained of all colour, she looked hard at Andrew and then back at the inspector. 'Oh my God! Who?'

'That we don't know yet, Ma'am.'

'Not the person who started the fire by any chance?' Andrew posed.

'That can't be ruled out, sir. However, if we knew who it was then we'd have a better idea as to what happened.'

'When will we know?'

'The forensic boys are working on that now. The body was pretty badly burned up.'

'Fried to a frazzle I'd have thought.'

'That's possibly what someone had hoped, sir.' He didn't move his eyes from Andrew's. 'Did you know who was staying there?'

'No one. It was empty,' replied Andrew.

'None of your workers or their families was there, sir?'

'Not that I countenanced. I'll have to check, but I think I'd have heard if anybody was missing by now.'

'If you'd do that, sir.' Greythorpe glanced around the room once more and then turned to go. 'Somebody had definitely been staying there, that we do know.' He walked to the outside door.

Andrew followed him. 'Why didn't you mention the body on Sunday morning?'

'Must have slipped my mind, sir.' Greythorpe opened the door and let himself out.

'What were you doing there in the first place?' Andrew asked as the policeman descended the steps to his car. 'Were you on a case?'

Greythorpe didn't appear to have heard. He got into his Mondeo, slammed the door and started the engine. Putting his headlights on full beam, he tooted his horn and accelerated out through the open gate.

'Hard of hearing as well,' Andrew said aloud, and waited until the light beams had disappeared into the darkness before gong back inside. He closed and bolted the door and turned towards the lounge. Dorothy was standing in the doorway, silhouetted by the light. He stepped up to her, and as she turned to go back into the room, he suddenly noticed the look of panic in her eyes. 'Don't worry,' he comforted her putting his arm around her shoulders and walking her into the lounge. 'Everything will be all right, just you see.'

CHAPTER TWELVE

Simon sipped black coffee and stared sightlessly ahead at an object a few feet away. He had much on his mind, problems not connected with writing, but with recent events that meant trouble for him. He blinked his eyes back into focus again as his watch momentarily distracted his gaze by playing a short musical ditty. In the centre of a small table was a small, square package. He reached out and picked it up. After turning it around in his fingers a couple of times, he turned to his desk, placed it down beside the telephone, picked up the receiver and dialled a number. While he waited for it to connect, he glanced at his watch. It was 11.00 a.m. and he'd done little of his morning's work.

He heard the telephone begin to ring at the other end of the line and eventually Rebecca's voice said, 'Pendle Court Farm.'

'Thought you'd be out working,' he said casually.

'What do you want?' Rebecca asked curtly.

'I wondered if you'd got my peace offering.'

'What peace offering?'

'The flowers! Did you like them?'

'My mother liked them very much.'

'And you? What about you?'

There was a pause on the end of the line as Rebecca wrestled to say the right thing. 'Yes, I thought they were very nice,' she replied eventually in an even tone. 'Is that all you rang for?'

It was Simon's turn to be silent. 'Can I see you this evening?' he asked eventually. 'Perhaps I could take you out for a couple of drinks? The village pub is quite nice.'

'No,' Rebecca said hesitantly. 'I don't think so.'

'It wouldn't hurt to meet though,' Simon suggested.

'I'm sorry. I'm rather busy at the moment.'

'Tomorrow night then?' Simon persisted.

'I'm afraid it isn't convenient.'

The phone went silent again. Rebecca felt uncomfortable. She didn't want to be the first to speak 'Are you still there?' she asked after another internal battle.

'I'll give you a ring later then,' Simon replied with as much enthusiasm as he could muster, and then hung up.

For a whole minute Rebecca stared at the receiver. She pressed the cradle and got a dialling tone. Her hand hovered over the dial and then she withdrew it, replaced the hand-piece and looked up. Garry Dealer stood patiently waiting in front of the office desk. Rebecca stood up. 'Come on then,' she said in a business-like manner. 'Let's get down to the beef unit.

'Me an' Dave can manage if you'd prefer not to bovver,' he offered.

'But I am *bovvered*,' Rebecca replied sharply.

'Sorry, I meant no offence Miss Hampstead. I just thought you seemed, well, a bit harassed with all your work an' all. It don't seem right you coming and helping us out with the vet when you have the whole farm to run, Miss.'

Rebecca smiled at him. She gave out a deep sigh and shook her head. 'Sorry Gary. I was being shitty. Bad night.' She rubbed her forehead.

Garry smiled broadly. Rebecca rarely swore and she had never had to apologise to him before.

'It's my business to be bothered, Gary. Perhaps I'll just come along this morning for a couple of hours.'

'Right'o Miss.' He beamed at her again before turning to leave.

Brian McCauley had already started inoculating the cattle when they arrived at the beef unit. David Ashton was guiding the cattle through the crush whilst McCauley injected them. David was a middle aged cattleman with a body, like a willow stalk, long, thin and pliable, against the pushing jostling cattle. A flat cap covered his bald head, and an elastic band was fixed around his spectacles to prevent them sliding off what was once a recognizable nose before it was crushed by a bull's horn. He handled cattle as expertly as any rodeo rider, he looked like a boxer and he swore like a trooper, only ever moderating his colourful language when Rebecca was around. Today, he wore his usual pair of newly pressed, blue cotton overalls zipped up to his chin.

Brian McCauley on the other hand was a chubby and ruddy faced man, with brown bushy hair and eyebrows to match. He was barely five foot in height, wore rubber leggings over his trousers, but nothing on top of his light blue, short sleeved shirt. He worked quickly and methodically with both hands, his hairy arms reaching for his tools and replacing them on a little folding picnic table which he carried as a regular part of his equipment. He was an extrovert, but nobody would have realized that if they had seen him working. He only spoke to give instructions. Rebecca stood and watched him as Garry took off his jacket.

'Are they all done, then?' he asked with a grin.

'Nearly,' David replied as he guided another steer into the cattle crush. 'Only another hundred and sixty seven to do after this one.'

'Oh good! That only leaves the outsiders for this afternoon then.'

Garry gave a mock groan. Brian McCauley worked on unperturbed. He knew there were as many cattle that grazed the fields outside as there were cattle that were kept inside.

Garry speeded the work up by taking over the task of releasing the caged animal when McCauley had finished with it. Rebecca took over McCauley's note book and wrote down each animal's ear tag number.

In the back of Rebecca's mind she had questions she wanted to ask, questions she didn't know how to broach, but which she had only gone there to resolve. She waited, biding her time until the right moment, then, as a gap appeared between the outgoing beast and a reluctant new arrival, she spoke 'I hear you were the one who called the fire brigade to the fire at Sunnybridge Farm,' she said casually.

'Ah yes,' McCauley said, straightening up and pressing his hand into the small of his back. 'Too late to do much good I'm afraid.' He placed his implements on his table and turned towards her. 'It was well alight when I spotted it. Looked as if it would have burned itself out before anybody got near. It's a good job it is well away from the grain silos.'

'You phoned in from the car did you?'

'No, no signal around here. I had to get to a land line.'

'It's quite a way to the booth in the village,' Rebecca acknowledged.

'Oh I knew that. That's why I went back to where I'd come from. It was much quicker.'

'You were on a call then?' Rebecca was surprised. 'I thought you'd been just driving by.'

'Not that night I'm afraid. I'd just left Thatch Cottage five minutes earlier. I went straight back there. I knew Simon Park would still be up and about.'

'Thatch cottage?' Rebecca's heart missed a beat. 'Simon Park?' she croaked.

Brian McCauley gave her an askance look as he picked up his syringes and examined the needles. Then he looked straight at her. 'That's right,' he said and fixed her with an inquisitive stare.

She felt the blood flush her cheeks as his eyes searched her face. She cleared her throat. 'I assume it'd be his horse then,' she delved.

'Well, considering I don't treat people I reckon you could assume that.' He continued his stare, ignoring the syringes, the men and the waiting animal.

Rebecca's cheeks went from bright pink to scarlet. Suddenly she felt uncomfortably hot. 'Nothing serious I hope.'

'If he'd called me out for nothing serious at that time of night, young lady, he'd have had the rough side of my tongue.'

It was serious then. 'What exactly was wrong with him?'

'The horse or Mr. Park?'

'You mean there was something wrong with both of them?'

'He seemed very edgy to me. Mr. Park that is! He'd been walking his horse around for hours before he could leave it to call me. While I was there he asked me to watch the animal until he'd made another call. He came back in a bit of a temper.'

'I see,' Rebecca lied. She tried to imagine what Simon was like when he was in a rage. 'What was wrong with Hassan?'

'Hassan? Oh, you mean the horse. Severe colic. Mr. Park let Freddie Hines' daughter go riding on him. She rode him till he was lathered and then she gave him a bucket of cold water to drink as soon as she got him back to the stable. It's lucky Mr. Park got back there early and knew what to do when he found the animal down. Don't think he'll let that girl near him again.'

'I wouldn't, that's for sure.' She could feel a lead weight in her stomach.

McCauley turned and started work on the next lot of cattle.

Rebecca watched that batch go through, documenting each one, and then, while the next batch was being herded in she turned to her enquiries again. 'What time did he call you out then?' she asked as if there had been no lapse of time between questions.

'He called about eleven. There was no trace of fire at the farm when I went past the first time.'

'That would be when?'

'Twelvish. Takes me time to get up and out of bed, and it's a twenty minute drive.' He paused a moment and then added, 'Say a quarter to. That would be nearer the mark.'

'I saw him out walking Hassan the following morning. He looked fine then.'

'I can't really take credit for his recovery, much as I'd like to. If he hadn't kept that horse on his feet I reckon he'd have been dead before midnight. Funny creatures, horses, you know. Not that everybody thinks walking them does them any good if they have a really bad bout of colic. Didn't do Hassan, or whatever you called him, any harm though, that's for sure. The body of opinion among the younger vets is...'

'I see,' Rebecca broke in, almost in a whisper. Suddenly the theories of veterinary practice no longer interested her. She ached inside. So Simon really couldn't come to see her on Saturday evening. She suddenly felt as if she'd been hit in the chest. The verbose vet continued to churn out the various ideas concerning twisted bowels caused by horses thrashing about on the floor in pain, but eventually, realising he had lost the attention of his audience, he turned and concentrated on his more immediate task in silence.

The remainder of the morning dragged on unbearably. Rebecca wanted to say she had to leave, but felt compelled to carry out what was left of her chore. After what seemed like an eternity, but what was in fact only three quarters of an hour, Brian McCauley's announcement that he was going to break for dinner came as a sheer relief. She stood up; a little too eagerly she thought afterwards, stretched, took a deep breath, and marched away without another word. Her mind wasn't on her work. She would get one of the other workers to take her place during the afternoon. She jumped into the jeep and sped off towards Pendle Court.

Neither was her mind on the cooked meal her mother had ready and waiting for her as she ran from the jeep and up the steps to the front door. By the time Dorothy had gone to meet her, Rebecca had already gone into the office and shut the door behind her. Dorothy shrugged. It wasn't usual for either Rebecca or Andrew to close the office door except when she was vacuuming.

Rebecca didn't need to look up the number as she lifted the receiver off the telephone. She dialled it. Endless seconds passed as she waited for the call to connect. Endless more seconds passed while she waited for Simon to answer her call. Seconds turned into minutes, until, finally, she resigned herself to the fact that he wasn't in. She replaced the receiver and went through to the kitchen.

'What on earth is wrong with you, young woman?' her mother asked when she saw her picking at her meal. 'Are you feeling ill or something?' She shook her head. 'If you ask me, you work too hard.'

'Oh mother! Don't go on. I only work as hard as I want to.'

'Then eat your food up or you'll have another job to do, making your own meals.'

Every hour on the hour, that afternoon, Rebecca dialled the same number, but there was no reply. Each time she dialled, she got a sinking feeling in the pit of her stomach. She knew he wasn't going to answer. In between times, she tried to turn her mind to some paperwork but with few results by the end of the afternoon. Finally, demoralized but not defeated, she went through to the lounge, informed her mother she was going out, and without waiting for a reply, went out to the garage. She opened the up-and-over door, got into her car, and started the engine. She sat there for over a minute, her hands tightly gripping the steering wheel, and her jaw clenched as she grappled to find the determination to drive away. The lump in her throat and the weakness in her legs only started to dissipate when she switched off the engine. Her pounding heart steadied as she thought through the events of the past few days. What could she say to him? She would just make a fool of herself again. She sighed in frustration and bit her lip to prevent the bubble of despair welling up from inside her and erupting as a sob. The dull ache was back in her stomach. She couldn't face him and tell him she was wrong again. She'd boxed herself into a corner and would just have to wait until he called her once more.

She hoped he would call again.

CHAPTER THIRTEEN

It was on her way back to the house that she noticed another car in the yard. She hadn't heard it arrive and a man was already on his way from it to the door of the house. As he turned towards her, she wondered where she had seen him before. As his eyes met Rebecca's, he smiled, and touched the brim of his royal blue trilby hat. He wore an overcoat of the same colour and thick, charcoal grey trousers that lapped onto a pair of shiny black shoes. 'Good afternoon. Would I be right in thinking that Mrs. Henson lives here?' He had an accent, not strong, but definitely Welsh.

Rebecca looked hard at his face. He was looking for her mother. 'I'm trying to locate Mrs. Henson,' he said as if Rebecca hadn't heard him the first time.

Rebecca walked up the steps past him and opened the house door. 'Who shall I say is calling?'

The man's smile disappeared like turning off a tap. 'Stubbs,' he said quickly, almost with a dismissive tone. Rebecca didn't like the cursory reply. Probably thinks I'm the stable girl or something, she thought, realizing she still had her working overalls on.

'Business is it?'

'That's right.'

'Have you known my mother long?' Rebecca watched for a reaction.

'Your mother? Ah, then you'd be...er...' He tried to remember the name of Billy Henson's little girl.

'Her daughter.'

The man managed a lopsided smile. 'Perhaps I should explain.'

About time, Rebecca just stopped herself from saying aloud.

'I'm a police officer. Chief Inspector. I was acquainted with your mother some years ago.'

How long since he knew her? Before my father's death, she thought, that's for sure...'Oh, eight years ago,' she stated.

'Yes.'

'I see. If you'll step inside.' She showed him into the office. 'Would you take a seat? I'll see if I can find her.' She turned and left him to pull up his own chair. She knew who he was now. She had been eleven years old at the time, but she should have remembered. The trouble was, he looked different somehow. He'd been a tall and dark haired plain clothed policeman. A detective inspector, that's it. But he wasn't like that now. He was still tall of course, and his eyes were still a dark grey colour. But his face was fatter now; he wore expensive looking clothes, and an even more expensive looking sun tan. His black hair was silver at the temples and yet, all in all, he didn't look a day older; just different. Top rank obviously agreed with him.

Dorothy was clearing up in the kitchen when Rebecca walked in. 'Mum, there's somebody here to see you,' she announced, unsure what her mother's reaction would be.

'Oh, who is it?' she asked and turned from the sink. She rubbed her hands on her pinafore and then brushed it straight again with the palms of her hands.

'Do you remember a policeman called Stubbs?'

Dorothy looked shaken. The colour drained from her face and she grabbed the back of a kitchen chair to steady herself. 'Stubbs,' she whispered. 'Inspector Stubbs?'

Rebecca nodded. 'Only he's a Chief Inspector now, apparently,' she stated and took hold of her mother's arm to help reassure her. 'I've shown him into the office. Come, I'll stay with you.'

'No!' Dorothy snapped. 'No,' she said again, more calmly. 'I'll see him alone if that's all right.' She straightened up and let go of the chair. She shrugged Rebecca's hand away, took a deep breath as if about to plunge into a bath of cold water, and paced out of the kitchen.

Stubbs had removed his hat, placed it on top of the computer monitor and was standing with his back to the door when Dorothy entered the room. He turned as she entered. She closed the door behind her and clenched the handle firmly leaning against it for support. Stubbs smiled a crooked smile. 'Mrs. Henson,' he greeted. 'How do you do?'

'Hampstead now. My name is Hampstead.'

'Ah! Right,' he said, his smile fading. 'Mrs. Hampstead. How are you?'

'What do you want?' she said, ignoring his greeting.

'Mrs. Hampstead,' he began, picking his words carefully. 'It isn't at all easy opening old wounds is it?'

'What makes you say that? What wounds are you talking about?'

Stubbs leaned over the desk towards Dorothy. 'Well, it isn't easy to talk about things that upset you in the past...'

'Oh, something's upset you, has it?'

Stubbs managed a smile. 'I am actually talking about your husband, Mrs. Hen...er Hampstead. Is there a Mr. Hampstead?'

'Yes.'

'You've remarried then?'

'No. It's my maiden name. As I have explained to your other police officer, he's my brother.'

'Yes, I see now.' He glanced around the office. 'Nice place this,' he said with a gesture of his left hand. 'Your brother's, this then?'

'Don't you talk to your men?'

'Ah, well I've not really had time to get the full details. I only just got in from my old patch this morning.'

'Been transferred have you?'

'No, no it's just a temporary posting pending a few enquiries, Mrs. Hampstead.'

'I'm sure you're going to tell me what those enquiries are.'

Stubbs shuffled some papers to one side on the desk and sat on the edge of it. 'That's what I was talking about when I mentioned opening old wounds. It's about the man who rented the cottage off you.'

'What cottage?' Dorothy's mind flashed to Sunnybridge Farm.

'Your Welsh cottage, Cil Cwm Farm, Mrs. Hampstead.'

'Oh, that cottage. You weren't too sure it was rented as far as I can remember. Reckoned my Billy was part of it, isn't that it?' she said, bitterness creeping into her voice from the controlled calm she had fought to hold.

'Well new evidence seems to have emerged, Mrs. Hampstead; evidence that could help to clear your husband's name.'

'Really?' Her voice was calm again. 'That's something else you didn't seem too bothered about either, clearing my husband's name. What makes it worth your while now?'

'We have a job to do, Mrs. Hampstead. We don't admit it's easy. In fact, at times, it's absolutely impossible.'

'And mistakes are made, is that what you are saying?'

'And, in anything where human error is possible, mistakes can be made.'

'Not by you though,' Dorothy said cuttingly.

'Perhaps we can find that out. All I need is the answers to a few questions.'

'And then, if you have made a mistake, you can sweep it under the carpet. You seemed to be good at sweeping the facts under the carpet from what I can remember. Like the fact that my husband went to the farm that day because of his cattle.'

'Mrs. Hampstead. That's not a very fair thing to say.'

'Not a fair thing for you to do either, if you ask me.'

'Perhaps if I can convince you I'm on your side and want to help you, you'd not be so hostile towards me.'

'Huh, and just how do you propose to do that?'

Stubbs put his hand in his pocket and took out his wallet. He opened it and slid out a photograph. 'This man,' he said, and handed it to Dorothy. 'Do you recognise him?'

'That's Creedy,' Dorothy said without any hesitation.

'The man who rented your cottage?'

'Yes.'

'He's dead.'

'Good,' she said harshly, tossing the photograph onto the desk.

'He died in the fire at Sunnybridge Farm.'

'What! No, he couldn't have,' Dorothy gasped.

'He could and he did. That's why I've been called in after all this time. He'd only just finished doing his sentence for his part in that drugs business and where does he turn up? A bit of a coincidence, wouldn't you say?' He smiled coldly as he retrieved the picture and placed it back in his wallet.

'So what do you want from me?' Dorothy said aggressively, sensing that he was trying to back her into a corner.

'I want to know what he was doing here, Mrs. Hampstead.'

'Well if he's dead, it's a bit late to ask him, I'd say,' she said evasively. 'You still haven't said how you want to help me.'

'He must have been here because of you, Mrs. Hampstead. It stands to reason.'

'Your reason,' Dorothy put in.

'So who killed him?' Stubbs stared hard at the frail woman in front of him.

'His pen pal for all I know,' she snapped. 'What do you really want?'

Stubbs fought to maintain his composure. He sighed, took a deep breath and then continued. 'If I can find what he came after, I might be able to show that you had nothing to do with his death.'

Dorothy turned to open the door. 'You must think I came up the river on a bike!'

Suddenly, a hand pressed firmly on hers, preventing her from turning the handle. 'Mrs. Hampstead,' his gruff voice whispered in her ear, 'a little co-operation, that's all I'm asking of you.'

'Or you'll arrest me, a poorly old woman, for battering that big fella to death I suppose! Knowing you, you'd convince everybody I had!' She struggled to turn the door handle.

'Mrs. Hampstead. Be reasonable! It's what he came down here for that we want to find.'

'And just what was it he came for? Did you ask him that? Did he leave you a note? Perhaps he came to pay the rent he owed me. Perhaps he came to bump me off! Just what *are* we talking about Inspector Stubbs?'

Stubbs released her hand, but she didn't attempt to open the door. 'Well, I'm sure you know,' Stubbs grated. 'He was overheard to say that you had it before his...accident. Yes, accident. That's what we could call it.'

'Could?'

'If you co-operate.' His voice was menacing.

Dorothy opened the office door and went to the outer door. She unlatched it and pulled it open. 'Goodbye Inspector.' She glared at him across the passage.

'You're making a big mistake Mrs. Hampstead,' he said and shook his head sadly. 'You will have to tell me what I want to know sooner or later, you do understand, don't you?' He turned back to the desk, scooped up his hat and swept out through the office doorway. He stopped at her side, took a look along the hallway to where Rebecca was standing, and then, without another word, turned and paced out down the steps to his car.

Rebecca joined her mother at her side and, together, they watched him drive away. 'What did he want mum?' she asked putting her arm around her mother's shoulders.

Dorothy began to tremble. Her face was pale and drawn.

'What he can't have, that's for sure,' her voice quavered.

'Come on mum.' Rebecca closed the door, led her mother into the lounge and eased her into her armchair. 'I've made some coffee. You can tell me all about it.'

Dorothy looked up at Rebecca with tired eyes. The visit from Stubbs had taken more out of her than she would ever admit. She wished Andrew had been there. He was strong. 'The coffee would be fine love, but I'd rather not talk about it. I'm a little tired. Another time perhaps?'

Rebecca patted her on the shoulder. 'Right, coffee it is.' She knew her mother would probably never tell her what had been said. She never talked about what happened eight years ago, and probably never would. She knew it had something to do with that.

CHAPTER FOURTEEN

It was two long days before a dark coloured Saab pulled into the yard at Pendle Court. Rebecca glanced out of her bedroom window but in the gloom of the evening she couldn't make out either the colour of the car or the occupant that emerged from it. A firm hand lifted the heavy brass knocker on the front door and rapped it hard against the door. The sound echoed through the house. There was a sound of a door opening downstairs and then, voices broke the silence.

'Hello, could I possibly see Rebecca?'

Rebecca's heart missed a beat when she heard Simon's voice. It missed another when she heard Andrew's reply.

'I think she's gone to bed. She gets up early you know. Is it important?'

'Oh, I would rather have liked to see her if I could. My name is Simon Park. It's a social call.'

'Ah yes, I've seen you in passing.' Andrew held out his hand and Simon shook it. 'Pleased to meet you,' Andrew said plainly. 'Would you step in so that I can close the door?'

Simon stepped inside and waited until Andrew had dropped the latch. 'Becki,' Andrew called from the bottom of the stairs, 'are you awake?'

'Yes,' Rebecca answered a little too quickly.

'You have a visitor, love. Can you come down?' He turned and smiled at Simon as Rebecca shouted back her reply.

'All right. I'll be down now.' Rebecca had already pulled on her dressing gown and was standing at her door, counting the seconds before emerging from her room.

Andrew ushered Simon past the yellow roses that stood on the hall table, and into the office. 'She'll be with you in a moment,' he stated and cracked his inimitable grin. 'Are you settled in all right down at Thatch Cottage?'

'Fine,' Simon replied returning a smile. Andrew turned and left him standing in front of the desk. He could hear Rebecca's footsteps on the stairs.

She entered casually but felt stiff and awkward when she saw Simon's back. The very sight of him seemed to affect her whole metabolism. Her chest felt constricted and a drum began to pound out an irregular beat in her ears. He heard her enter the room and turned and smiled softly. It was a smile that did nothing for Rebecca's condition except to make it worse. Their eyes locked momentarily and she felt her cheeks turn pink as the heat flowed into them. She controlled her breathing and spoke. 'Hello,' she said softly. 'You just caught me before I went to bed.' The last word made her heart flutter. She knew she would have got up at midnight to receive him, but tried to be as casual as she could.

'Hello,' he replied plainly. 'I saw you go past in your car an hour ago so I thought I'd drop this in for you.' He handed her a small package. 'I know it's hard to forget that I stood you up, but I thought perhaps this would keep us on neighbourly terms.'

Hesitantly, Rebecca took the package from his hand. 'What is it?' she asked curiously. She took the package and turned it over with her fingers.

'Your birthday present.' He looked a little uncomfortable and turned to leave.

'Hang on,' Rebecca called but controlled her voice to prevent it becoming a desperate shout. 'I haven't told you that you can go yet,' she said firmly but lightly and smiled at him as he turned back towards her.

Simon chuckled. 'Well, aren't you going to open it then, and see,' he asked, nodding at the packet in the palm of her hand.

She looked down at the present and then glanced back up at Simon's face. Seeing him watching her, she quickly diverted her eyes back to the gold and red package, tied with a silver bow on top. She was still smiling. Her face wanted to break into a beam, but she felt her bottom lip quiver nervously as her lips parted to speak. 'Thanks for the flowers, by the way,' she whispered.

Simon grinned, his apprehension lifting. He watched as Rebecca carefully pulled at the ends of the bow, undid the ribbon and removed the wrapping paper. A black-spotted, silver box remained. She lifted the lid and looked inside, then took a short breath as she saw the ivory face of a bronze ornament. Carefully, she lifted out the figure.

He watched her looking at it and then she glanced up at his face. Again their eyes locked momentarily and then she glanced back at her gift. 'I should have brought it, I know...'

'Yes, well...' Rebecca broke in. 'Better late than never.'

'The *Lace Maker*,' Simon announced. Rebecca held it in front of her face and looked at the minute detail of the tiny sculpture.

'It's beautiful,' she said and placed it down on the desk. She stepped back to look at it from a distance.

'Made by Charlotte Monginot,' he explained.

'Never heard of her,' Rebecca said with a slight shrug. She smiled and looked up at him.

'She worked in Paris around the beginning of the twentieth century,' he explained, his eyes settling on hers.

'Oh, that accounts for it,' she said and quickly averted her gaze. 'Slightly before my time,' she chuckled. 'Come on.' She scooped up her gift and led the way. 'You can have my celebration gift now.'

'Better late than never,' Simon said, dryly. They both chuckled together like naughty school children. Rebecca looked straight ahead. She could feel his smile as he followed her through the hall to the kitchen where she placed the ornamental figure on the table. He watched as she searched inside a couple of cupboards before discovering what she was looking for.

'Mother never leaves things in one place more than a week,' she stated and brought out a bottle of Moet et Chandon. Simon waited until she had found the drinking glasses, and then he held out his hand for the bottle.

'I'll open it,' he said, and began to untwist the wire. He plied the cork loose and it came free with a resounding *pop*.

Rebecca held the glasses beneath the frothing liquid. 'Can't stand people who waste it,' she stated. 'You might as well give them lemonade if they want to squirt it all over people's best clothes.'

Simon grinned. 'I take it you're accustomed to champagne.'

'Only down my best clothes!' They both burst into laughter.

'Cheers,' said Rebecca radiantly. At that moment it felt as if she were dreaming.

'Happy birthday!' he said quietly and looking at her rather strangely.

They both sipped silently at the bubbly liquid. 'Not got around to having it with kippers for breakfast, then?' Simon asked and refilled their glasses.

'Ugh! Does anybody?'

'It has been known' He said softly and moved closer to her. Rebecca felt as if she were going to drown in the dark pools of his eyes, and for a moment she thought he was going to kiss her. Suddenly flustered, she blurted out, 'I like my stomach too much to even try it! Come on,' she said, and moving aside, she grabbed the bottle and pushed Simon through the doorway. 'Let's celebrate in comfort.' She guided him by his elbow into the lounge where Andrew was sitting reading *The Farmers' Weekly* and Dorothy sat knitting.

'This is Simon,' Rebecca announced as they came through the doorway. They both looked up. Andrew nodded, having met him at the door.

Dorothy looked at him through her reading glasses and gave him a friendly smile. 'Lovely flowers you sent,' she complimented. She took off the spectacles and gazed at the young guest, scowling for a moment as her eyes adjusted to the range.

'Thought somebody must have appreciated them,' he said and smiled awkwardly as their eyes met.

'They are still out there. We all like flowers,' she said, her voice suddenly sharp. An uneasy silence followed for a few seconds while Dorothy and Simon looked at each other, and then Rebecca spoke.

'Would you like a glass of bubbly, mum? We're celebrating'

'No thank you.' The reply was brief and to the point. She put on her reading glasses and finished off the last few stitches of a row of knitting. Rebecca shrugged. She looked up at Simon's face. She could tell he felt awkward too. Perhaps introducing him to her mother hadn't been such a good idea after all.

'I must get to bed now,' Dorothy announced. She packed up her knitting and brushed past Rebecca and Simon. 'Good night,' she said and disappeared up the stairs.

'Mother!' Rebecca gasped. She turned to Andrew hoping that he would help her cover her mother's behaviour. 'What about you?' she asked her uncle and proffered her glass.

'No thanks Becki love. I'll give it a miss tonight and let you have a bit of peace and quiet.' He stood up, put down his magazine, and prepared to follow the path taken by his sister, only first, he kissed his niece on the cheek, and then held out his hand to Simon. Simon took the hand and shook it warmly. 'It's nice to have finally met you,' Andrew grinned. 'Perhaps you will call again.'

'Yes,' Simon agreed.

'Got to get to bed early, otherwise Becki will have done all the work before I get up,' Andrew joked. He patted Simon on the back before finally leaving.

'Mum's always a bit abrupt with strangers,' Rebecca lied to excuse her mother's behaviour.

'No need to explain. I forgot you were all early risers. I work the opposite way round.'

'Never mind, it gives us chance to finish off the champagne together,' Rebecca remarked and walked over to the sofa thinking he would follow her.

Simon finished off his glass. 'Better make it another day, I think.' and handed the empty glass to Rebecca who had turned to face him. 'Thanks all the same. I didn't mean to upset your routine.'

'Oh that doesn't matter,' Rebecca began to say, but Simon had already turned back into the hallway and was well past the flowers on the hall table when Rebecca caught up with him. She was bewildered. Everything had seemed wonderful a few moments ago. She could not understand what had happened.

'I'd better be getting along,' Simon said as he unlatched the door and pulled it open. The cold night air wafted inside, making Rebecca pull her arms in close to her breast. 'Good night,' he said, before descending the stone steps.

'Good night,' Rebecca said after him, desperately thinking of something to say that would make him stay a little longer. But it was no use. His manner was as cool as the night air. It was so unexpected. She had thought he would *want* to stay. In fact, a moment ago she could have sworn he had wanted to kiss her. She had almost longed for him to kiss her.

'Thanks for the present,' she called across the gravel, her voice beginning to break up. 'It's lovely.'

Simon smiled from the distance. 'You're welcome.' He sank into his car, started the engine and gave her quick wave from the open window before switching on his headlights and accelerating out of the yard.

Devastated, Rebecca watched after the beams of light until all traces of them had disappeared, then, with a deep sigh and a shiver, she went back into warmth of the house. She tidied away the champagne and the drinking glasses, and then sat in the room by herself, curled up on the corner of the sofa. She was totally confused. They had been getting on so well before she introduced Simon to her mother. She couldn't understand why, after all her mother had said to encourage her to make up with Simon, she had suddenly been so cold and unwelcoming to him. She had taken a great deal of her time to arrange the yellow roses in an attempt to bring Rebecca around, and yet couldn't spare five minutes for a celebratory drink with them when finally they had made friends. It just didn't make sense. And Simon! Well he was as bad! He'd said he wanted to remain neighbourly, but he must have meant more than that. He *must* have! She had received him in as friendly a spirit as possible. Too friendly perhaps? Maybe she had been mistaken about the feelings she had sensed between them when they were alone together earlier. Perhaps she had read signals that weren't there and had made a fool of herself yet again.

Finally, feeling the tendrils of sleep begin to clutch at her, she got up and went to the kitchen, picked up the ornament, switched off the light and went upstairs. She lay on her bed, the gift held tightly in her hand, and mulled over what had gone wrong. Again and again she replayed the events of the evening in her mind. 'But nothing did go wrong,' she said aloud to the blackness of the ceiling. 'Nothing did go wrong!'

Yet the evening finished before it had got started. He never even asked if he could see her again. His manner had cooled like a sudden ice age, his face even, seemed to lack the warmth it had held when she opened his present. And it all started when she introduced him to her mother. But her mother's rudeness couldn't have been solely to blame. The more she thought about it, the more she came to the conclusion that, instead of a growing bond of warmth and affection all that developed between them was a sure and inexorable glacial chasm.

CHAPTER FIFTEEN

'Come in Arthur,' Simon greeted in a business-like manner. The serious look on his face masked any pleasure at seeing an old friend. He shook hands vigorously with the man at the door and then stepped back along the narrow passageway and led to his lounge. His visitor closed the outside door behind him and silently dogged Simon's heels. 'Here, let me take your coat.'

'Thank you.' While Simon hung the coat in the hallway, Arthur took his first look around the lounge. It had a warm comfortable look to it, characteristic of Simon's tastes, he thought. The evening sun illuminated the left hand wall against which stood a small bureau bookcase with several hardback novels by Simon Park among a selection of other books, and three ornamental figures. He glanced at the two old oak beams that supported the ceiling and a dozen or so horse brasses that were pinned on them, and nodded his approval. As he stepped past the plain blue sofa and matching armchair which practically filled the whole room his gaze fell upon couple of paintings adorning the right hand internal wall, and a photograph of a young woman which hung next to the mullioned window. He studied the photograph for several moments, trying to recall who she was until, eventually, his concentration was broken as his friend entered the room.

'I was just about to have a drink' Simon stated, bending his tall frame to avoid banging his head on the oak beam. 'Will you join me?'

'I try not to drink and drive, you know that.' Arthur's eyes followed Simon as he went over to a tray of glasses which seemed to have been strategically placed on top of a small pie-crust table.

'It's been a long time,' Simon said, 'things could have changed,'

'Could they?'

'It would have been a change if you'd asked for a large one,' Simon stated, his lips curling at the edges just enough to reveal the humour that was absent from his voice.

Arthur just smiled a rare smile back. That, from his old friend, was, in itself, acknowledgement enough. 'I'll just have lemonade.'

Simon waved him over to the sofa, where he settled, with a look of satisfaction, amongst an array of comfortable coloured cushions, whilst Simon poured some drinks, handed a glass to Arthur and took up his position facing him from the old, well worn, but comfortable arm chair. He crossed his legs and stared into a pair of penetrating eyes and waited for Arthur to speak. 'Thought it was all dead and buried,' Arthur stated eventually.

'So did I until I saw the newspapers four weeks ago,' Simon said in a similar monotone. They looked at each other, a silence of uncertainty falling between two friends who hadn't met for years.

'So,' Simon said to break the uneasy silence, 'what progress have you made?'

'Very little,' Arthur answered, examining his glass intently.

'By that I presume you aren't going to tell me.'

Arthur lifted his head and looked hard at Simon. 'I mean very little,' he insisted indignantly.

'You don't know who killed Prosser then?' Simon asked uneasily. If Arthur was here to discuss Prosser then the least he could do was stimulate the conversation.

'You said you read all about that in the newspaper,' said Arthur, still holding his gaze.

'All I read was that Prosser was killed within hours of his release.'

Arthur took another sip from his glass. 'That's quite true. He was.'

'Eight years in jail and then bumped off as soon as he gets out,' Simon exclaimed. He shook his head at the incredulity of his own statement. 'I thought you might know who.'

Arthur deliberated before answering, and after a long silence he said, 'I'm not sure.'

'How then? Can you tell me that?'

'By an expert; knifed from behind. The blade was skilfully placed between the ribs, straight up through the left ventricle.

'Simon pondered for a moment. 'Creedy?' he suggested eventually.

'Good heavens no!' exclaimed Arthur seemingly amused.

'He'd be my first suspect,' said Simon, puzzled by Arthur's confidence.

'Mine too,' Arthur agreed, waving his hand, 'but it just wasn't his style.'

'Style? I didn't know he had a style,' Simon replied even more surprised.

'Don't fool yourself. Creedy wasn't just a small time crook that got caught handling drugs. He was a professional.'

'Yes, I know that much,' said Simon, suddenly feeling that the conversation was leading nowhere.

'He paid other people to do his dirty work,' Arthur stated and held out his glass.

Simon stood up. 'Another drink, Arthur?'

'I'm fine thanks.' Simon took the glass and placed it on the table while he topped up his own and then stood for a while, looking out at the back garden. It looked bare now that winter was on its way. The deciduous trees were beginning to defoliate, and the roses were all finished for the year. I'll have to start pruning soon, he thought, his mind not really on what Arthur wanted to discuss. He had tired of it eight years ago, and now, it had raised its head again in more than one quarter, just when he'd least expected it, and, more importantly, just when he least wanted it. Finally, after wishing that the whole affair had remained dead and buried, he sighed, turned and stood in the middle of the room.

'Well?' he said eventually, hoping that Arthur would realize that his voice showed a complete lack of interest.

'What I'm getting at,' Arthur began, 'is that your article all those years ago...'

'Eight,' Simon interrupted and rubbed his eye with bored indifference.

'Your article eight years ago,' Arthur fought on, 'only made a broad assessment of the situation. There was nothing specific in it at all.'

'I could only write the facts as I knew them then.' Simon shrugged his shoulders. 'Anyway, you didn't believe me.'

Arthur grinned. 'Ah, that's where you're wrong. I did believe you. The trouble was you had been proved a liar.'

'Not proved Arthur,' Simon said, anger rising in his throat.

'Well, you know what I mean,' Arthur said with a conciliatory wave of his hand.

'What I do know is that I did a lot of work on that job. All wasted. One man's word against mine and that was enough to discredit all the information I had gathered.'

'I agree Simon.'

'Well if I was telling the truth, what does that make him?' he growled.

'Look, Simon,' Arthur tried to explain; 'you were a discredited witness. All you could say is what somebody else had told you, and he was dead. It wasn't enough to arrest and hold an arch villain, especially when the police refuted your story.'

'What about the story Prosser gave me when I interviewed him in prison?'

'Hearsay again Simon. He denied telling you anything when I questioned him. For all anyone knows, you could have made that story up as well.'

Simon sat down heavily in the arm chair. His anger was growing. 'But that's why I contacted you in the first place, Arthur.'

'I know, but I wasn't involved in the case. I had no portfolio to just walk in and take over the investigation.'

'The facts were there Arthur, but nobody seemed to be taking a blind bit of notice of them. I notified the local police about the drugs deal and they didn't net the place until half the people had left. I told them what Henson had said to me, but I was called a liar. How was I to know he'd kill himself? How was I to know Prosser would bottle up after he told me his story?'

'Prosser was afraid, Simon, you have to understand that. He was afraid of whoever it was who got him in the end.'

'His silence didn't do him much good then, did it?'

'That's why, at first, I did suspect Creedy of killing him,' Arthur stated. 'He or somebody must have put pressure on Prosser to keep him quiet. If Creedy was afraid of what he might say then, he had good reason to silence Prosser when he was released, especially if Prosser was going to tell everybody that another deal was going to go down later on that day when they were arrested.'

'If you believed what I told you.'

'There's a marked difference between believing and proving.'

'There's even more difference between *knowing* and proving.'

'Exactly! And I know Creedy didn't kill Prosser,' Arthur said waving his finger in emphasis.

'Then who did?' Simon asked as he raised his glass to his lips.

'The same person who killed Creedy.' Arthur's dark eyes watched the reaction on his friend's face. Simon's head jerked up. Now his friend had stimulated his interest.

'Am I hearing you right Arthur? Creedy's dead?'

A rare smile fluttered across Arthur's lips before disappearing into his mask again. 'It has happened on your own doorstep as well.' Arthur shook his head. 'Tut tut, Simon.'

'Where exactly do you mean?' Simon asked impatiently, leaning forward now that his interest had been tweaked.

'Sunnybridge Farm of course.'

Simon looked startled. 'Next door! In the fire you mean? He was in the fire?'

'I believe he was.'

'Murdered?' asked Simon, his face unable to hide his astonishment.

'I believe so,' Arthur nodded.

'Believing is not proving. We have just established that.'

'Quite!'

Simon stood up and paced the length of his room while Arthur's eyes tracked him. So his friend was here because of the fire, not because of Prosser. Now *that* was unexpected. He stopped and turned to Arthur. 'So, who do you suspect?'

'You have a good alibi for the night of the fire, but it could still have been you.'

'Me!' Simon gasped.

'He *was* after you, wasn't he?'

'No.' The answer was emphatic. Simon put his glass down on a side table beneath the framed photograph of the young woman, and then stepped to the middle of the room. He waited for Arthur to speak.

'No? You seem sure of that. You've just heard about him this very minute, and yet you have no doubts why he was here. You know something, Simon, you answered too quickly.'

'What I said, Arthur is that he wasn't after me, plain and simple. I doubt if he ever knew I was here. You didn't until the local copper called in the course of your enquiries, yesterday.'

'Bit of a surprise, I must admit.'

'Now I know why you really called,' Simon said with a hint of sadness in his voice and nodding that he understood now. 'I bet you called me as soon as he told you. I thought for a while that it was because of the old days. Remember them do you?' A note of bitterness crept into his voice. He turned and looked out of the window. The old days. Simon remembered them. He remembered the friendly little policeman who found the seven year old boy who was crying and alone, and took him back to his father and mother, a boy who had run away from home, determined to make his own way in the world, a boy whose big sister had been killed by drugs because of the indifference of her wealthy parents to the real needs of their children. They only had time for their social lives. Even after the loss of their daughter, they still carried on the same regardless and self-interested way. It was only the policeman who had drummed into Simon the necessity of his accepting life as it was until he was big enough and old enough to do anything about it. Take what they have to offer, he had said. Use it to your own advantage. Then, it had been Arthur who had been his closest friend, writing to him occasionally, and even visiting him at boarding school. It was to Arthur that Simon turned when he needed somebody to talk to, and it was to Arthur he had turned, years later, when he needed somebody to help expose the truth in what was later called the Welsh Drugs Affair. But Arthur had changed. So had he. There was no turning the clock back now.

'After the initial surprise, it all began to fit,' said Arthur.

'Fit! What the hell do you mean?' Simon swung around to face him.

Once again Arthur carried on, oblivious of Simon's protestations. 'Why would he be squatting in an empty farmhouse next door to you, I asked myself?'

'Coincidence,' Simon dismissed the question with a wave of his hand.

'I can't really believe it was just coincidence,' Arthur said as if Simon hadn't spoken.

'Don't you think you're scraping the barrel suspecting me Arthur?'

'Not at all,' Arthur replied, finally conceding it was a two way conversation. 'We go back a long way, but calling it a coincidence is stretching things a bit far isn't it? Coincidences like that are few and far between. It isn't such a small world as people would have us believe.'

Simon could hardly believe his ears. Was this really his old friend speaking? 'Isn't it?' Simon rasped, glaring at Arthur. His voice was raised. 'You don't know the half of it.'

'Oh?' Arthur's tone was still flat. 'I suppose you will tell me the rest then.'

'How long is it since you had anything to do with that affair?'

'You said it yourself, eight years.'

Simon laughed coldly. 'Well in eight years things have changed so much that even I can't believe it,' he said and turned away again towards the window.

'I'm sure you're going to tell me what *it* is.'

'As you said, my article only made broad assertions,' Simon replied, turning back to the tranquil and calming view outside the window. 'There was nothing specific and it was just as well since obviously there is still something I don't know.'

'No use asking you what that is then,' stated Arthur blandly.

'If Creedy was at Sunnybridge Farm, then he wasn't after me.'

'If he knew Prosser had spoken to you, then he would want both of you dead. It stands to reason,' argued Arthur.

'But *he* didn't kill Prosser, you said so yourself.'

'I don't believe he did, no.'

'And you couldn't think I killed Prosser.'

'Not a lot of motive there, I must confess.'

Simon thought for a moment. 'What about the Hampsteads?' he asked casually, and then added, 'He was on their land.'

'I've looked at that possibility.'

'And?'

'And Andrew Hampstead knew how to use a knife. I do know that much. I've looked into his background and discovered he was a crack commando as a young man. But he seems unconnected. Creedy was squatting at the farm. I don't believe Andrew Hampstead knew anything about his being there. I just don't see any connection. Can you?'

Simon's brow furrowed into a deep frown. After a long silence, he answered. 'No,' he lied. 'But are you sure it was Creedy at the farm?'

'As sure as I can be. Very little to go on though.'

'There has got to be more to it than Creedy wanting Prosser dead to prevent him telling what he had already told me,' Simon insisted, trying to list the facts clearly in his mind. 'Somebody must have thought Creedy was just as dangerous to be alive as Prosser. Somebody connected with that other deal perhaps; that other deal,' Simon emphasised, 'not connected with exchange of drugs for money.'

'Perhaps,' Arthur conceded.

'Or somebody else found out about that other transaction.' Simon gave Arthur a knowing glance.

'I know what you mean,' Arthur replied and then stood up. 'But believing isn't proving, is it?' He walked into the hallway and collected his coat. Something told Simon that his old friend was holding back on him. He couldn't be sure if he really did suspect him. He followed him out of the room and held his coat for him while he slid his arms into it. They both walked to the door. 'By the way, Simon,' Arthur turned and asked, 'what brought you here?'

'That's the coincidence I was talking about,' Simon replied evasively. He leaned forward and opened the door.

Arthur stepped outside and looked around 'I see,' he said and walked to his car. He ducked into the driving seat and slammed the car door.

'You'll keep in touch, won't you,' Simon called after him. There was a mark of sarcasm in his voice.

'Oh yes!' said Arthur, with an imperceptible movement of his lips. He wound down the window and started the engine. Simon thought he could see a smile behind the deep eye sockets of the inspector. 'And if you have anything you'd like to tell me,' Arthur called, as the car pulled away, 'you'll be able to locate me at *The Windsurfer*.'

He knows more than he's letting on, that's for sure, thought Simon as he watched him drive away. Arthur Greythorpe always did play his cards close to his chest.

CHAPTER SIXTEEN

In the three days after Simon's visit, Rebecca drove along the road near Thatch Cottage a dozen times, hoping that she would 'accidentally' meet him, but he was nowhere to be seen. She felt empty inside. She ached and her mother was to blame. It had to be her mother's unreasonable behaviour that had made Simon leave, and until an explanation was forthcoming, she felt no compunction to speak to or even be in the same room as her.

To Dorothy these three days had been unbearable. She hated making her daughter unhappy. She hadn't wanted to explain her reaction when she'd seen Simon, but now she had decided that enough was enough. Rebecca was hurting, and what her mother was going to tell her would only compound the injury. But there was no alternative now. She had to tell her daughter who Simon Park the novelist really was. Rebecca had to know the truth and now was the best time to face her with it; in the evening; in her bedroom; no interruptions; no phone calls; no workers popping their heads around the office door and asking for a word with the boss. A quiet motherly chat would put things straight, and then all would be well again between them. She knocked lightly on the door.

'Yes,' said Rebecca faintly.

Dorothy opened the door and stepped inside the bedroom. Rebecca looked up to see who was coming in, and then, seeing her mother, turned her head away abruptly and gazed resolutely at *The Lace Maker* which she had positioned beside the bronze Shetland pony, nearest her pillow. 'Darling, we've got to talk,' Dorothy said trying to get Rebecca to acknowledge her, but Rebecca stiffened and fixed her stare even more firmly on her ornaments. 'Believe me love, I don't want to make you unhappy.' She stepped over and sat beside Rebecca.

'Then tell me why you acted like you did.' Rebecca glared indignantly at her mother.

'He's no good for you, no good at all.'

'Oh, you're suddenly an expert are you?' Rebecca said bitterly, her chin stiffly emphasising her cold hard stare. 'It wasn't so long ago that you couldn't wait for me to get back on friendly terms with him. And when I did, what happened!' She stood up and moved away from the bed angrily.

'Darling, I do know something about men. He's a bad lot, believe me.'

'Mother! You couldn't tell a bad lot if it were labelled and stuck on your nose!'

'I can tell when a man's no good,' Dorothy protested, desperately trying to avert a full blown row.

'That's why you married a weak, spineless man is it?' Rebecca stabbed. 'A man who killed himself and left us both alone in the middle of nowhere.' As soon as she had said it she hated herself for the pain it had inflicted. A cloud seemed to pass over her mother's weary face, but Rebecca had already said it and even now, she felt compelled to stand by what she had said.

Dorothy's bottom lip began to tremble. The wound had gone deep. Tears filled her eyes. She blinked and cleared them away, only to have them fill her throat. 'Your father loved us both very much.' she choked with emotion.

'Well I hate him!' Rebecca grated.

'Well I still love him. He was a good man and...' She broke off and bit on her lip to stem her emotions.

'And that's why you want me to be unhappy is it? Because I don't like him for what he did.'

'You aren't giving me a chance,' Dorothy said, stifling her tears. She fluffed a tissue out of the top of a square pink box that stood behind Rebecca's ornaments. After wiping her eyes, she continued against Rebecca's stony glare. 'You know nothing about your father, or what happened to him.'

'I saw him. Remember mother?' Rebecca shouted, 'I was with you.' She turned away, and picking up a brush from the dressing table that stood in the corner of the room, she began to brush her hair furiously.

'You saw him dead. That's all you saw.' Dorothy's voice became bitter. 'You never once looked at his good side did you? Well I'll tell you something. Your father might not have been the most successful farmer in the world. He might not have really been suited to anything but working for somebody else, but he worked hard to keep us both.' Dorothy took another paper tissue from the box and dabbed her eyes.

Rebecca had turned and was staring at her silently. She was confused. She was aching with years of pent up emotion. Deep down inside her she knew she hadn't hated her father, but her despair had only flowed out of her as revulsion. It was the only way she could cope with the memory of seeing the way he died. To continue to love him would have killed her for sure. Somebody was to blame and he fitted the part. Who else was there?

'No father ever loved a child more than he loved you, you should know that,' Dorothy continued. 'And nobody loved a father more than you loved him. You did everything and went everywhere with him.'

Rebecca turned her head away. She didn't want to hear it. 'I'm not interested in being psycho-analysed, mother' she said angrily, banging the hair brush down on the window sill.

Dorothy stood up and went over to her daughter. 'Do you remember,' she said softly as she took hold of Rebecca's hand and squeezed it gently, 'when he used to bring us here on holiday?'

For a moment Rebecca froze, and then, after an internal struggle, she responded and squeezed on her mother's slender fingers. She nodded, bowed her head and sniffled as tears filled her eyes. 'Yes. I remember,' she choked.

'He used to rent the farmhouse out for three weeks in the summer, and come over here to drive the combine for your Uncle Andrew.'

Rebecca nodded. She remembered him saying that renting the house out for three weeks paid better than farming for three months. At the same time, he would earn good wages combining grain for Andrew and give his family a holiday into the bargain. Rebecca would ride in the cab with him all day, stopping only when her mother had brought out flasks of tea and cartons of sandwiches to keep them going until darkness fell. They were long hard days, but she had loved every second of them. And after the harvest they would stay an extra week or two. When she wasn't out riding her Shetland pony, she'd be helping her father as he worked on repairing the machinery ready to be stored away until the following year. Those happy times had been forced to the back of her mind. She had tried never to think of them. The pain would have been too great. 'So what went wrong mum?' she sobbed. She clenched hard at her mother's hand.

'Everything love.' Dorothy frowned and sucked in a deep breath. She slapped her knee with her free hand in a gesture of complete frustration. 'Everything!' she groaned and stared into her daughter's eyes. Rebecca could see her own pain reflected in her mother's eyes. After all these years of pretending, Dorothy still mourned for her husband.

'I'm sorry mum,' Rebecca whispered, and put her other hand on her mother's arm, comfortingly. 'It's all right, you don't have to say any more,' she soothed.

But Dorothy was determined. It was already too late. She should have told Rebecca years ago. Now it *had* to be out in the open. The choice had been made for her. She took a couple more deep breaths, and exhaled loudly. The tears had dried up now. No need for emotion any longer. The whole thing was a matter of fact. 'Come,' she urged, leading Rebecca over to the bed. They sat down together, still holding hands and then, when she thought Rebecca was ready, she spoke. 'Those few weeks' holiday were the best part of our lives,' she started. 'The rest of the year was just hard slog.' She paused a moment to think, and then went on slowly, in her mind, re-living the past as she spoke. 'No days off, no week ends, nothing. Once a year, in the best months of summer, he'd open all the gates in between the fields, and give the cattle the run of the farm. Then we'd have a holiday. It was always after he'd done his hay making so that all the fields could be opened up for grazing.'

Rebecca nodded.

'The rent from letting the farmhouse was good money. The same man rented it in August each year for a holiday. Your dad couldn't believe his luck when he met the man in a pub. He offered him more than double what he'd have dared ask for. Paid for our Christmases that, remember?' Rebecca nodded silently, her eyes filling with hot tears again as she remembered the good times they had shared. 'Things never were as good after that, were they?' Dorothy said, looking down at the floor, with a deep, unhappy sigh.

'No.' Rebecca sniffled.

'Christmas without your dad was like...like a day without daylight!' Dorothy's voice broke, and for a moment she found it impossible to go on, as the pain of remembering became too much to contemplate.

Rebecca squeezed her lovingly. 'Don't, mum,' she pleaded.

Dorothy patted her on the hand. 'I'm all right love,' she said eventually. 'It's just that at times like that, you miss people the most'

'Yes, something has definitely been missing, hasn't it mum?' Rebecca managed a weak smile.

'Everything that meant the most to us, yes love.'

'But we got by mum. We managed didn't we? We aren't too badly off now.'

'Oh, it wasn't money!' Dorothy exclaimed, the grief beginning to dissipate from her face. She clutched Rebecca's hand again. 'We were never really poor you know.'

'It seemed like it to me,' Rebecca stated calmly. 'We always seemed to be skimping and scraping.'

'We could have been better off,' Dorothy stated emphatically.

'Then why weren't we, mother?' Rebecca exclaimed staring at her mother in disbelief. 'Why weren't we?'

Dorothy lapsed into thought before speaking again. Eventually she had sorted out in her mind what she wanted to say. 'You remember we changed our names?'

'Yes, of course!' Rebecca replied impatiently.

Dorothy frowned and thought again before speaking. 'You know, that was the hardest thing we had to do,' she reflected.

'But I remember you saying you hated his name,' Rebecca protested.

'I was lying.' She looked Rebecca straight in the eyes. 'Oh, I know I said I was ashamed of him. But it wasn't his name I was ashamed of. No, it was the stigma. First the police, then the charges, then him dying like he did, then... Oh well, I changed our names because *I* wanted to forget. *I* wanted to put what had happened behind me. But it isn't as easy as just changing a name. I found that out. Everyone for miles around knew what had happened. They all knew better than me to hear them talk. Not that they ever talked to me about it. It all came back to me as gossip six months, a year, two years later. They were still talking amongst themselves about it when we left! I ought to have known they would never let the matter drop.' She lowered her voice again and spoke almost as if talking to herself. 'It was in their eyes when we walked past them in the streets. Oh yes, *they* knew for sure what had happened. No doubts in their minds who it was that was guilty.'

'Guilty?' Rebecca cut into her thoughts. 'What had dad done?'

Dorothy sighed again. 'It's such a complicated story love. And I'm not sure I understand it myself.'

'Try mum.' Rebecca urged, gently stroking the silken skin of her mother's hand. 'Tell me what happened mum. Please?' But Dorothy needed no prompting. She had already braced herself to carry on.

'Well, you know about the holidays.'

'Yes.'

'And the man renting the cottage.'

'Yes.'

'His name, do you remember his name?'

Rebecca frowned. 'No, I don't think I ever knew it.'

'The man was called...' She paused and sucked in a breath. 'His name was Creedy.' Dorothy waited until she thought the name was thoroughly etched on Rebecca's mind.

'Go on mum,' she urged gently.

Dorothy's voice faded slightly as she recalled him to mind. 'He didn't seem such a bad man, I thought. He always paid his rent up front and he was always polite and never short of a humorous word. Always telling jokes, he was. And he was clean and tidy. He never spoilt or broke anything while he was there; left it as he found it. I used to give the place a good going over before going away of course, but it was always as if nothing had been taken out of its place when we returned. And spotless! Well I cleaned the place before we left and it would be spotless when we got back.

In fact I sometimes wondered if he hadn't been around with a duster and polish again for us! It really was pleasant dealing with him. He even assured us he would give us a ring if the cattle got out, not that he ever had to. Your father's fencing was first class.'

Rebecca huffed. 'Few and far between, holiday makers like that!'

'Like him? Very few and far between!'

Rebecca noticed a satirical note as her mother's voice became louder. 'What do you mean?'

'He wasn't exactly what we thought he was that's what.'

'But what did you think he was?'

'A holiday maker of course! That's what he told your dad when they met. That's what we believed. He'd come for three weeks' holiday from the hustle and bustle of the city. Walking in the countryside; fly-fishing on the river. He had a rod you know?'

'Did he?'

'Oh yes. Said he was a real fishing enthusiast,' she said, sarcasm ringing in her voice.

'Should have suited him then,' Rebecca commented wryly.

'That's what we thought, until...' She stopped and glared angrily at the wall. She closed her lips tightly and exhaled hard and angrily through her nostrils.

'Until?' Rebecca prompted.

'Until...Until that last summer. You remember that summer? It was hot, very hot.'

'Yes, I remember. We were over here and Dad was worried that the springs had dried up in the fields so he drove all the way home to open up the fence into the woods so that the cattle could get down to the river.'

'That's right love, that's exactly what happened. We were over here, but the rain that had been forecast never came. Your dad was worrying himself silly about the cattle, so I told him he'd best go home and check them. He should have been back the same day.'

'He wasn't though.'

'No, he was in jail,' her mother said vehemently, 'in a bloody awful police cell with a load of criminals. That's where he was.' Dorothy was almost shouting.

Rebecca's eyes showed disbelief. She had never known that. She had never heard her mother swear either and stared at her incredulously. 'But...but why? You told me he had never done anything wrong in his life,' she gasped.

'He didn't. But he got put in jail all the same, and for what? For going back to check his cattle, that's what.' Dorothy's face was becoming flushed with anger.

'But why mum? None of this makes any sense.'

'Not yet it doesn't love,' Dorothy said, trying to bring her rage under control. 'But I haven't told you what that man Creedy was really up to. A holiday maker!' She raised her voice again. 'Huh! I reckon he had his holidays in the Bahamas, not on a piddling little Welsh farm!'

'What was he doing there then?'

Dorothy released her hand from Rebecca's and clasped her palms together between her knees. 'He was a crook,' she said flatly.

'He was a crook?' Rebecca could hear her voice parroting the words as she watched her mother's lips go tight with contempt.

'That's what I said. A crook. A crooked malicious evil one at that! He used us and he used our house to transact his crooked, evil deals.'

'Deals?' mimed Rebecca.

'Drugs,' Dorothy stated.

'Drugs?' Rebecca parroted again.

'Drugs,' Dorothy nodded. 'Each year he'd rent our farmhouse on the pretext of having a holiday and wait for a delivery of drugs. Heroin it was.'

'But why rent our place? I can't see the sense in that. A back alley would do just as well.'

'I couldn't see the point either. Not until the police explained it. The drugs were being brought in from ships off the coast of Wales. Men in rubber power boats would go out before dusk, no fishing tackle, nothing, just wearing their wet suits. They would go out beyond the horizon where they'd meet a bigger boat, a sea going trawler or a ship of some sort.' Dorothy fluffed out another tissue and blew her nose.

'And?' Rebecca urged impatiently.

'And they'd collect the package of drugs, bring it ashore after dark, and deliver it to the buyer. Seems like they insisted on the big city men coming out to them.'

'But weren't there any customs boats about?'

'From what I've heard, there aren't more than half a dozen to patrol the whole of the coast of Britain,' Dorothy said raggedly. 'The smugglers must have each one pinpointed!'

'So, Creedy rented our place to get deliveries of heroin off them. I see. But why rent the place for three weeks. Why rent a farm at all?'

'He used to get a year's supply of drugs for his own night clubs, and on top of that he would get drugs for his other contacts, using our cottage, and possibly other cottages elsewhere, as distribution points outside the city. He was like a wholesaler. The stuff went straight there, no towns to go through, well away from any main road. It was ideal, and his being around for three weeks each year didn't look suspicious to the neighbouring farmers. They'd see him with his pipe in his mouth, wading into the river with a fly rod, or walking through the woods wearing a deer stalker. To them he was just a holidaymaker just the same as we thought he was. But he was a clever man. Very clever.'

'But what had dad got to do with it?'

'He was unfortunate enough to turn up just before the police raided the house.'

'But surely they knew he rented the farm to Creedy? Dad couldn't have known anything about it.'

'As far as the police were concerned, love, he was still technically in possession of drugs. Strict liability it's called. You don't even have to know about it. It was his farm and the stuff was found in it, plain and simple. It would be the same if somebody put some in your pocket without you knowing it. Bang! You are in possession. Strict liability!' She flicked her fingers in a derisory manner and sneered.

'It doesn't make sense.'

'It did to the police. He was arrested and charged, anyway. Open and shut case as far as the chap in charge was concerned. Your father proved his connection by being there, he said.'

'They convicted him!' Rebecca exclaimed.

'No, he was dead before they could try him. Out on bail he was, when it happened. As far as everyone was concerned, he'd proved his guilt by killing himself.'

Rebecca stood up and stared at her mother. 'No wonder you wanted to change your name! I don't suppose there was a single person within a radius of fifty miles who didn't know all about it.'

'Everybody knew! *Everybody!* I felt I could crawl away into a hole.

'But why did he do it? If he didn't have anything to do with the drugs, why did he kill himself?'

'Kill himself? Kill himself!' Dorothy growled. 'Your father never had any intention of killing himself. I know that. I know it as sure as I know birds whistle.' She lowered her voice to a barely audible pitch. 'He was murdered love. They killed him.'

'But I heard the policeman say that it was as obvious a case of suicide as he had ever seen. They couldn't have all been wrong.'

'Well I'm telling you they were wrong. The police, the doctor, the coroner. All of them!' She sighed wearily. 'But nobody would believe me. Nobody! And why? Because that one damned policeman who was in charge of the case had branded him as one of the crooks, that's why. His so-called suicide put the lid on it. Proved he was in with them, that policeman said.' Dorothy's voice became sharp and bitter. 'They were all fools. What did they know! And because of them, we were to be branded as the wife and daughter of a crook. Not many neighbours liked the idea of living next to us, I can tell you.'

'But they all knew us,' Rebecca protested. 'What was the point of changing our name?'

'Well, I suppose it helped to convince a few of them that we had nothing to do with it; *Innocently implicated* I'd reckon they'd call it. And then there was you. I thought it better not to bother your young head with the truth. You started secondary school that year and I got you in at St. Jude's at the other side of town. I knew that most of the kids wouldn't know you or connect you to the police thing or the gossip if you went there as Rebecca Hampstead. It would have only made things worse for you at school if you had gone to the same school as all the other kids from the junior school; and it wouldn't have helped if you had kept telling everyone what they didn't want to hear. It was enough to convince most of them that we were decent folk. Decent! Huh! I'd have left there straight away if I'd known.'

'Known what?'

Dorothy looked uncomfortable. 'Known? Did I say known? I meant if I'd had the chance.'

'You mean if Uncle Andrew had offered to let us move here earlier?'

'Yes, that's what I meant, love.' She patted Rebecca on her arm. 'That would have been nice, wouldn't it?'

Rebecca thought for a moment. 'Yes it would,' she nodded and smiled. Then she frowned deeply. 'You really think dad was murdered mum?'

'Yes darling, I know he was. And that's where that novelist chap came into it.'

'Simon!' Rebecca had forgotten how the conversation had started in the first place. 'What had Simon to do with it?' she asked eventually.

'Simon Park the novelist,' she stated as if reading it off the back of a book, 'is a pen name. He was an investigative journalist by the name of Simon Pears, trying to make his fame and fortune by claiming the benefit for uncovering the Creedy gang. That policeman proved him a liar.'

'Like he did dad?' Rebecca said sceptically, looking straight into Dorothy's eyes and waiting for a response to her innuendo.

For a brief moment Dorothy looked stunned, but then, regaining her composure as quickly as she lost it, she ignored Rebecca's question and went on. 'Pears said he'd tipped off the police, and he hadn't. He said he would help your dad, and within a day your dad had been murdered. And he was murdered only because of what he told Simon Pears. It was Pears who killed your dad. If your dad hadn't talked to him, he'd be alive today!' She took a hold of Rebecca's sleeve and tugged on it desperately. 'You must not let that man fool you with his clever talk. You mustn't, do you hear? He fooled us; you mustn't let him fool you.'

Rebecca was devastated. She took a sharp breath and looked in to her mother's sad and weary eyes. 'But I still don't understand mum. What had Simon got to do with Dad's death?'

Dorothy shook her head. 'It's so difficult to explain.' She said and composed her thoughts before speaking again. Rebecca gave her time, neither speaking nor urging. 'You see, he tried to make his name by claiming the credit for being the one who had tipped off the police about Creedy and his shady goings on at our farm. Only, Pears had nothing to do with it. The policeman in charge of the case had done it on his own.'

'But what about dad? What had he got to do with dad?'

'Pears came to see him after he'd been released on bail. You see, your dad got bail because our lawyer managed to convince the magistrates that he wasn't likely to run off, having a farm and a family an' all, unlike Creedy and his lackey who were well known crooks apparently. They were held in custody. Never saw light of day them! Straight to prison after the trial. Serves them right!

Blamed your dad they did. Tried to say they knew nothing about the stuff the police found in the house. Anyway, as I was saying, that Pears chap came nosing around asking questions and like a fool, I let him in when he called. Didn't know what he was then! *Can I go over what happened?* he asked. I said there wasn't much use as we'd already told the police everything. But he still insisted he might be able to help, so I called your dad in and left them to talk while I went into the kitchen to make some tea.'

'So you don't know what was said then?' Rebecca asked, noticeably irritating her mother.

'Know? Of course I know,' her mother retorted. 'You could hear everything in that house from the kitchen, you know that. Anyway, your dad discussed it with me after that man had gone.'

'And?'

'Well, that Pears chap, he asks your dad to go over what happened right from the beginning. So your dad explained that when he arrived at the farm, he had no sooner gone into the house than there was a knock on the door and the police were there. *No*, that chap says. *I want to know what you saw as you drove up the road. Were there lots of cars parked around?*

Just the one, your dad said. Then Pears asked him if anybody was in it and your dad said that there was a man in the driving seat and that he had also seen another chap coming across the fields towards the car carrying a bag.

And you mentioned this to the police' Pears asked.

*No. Why should I? They **were** the police,* your dad said. Well, it stood to reason. They were staking the place out. It must have been the police. But this Pears chap, well he got really keen on all this about a car. Did your dad remember anything about it or the driver, he asked. Well as it happens, your dad did recall something. He thought it seemed a big car for policemen to use, a silver BMW. Of course, with it being parked on the road above the farm, your dad had a good look at the driver to see if he recognised him. You know how it is in the country. See who's going up in the world, driving about in a big new car.'

'And did he recognise him?'

'That's what Pears asked. *No. Never seen him before*, he said. So this Pears chap asks him if he could describe him, which he did. Pretty good description I thought. Then he asked about the car. Well, your dad remembered the numbers of it because he'd had a car with the same letters in its number plate years ago. MNV. Only this one had a new 05 plate, of course. Didn't have dates on number plates when your dad had his old Granada estate.'

'No,' Rebecca agreed. 'So what happened then?'

'He suggested your dad ring the copper in charge and tell him what he had just told him. Could help clear him, he said. He was just leaving when I came into the room with a tray of tea and Welsh cakes. He was smiling to himself. Then, as he left, he turned and said: *Oh, by the way, it would be better if you don't tell anybody you told me about the car first.*

'Why would he say that?'

'We didn't know at the time. It seemed a little strange, but when your dad rang Stubbs about the car, he seemed a bit offish. He said he was too busy to discuss it at that particular moment because he was on his way out. But he suggested that if your dad really felt it was important he could meet him and discuss it.'

'Which he did?'

'Apparently not. Your dad went out and that was the last time I saw him alive.' Dorothy's eyes began to fill up again. 'You and I found him later that day when you came home from school.' Her voice shook and her lips trembled. Rebecca put her arm around her shoulder to comfort her. Dorothy went on. 'Stubbs said that your dad had never turned up where they'd arranged to meet. So after that, Stubbs decided that your dad had been lying and that he'd killed himself.'

'Didn't you tell them about Simon?' asked Rebecca, desperately trying to hold back her own tears.

'Well, you see, Stubbs had asked your dad on the telephone why he hadn't told anybody about the car, and your dad, remembering what Pears had asked, said he had just thought about it and thought that Stubbs should be first to know. I'd had enough of people calling your dad a liar, and after he'd been killed, I couldn't think of any reason to let them add another time to their list. I just never said anything. It wasn't till later, a lot later, after the funeral, that I got to thinking about Pears again and why he hadn't wanted anybody to know that your dad had spoken to him.'

'So why didn't you tell the police then?'

'Because I was afraid. Not just for myself, but for you, my love. I knew your dad had been murdered, although at first, I must admit, I did begin to believe Stubbs was right. But, gradually, as I put two and two together, I realized what had happened, and, if I'd said I'd heard the whole conversation, then who knows what that man would have done next.'

Rebecca's face was drawn by the time her mother had finished speaking. 'Stubbs,' she asked. 'Is that the man who came here last week?'

Dorothy nodded silently.

'He's after Simon Park is he?'

Dorothy jerked her head up as if surprised. 'After *him*?' She fell silent again.

'Is he after Simon, yes?' Rebecca pushed for an answer.

'I'm not sure,' her mother replied awkwardly. 'Perhaps.'

'Well what did he want then?'

'As I said, I'm not all that sure.' There was a strange firmness in Dorothy' voice, a firmness that had been absent before. She stood up and brushed the wrinkles out of her dress. 'Are you having any food tonight?' she asked in a more commanding tone. She walked over to the door without waiting for her daughter's answer. She had decided that the conversation was over.

CHAPTER SEVENTEEN

The telephone rang and rang. Rebecca was the only person in the big sprawling farmhouse. Eventually, tiring of the constant disruption to the peace and tranquillity, she pushed back the office chair, reached over the computer, and picked up the telephone receiver. 'Hello, Pendle Court Farm.'

'Hello, Rebecca?'

Rebecca recognised the voice instantly. 'Yes,' she answered curtly.

'Simon here. I thought that if you weren't doing anything, I'd ask you out for dinner tonight.' He waited for a reply.

'You needn't bother yourself,' she said eventually. 'I've made other arrangements, thank you.'

'There's something I want to talk to you about, Rebecca. It's important.'

'It can't be that important if it can wait until tonight,' she said, doodling erratically on a piece of paper as she spoke.

'But there *is* something we ought to discuss,' he insisted.

'Sorry, I really don't have the time,' Rebecca said in a business like manner.

'Tomorrow then?' Simon persisted, unruffled.

There was another pause while she composed herself for what she had to say. 'Look, I don't wish to see you tonight, tomorrow, or any other time. Is that clear?' Her voice was cold and abrupt.

'Quite clear.'

'I don't even want to know you,' Rebecca added bitterly, 'so please, don't bother me any more.' She slammed down the receiver.

Simon stared at the dead hand piece. 'Hell fire!' he cursed, pressing the cradle and dialling the number once more, but the phone on the other end of the line rang on. She did not answer. He left it ringing for three whole minutes before hanging up, then dialled once again, determined to get Rebecca to listen to him. 'Off the hook,' he murmured, as the engaged tone beeped back at him through the hand piece. He drew a deep breath and slammed it down.

Three loud knocks against the heavy wooden door with the brass knocker, and the resulting sound, but for the heavy mist, might have been heard six miles away in town. The still, grey blanket lingered over the fields, and closed everything in, enveloping sounds like a padded cell. A fine, clothes-drenching drizzle filtered down through the air and settled everywhere that Simon looked, counterfeiting everything with silver gilt. A curtain moved at the kitchen window, but no face appeared. The whole place was silent and grim.

Simon turned his back to the door and looked around the yard. A sound of a tractor chugging somewhere in the distance, and the lowing of a single milk cow, newly separated from its calf, broke the dull silence. The droplets of rain began to trickle down his temples as he turned to give the door one last rap before giving up. As his hand lifted the brass knocker, the door opened and Rebecca stood before him. She looked pale. Her eyes had shadows around them, as if from loss of sleep. In her hand she held a small, black spotted, silver box. 'I suppose you called for this,' she said, and held out the parcel. Her voice wasn't what Simon had expected. It sounded brittle, and bitter. But her eyes didn't show the same malice. They were not full of hatred, but full of pain.

Simon looked at the box but kept his hands by his side. 'When I give someone something, there are no strings attached,' he replied sharply.

'I wouldn't have accepted it in the first place if I'd thought there were.'

'So why hand it back?'

'I think you know very well,' said Rebecca, staring at his face, her voice breaking up until it quavered.

'Do I?' He asked softly, 'What about you? Do you know why you're handing it back?'

'I try to always be aware of what I'm doing.' Rebecca's voice gained a firmness that it had lacked a moment or two earlier. Her eyes began to gain the life and fire they had shown when she had first met Simon. 'The problem is getting people to tell the truth in the first place,' she said resolutely, pushing the box into Simon's chest. She let go, predicting his reaction precisely. His eyes left Rebecca's as he clasped the box before it had chance to fall, and by the time he looked up again, Rebecca had already turned away. Simon, realising he was going to lose his chance to speak to her again, put out his free hand to stop the heavy door from closing, but he had barely got his palm to it before it slammed shut.

'Rebecca!' he shouted angrily. 'We have to talk.'

No reply came from inside.

'Rebecca!' he called again as loud as he could. 'For God's sake be reasonable!' He hammered his fist against the door. 'Rebecca!'

'Reasonable!' Rebecca hissed as she leaned with her back against the door. But she stifled the sound from reaching Simon.

'Bloody stupid woman!' she heard him curse. 'I knew you were trouble from the very first moment you tried to kill me!'

Rebecca clenched her jaw tight and gripped the door handle behind her. She felt like telling him exactly what she thought of him, but some inner strength restrained her.

'You're going to regret this,' Simon called over his shoulder as he stormed away to his Saab.

When Rebecca heard him slam the car door shut, she turned, opened the house door slightly, and peeped out of the small crack. Seeing him at a safe distance, she flung the door back on its hinges. 'Threats now is it?' she called after him, the anger now clear in her voice, but Simon was already speeding out of the yard and was gone in a blink.

Rebecca stared for ages before going back inside. She knew she should have felt better for what she had done and said, but she didn't. Instead, she felt a heavy weight inside her, dragging on her, sapping her energy. She went through to the lounge and flopped into the soft sofa, cradling her head in her hands beneath the soft hair that had fallen about her face. Eventually, she lifted her head and combed her hair back with her fingers. The whole place was silent. It felt empty without Andrew or her mother in the house; and looking around now, she regretted ever going to Pendle Court. She regretted ever having a holiday there when she was a child. If it hadn't been for those holidays, her father might well be alive today, and if it weren't for Simon Park!

Because of him, she had hated her father, the one man who loved her more than anything in the whole world. A small tear ran down her cheek but she rubbed it away, angrily. She would never forget what Simon Park had done. Never!

She stood up and went to the bathroom to wash her face. The water felt cool and soothing on her skin but she felt no relief inside. She picked up a towel, and as she dabbed her face dry, a stranger looked back from behind the mirror. Through tousled hair, a pair of empty eyes watched her. 'Just think,' she said to the stranger, 'I nearly fell in love with that man! My God!' But the stranger had nothing to say to console her. Minutes passed as Rebecca studied the reflection, then, suddenly, as if everything had become crystal clear, she swept out of the door and ran to the office. A quick search under some papers uncovered the telephone directory. She thumbed through it until she found what she was looking for, jotted down a number, threw the directory to one side and dialled.

CHAPTER EIGHTEEN

Rebecca looked around the street as she walked along it. It was a street full of solicitor's signs, and estate agent's window displays. Eventually, as directed, she came upon a large brass name plate with the name *Goring Polson and Speak, Solicitors.* Beneath it, almost one tenth of the size was the name plate she was looking for.

JOHN COWLING

PRIVATE DETECTIVE. 2nd FLOOR.

She looked up at the Venetian blind in the second storey window. The place looked unused from the outside, but the outer door was open and, with a glance at her watch, she walked straight in, past the solicitors' inner door, and up a flight of steps that led to a landing two floors higher. The staircase to the second floor led to a single teak door. On it was a small plastic plaque with the name of JOHN COWLING inscribed on it in capital letters, and beneath his name, printed neatly in black lower case letters, *discreet enquiries and private investigations.* She looked at it for a moment, considering what she had set out to do, and then, reassured, tapped on the door lightly. It was ajar, and there was no mistaking the reply.

'Enter,' a man's voice commanded almost immediately. It was an unexpectedly deep and rasping voice. Rebecca hesitated slightly, then, deciding that it was too late to go back now, she pushed the door open with the palm of her hand and peeped inside.

Looking past a cream coloured screen, she saw a large window, shaded by the Venetian blind, and to the left of that was a large oak, knee-hole desk piled high at one end with different coloured folders and providing a resting place for a single green folder at the other. The reproduction captain's chair behind the desk was empty.

The door closed behind her with a click, and as she stepped past the dividing partition into the room she saw a steel filing cabinet that had a yellow ring of rust on its top. Above it hung a single framed certificate of some kind. The reflection of the light from the window, on the glass, prevented her from seeing what was written on it but, in the bottom right corner of it, a big red seal looked reassuringly impressive. Her eyes dropped down behind a ficus planter and there, on one knee, stooping over the green foliage and busily dampening the soil with a small hand sprayer was a man. He didn't look up, but continued the spraying, gradually straightening up and pushing up off his knee, and circling until he had sprayed every leaf of the plant. Finally, his mission accomplished, he stopped, placed the sprayer on the top of the filing cabinet, and turned to his visitor.

'Got to give her her weekly wash,' he said, stepping forward and lightly touching Rebecca's elbow. 'Would you like to take a seat?' He waved her towards the desk and fetched a small cane chair from the far corner of the room. He placed it facing his desk, let Rebecca sit down and walked around to his chair. 'There,' he said, pulling his seat forward. He put his elbows on the desk, folded his hands beneath his chin, and looked Rebecca in the eyes. 'Right, ready when you are.'

Rebecca felt relaxed by the courtesy of his easy manner. Going to visit a private detective wasn't as easy as she had first imagined. There was something very personal about it. She unbuttoned the top button of her coat and leaned back against the chair. It creaked a small protest, but then submitted to her meagre weight with no further complaint. She clasped her hands together on her lap and cleared her throat before speaking.

'I want to find out all I can about somebody.'

'Ah, right.' Neither Cowling's voice nor his face showed the slightest glimmer of surprise. He took hold of the green folder, opened it, took out several sheets of foolscap, and placed them down in front of him. He opened a drawer and sifted through it, eventually locating a propelling pencil. 'First of all, I need particulars about yourself, your name, address, where I can contact you, and so forth,' he said, pressing the top of the pencil to adjust the length of the lead.

Rebecca nodded and gave the information he required.

'Good,' he said, almost to himself as he wrote the word 'client' at the head of the paper, placed it to one side and headed the next sheet '*Target*.' 'Now, who are we investigating?'

Rebecca hesitated. So far it had been easy. Cowling waited patiently. 'Simon Park,' she said eventually.

'Simon Park?' Cowling asked as if to confirm the name before he wrote it down.

'Yes.' Rebecca watched the propelling pencil as it hovered over the paper. Cowling still didn't write. He leaned forward on his forearm.

'The novelist?' he asked quietly

'Yes.'

'I see.' He searched Rebecca's face but drew nothing from it. 'You do realize that that is his pen name, Miss Hampstead?'

'Yes.'

'Do you know his real name?'

'Simon Pears.'

'That's right,' he said confidently, and raising an eyebrow to support his reflex of mild surprise.

Rebecca watched his hand. It was still motionless.

'Don't you want to write this down?' she asked.

'Not yet,' Cowling answered in a serious voice. 'What do you want to find out about him?'

'Everything I can,' she replied uncomfortably.

'You'll have to be more specific I'm afraid, Miss Hampstead.'

'Well, everything!' This wasn't going to be easy. 'Where he comes from, his family background, what he did as a reporter, how and when he became a novelist, you know...'

Cowling nodded.

'And anything that has been written by him and about him,' Rebecca added.

'I have two of his novels at home to start you off with.'

Rebecca couldn't tell if that was a facetious comment.

'I want all the information I can get,' she said, forcing herself to be firm. She paused and then, 'I would like you to concentrate especially on what he wrote about The Welsh Drugs Affair eight years ago and anything else about that case that you can find out, be it written or verbal.'

Cowling smiled. 'I see,' he said and began to write. When he had finished, he looked up. 'Anything else?'

'I want to know what he's doing living at Thatch Cottage, a mile and a half from Pendle Court. I want to know who he sees and where he goes.'

Cowling scribbled some more notes. 'Now, I'm going to have to explain something.' He put down his propelling pencil and placed his hands palm down on the desk. 'Investigating ordinary people is one thing, investigating somebody who is well known or in the public eye is another, especially if they are reasonably wealthy.'

'Oh, why?'

'Simply because they have clout Miss Hampstead. They can quite often afford to sue people like ourselves for invasion of privacy.'

'Not if they are public figures,' Rebecca argued.

'That argument only runs so far. There is a line at which even such people have a right to privacy.'

'What are you saying?' asked Rebecca frostily.

'I am simply explaining that it could be an expensive job,' Cowling stated patiently.

'You want paying in advance, I presume?'

'When I know what the job entails, you will be quoted a price accordingly. You see, you have not yet explained why you want me to undertake this investigation. Without any such explanation, I am unable to commit myself fully at the moment.'

Rebecca was unsettled by the detective's attitude. 'But information is information, Mr. Cowling. That's all I want you to collect.'

'And I say again, Miss Hampstead, for what purpose? Are you emotionally involved?' He stared at her intently. The question came like a bomb blast.

Rebecca felt like getting up and leaving, but she had gone too far to back down now. She held her head up, pushed out a determined jaw and spoke. 'No, I am not emotionally involved. Not in the way you mean it, anyway. I dislike the man intensely.'

'Why?' Another blast.

'Because...because I happen to believe that he had something to do with the death of my father.

'Cowling frowned and lifted his eyebrow again. 'When?'

'My father's name was William Henson. He supposedly committed suicide because of the case I have mentioned.'

'Henson? I don't quite see...'

'Hampstead is my mother's maiden name.' She looked away from Cowling's probing eyes.

'Ah right! Well now I have something to go on. If you can see, I can angle that side of my investigations accordingly. As for what Mr. Park is up to now, that is a different matter.' Cowling explained what he was going to do and then, after sifting through the left hand drawer of the desk, handed her a pink sheet of paper.

'What's that?' she asked as she reached to take it from a well manicured hand.

'A list of my charges. It's also a contract. If you'd date it and sign it, then we can get down to business.'

Rebecca read it and then placed it on the desk and signed it with a pen already held out by Cowling. Beneath her signature she wrote down her telephone number. 'That is to let me know when you have anything to tell me. If I don't answer the phone, then, try the mobile number, but depending where I am you may not get through to me as the signal is sometimes non-existent. You'll of course not mention your name or your business to anyone else. I'll come and collect any reports you compile.'

Cowling looked faintly amused. 'Reports?' he said raising his eyebrow again, 'I rarely put my findings in writing, Miss Hampstead.'

'Then I suggest you start Mr. Cowling. I expect there to be more than just a few casual comments for that kind of money. In which case, I don't intend taking my own notes when I come to see you.' Cowling was suddenly aware of an authority in Rebecca's voice, the authority of a principal over an agent. She took out a cheque book and wrote out a cheque. She tore it out and handed it to the investigator. 'One thousand five hundred pounds for one week in advance. I believe I read it correctly.'

'That's right. Of course, that includes my other man.'

Rebecca seriously considered asking him about his phantom helper, but restrained herself at the last moment. She knew he was using that as an excuse for handing her the contract with the highest rates charged on it. No doubt he had a yellow or a blue one, or perhaps several colours of priced contracts that he handed out according to what he thought customers could afford, or when, like he probably wanted to do in her case, put her off employing him in the first place. She stood up and pocketed her cheque book. She held out her hand. As Cowling was about to shake it she said, 'My copy please?'

Again, Cowling was taken aback by the forcefulness of this wisp of a young woman. He'd expected her to balk at the prices and walk out. He had no stomach for getting involved with any best selling novelist. At best he could get sued. At the worst, Simon Park could write about the small time detective, expose his little practice, and just about ruin him. He'd heard of Simon Pears long before he bought the novels by Simon Park. The only advantage of that was that he knew where to start looking for copies of his newspaper reports. He scribbled out a receipt in a little blue book, peeled off a copy of the contract and handed them to his client. 'All right?'

'Thank you. Goodbye for now.' She turned and walked to the door. 'Value for money Mr. Cowling,' she said as she went out. 'I expect value for money.'

The next moment she was gone, leaving the door ajar as she had found it. Cowling watched the door. He knew that he had no choice but to do his task or return the money. One and a half grand was too much to let slip through his fingers. He knew that the young woman was after Simon Park's skin, and seemingly had enough money to do it. He had a feeling she might be more dangerous to oppose than the novelist.

'Okay!' he said and unleashed one of his broad grins. 'See what we can do for you Miss.' He chuckled and shook his head. Anything was better than divorce cases. He went behind the partition and reached for his jacket and overcoat. Well at least in this case he knew exactly where he was going to start.

CHAPTER NINETEEN

The Windsurfer Hotel was one of many small but pleasant hotels in and around the towns of Hampshire. It was only six miles from Pendle Court Farm, on the main road to town, nestling between a narrow belt of evergreen oaks and its own grounds which extended up to the main road at the front. A mile and a half to the left, the main road reached the country lane that led past Sunnybridge Farm, Thatch Cottage and thence on to Pendle Court Farm. At the back of the hotel lay a wide expanse of fields, now ploughed and re-seeded with next spring's crops. The grounds of The Windsurfer were laid down to lawns and gardens broken by well matured belts of rhododendrons and lilac bushes. It was a welcoming and relaxing place to stay.

The brightness of the floodlights during the evening broke into the darkness of the surrounding countryside like some supernatural craft that had just landed, and as one approached along the main road, the full effect of the light upon the half timbered walls enhanced its character and gave the whole place its own individuality. The lights had been on for a couple of hours when Simon drove up the avenue of trees and bushes, and brought his car to a halt in the hotel car park. He knew the place well, for it was there that he had stayed when he first came to the area to see what it was like. Before buying his property, he had boarded there for two and a half weeks, plenty of time to research, plenty of time to come to a decision.

The receptionist he also knew well. Mary Blandford was the daughter of the ageing proprietor. She was in her mid thirties, had a round body, three chins which increased in number when she laughed, and thick-lensed spectacles which, while covering a pair of pale blue myopic eyes, lended support for a frizzy, fully permed mop of natural black hair. Her cheery, outgoing manner had played an integral part in building up the customer base in the hotel after the death of her mother six years ago. Until then, she had played no part in the running of the business. She was married to a local tenant farmer who, no doubt, missed her about the farm but welcomed the extra income when she agreed to work for her father in the hotel. She always had something to say to the guests, and invariably had them doubled up with laughter. Simon liked her. During his stay they had spent hours talking about the local people and the various farms in the area.

A mahogany, glass-panelled door opened onto a thick red Axminster carpet in the hotel lobby. Mary looked up from *The Times* and, straight away, her chubby face was cracked by a broad grin. Her eyes glinted mischievously at Simon who nodded and smiled back affectionately. Of all the people in the area, she knew as much about him as anybody. She knew why he had come to the area in the first place, that he had bought Thatch Cottage, and even that his horse had been ill. Since she had kept her ear to the ground - something that she'd always done - there was very little she didn't know about what was going on in the district, and that included Simon's activities.

'Hello sailor,' she chortled. 'How's your new book coming along?'

'Too many distractions, Mary. Can't keep my mind off you.'

Mary chuckled again. 'Who brings you here then? Can't be just me and my good looks.'

'*Who?* Simon raised his eyebrows interrogatively. 'People usually ask *What*.'

'Oh, I still think it's who,' said Mary, still beaming like a headlamp.

'Who do you think?' asked Simon casually as he glanced around the lobby.

'How about Mr. Greythorpe?' Mary probed. Her grin subsided to a smile as she waited for Simon's reaction.

'Hmm,' Simon muttered. He scowled and thought for a moment. Mary was astute. 'Is there a Mr. Greythorpe staying here then?'

Mary's smile vanished. 'Hell, don't say I'm wrong!'

'Well...' Simon tilted his head on one side. 'How about another guess, seeing that you're my favourite person around here?'

Mary opened the register and ran her thumb down the list of guests. 'Got to be him,' she said firmly. 'Unless...No, it can't be that old grey haired man. Not your sort him,' she half asked and half stated.

'Hmm. Depends what his name is.'

'Herbert Stenton. Is it him?'

'Stenton,' Simon said slowly. 'Grey haired you said?'

'Yes,' Mary nodded.

'Nope. Never heard of him.' Simon beamed as Mary pursed her lips in mock injury. 'You're having me on, aren't you? You Devil! It was Greythorpe all the time, wasn't it?' Her confident grin returned to full beam.

'Afraid so, Mary. Had you going there for a moment though, didn't I?'

'You wait,' she threatened, and wagged her finger at him. 'He's in room 27. Shall I give him a buzz?'

'No, I'll surprise him, if that's all right.'

'All right by me. Third door on the left at the top of the stairs.'

'Thanks Mary.'

'You're welcome,' she replied and rested her chins on her hands as she watched him run up the steps taking them two at a time.

Simon stood outside the door of room 27 and listened for a minute to the sound of one of Bach's flute concertos before knocking lightly with his knuckles. A moment later the door opened wide and Arthur Greythorpe was facing him, standing in his shirt sleeves and slacks. and holding a newspaper in one hand. His face was the usual expressionless mask, except that his gaze, somewhat unusually, was directed through a pair of steel rimmed reading spectacles. He slipped them off to one side with his free hand and spoke evenly and softly. 'Don't tell me you've come to confess!'

'Going to ask me in Arthur?'

Arthur stepped back and gestured for Simon to walk inside. The flute concerto still played in the background and Arthur stood with his head tilted slightly, in order to capture its final bars before the CD came to an end.

'Often wondered what we had in common,' Simon remarked, with a serious face, when the music ended.

'A little more than just our taste in music I think.' Arthur went to the player and pressed the *play* button again. He waited until the music started and then adjusted the volume down slightly. 'However, that doesn't tell me why you've graced my humble lodgings with your presence.'

'Still think I could have done it, don't you, Arthur?'

'Doesn't make any difference now. Can't identify the remains.'

'That rather lets me off the hook then.'

'If you were on it Simon, yes.' He settled onto the edge of the bed.

'I wasn't.'

Arthur looked straight into the eyes of the man who had once been the heart-torn little boy he had known so long ago. 'Sit down,' he said eventually, and pointed to the chair by the television. 'Can I order you a drink or something?'

'No thanks. I need my senses where you are concerned.' Simon sat down.

'Afraid I might be setting a trap are you, Simon?'

'If your idea of falling into a trap is being followed by one of your lap dogs, then you're right.'

Arthur glanced at Simon. His eyes burned into him as if they could read every thought in his head. They stared at each other in silence. 'Lap dog, heh?' Arthur repeated eventually.

'Walks to heel more precisely. Can't turn around without him nearly tripping over me.'

'I see.'

'You do, do you? Going to have to have a word with your men? Not the calibre you are used to are they?'

'You're the sort of man who could sense somebody following you whether you could see him or not, Simon. In this particular case, however, your senses must have gone haywire. I don't have any men working with me over here.'

Simon breathed a sigh of disdain. 'Why can't you be straight with me Arthur? Why can't you admit it? I know anyway.'

'No, Simon, I can't admit anything. You're mistaken.'

'Mistaken!' Simon's voice rattled with anger. He stood up and pointed his finger at the inspector. 'Believe me, Arthur, I'll tread on his tail if he doesn't get off mine. Do you hear me?'

'I hear you all right. Close the door on your way out won't you?' Arthur said sharply. The visit was over.

Simon emerged from The Windsurfer knowing that the bond of friendship that had once existed between Arthur and himself was now dissolved. If Arthur suspected him of murder then nothing would stop him from investigating to the full. Nothing. Arthur Greythorpe was like that. But it wasn't like him to use unskilled men to do his footwork. He was slipping, and Simon knew he knew it now that he'd told him in no uncertain terms. The muscles in his face were still taut with anger as he descended the stairs at a trot. He forced a smile, and with a simple, 'Good night, Mary,' he went out to his car. With a spin of the wheels on the drizzle-dampened tarmac, and a squeal as the radials hit the edge of the main road, he sped off into the night.

The road seemed bare and empty but for a couple of pedestrians lit up by the full beam of his headlights as he accelerated away past the side road and towards town. The traffic was light as he drew nearer the built up area. A seemingly familiar pair of headlights stuck in his rear view mirror, following him at a distance. Simon clenched his jaw, turned left down a side road and right again to loop back to the road he had left.

The headlights still followed. 'Damn him,' he cursed as he built up his resolve to sort the matter out once and for all. He drove for another mile until he reached the road that ran beside the edge of the municipal park. He slowed down, turned left down the next side road and parked his car. He had lost sight of the car behind now, but he knew it was still there. He walked through the large open wrought iron gates that led to the bandstand. The light was poor there and anybody following would soon lose sight of him as he disappeared behind the small ornamental pavilion.

CHAPTER TWENTY

Thick dark clouds began to pile up in the sky, bringing darkness even earlier than usual. Rebecca finished her work at six-thirty and went to her room. She changed out of jeans into a woollen skirt and jacket, and pulled on a pair of red leg warmers and a pair of brown, leather, knee-length boots before going down stairs. Throwing her beige overcoat around her shoulders, she left the house without a word.

The traffic into town was light compared with the heavy tea-time traffic flooding away like an overflowing spring. She had no trouble finding a parking place at that time of the evening. Few shops remained open, and it was still too early for the night life to begin. There were a few young courting couples about, meeting after work and as she approached the pedestrian precinct, she could see a group of teenagers sitting listening to music from a portable radio.

She glanced at her watch and realising she was running late for her appointment, she decided to take a short cut which left the precinct and led around the back of the shops. Quickening her stride she walked up the back street between empty dustbins and piles of empty cartons that had been left outside the rear entrances of the shops. A stray dog rummaged unperturbed as she strode past in the darkness; a cat ran out of the shadows and across the opening to another alleyway up ahead. The light from three small lamps cast long shadows behind each pile of rubbish and, as she walked on, the dim light fell on the faces of a group of youths, chatting and leaning against the wall. They stirred; their conversation lapsing till a passer-by went out of earshot. As Rebecca approached them they drifted away and disappeared around the next corner.

She glanced behind her as she approached the bend. She had a feeling about it, nothing definite, but a foreboding, all the same. She glanced back just as a shadow moved behind her, but it melted back into the darkness and was gone as suddenly as it appeared. Up ahead, some distance away, she could see the bright lights of the precinct. The youths were in front of her again. They stirred and chatted as she drew nearer to them. Suddenly, one of them chuckled loudly and stepped out in front of Rebecca. He side stepped as she stepped sideways to go around him and before she could move away a jostling and intimidating circle had moved around her small figure. One of the gang, possibly their leader, caught hold of her arm and a rough hand clamped onto her jaw. She struggled as an unshaven face drew nearer to hers and a beer-laden breath swilled over her.

'Hello Rebecca!' a loud and familiar voice said as the unshaven face suddenly swivelled around. The hand relaxed and she pulled her face clear. 'This is what you get up to, is it, when I'm waiting for you?' The circle broke completely and Rebecca saw Simon pushing towards her. 'He doesn't look your sort,' he said eyeing the hooligan and, at the same time, grasping hold of her arm. 'I've told you before about being late!'

The youth stared as Simon pulled her away. He didn't want to be made a fool of in front of the others, but he had no stomach to argue with the tall stranger. His bravado had melted, and shrugging his shoulders, he let Rebecca glide away. The others all laughed and he joined in before sauntering away at the head of his gang. Simon ignored them, put his arm around Rebecca as if he really had arranged to meet her, squeezed her body to his and, holding his head close to hers, walked with her towards the bright lights of the open street.

'Damned fool thing to do,' Simon said angrily as they reached the lights.

'What is?' Rebecca asked, reluctant to pull away.

'Walking up dark back alleys. You should keep to the precinct.'

'Never had any trouble before,' Rebecca replied chirpily.

'Neither did King Harold,' growled Simon.

Rebecca scowled. 'What are you on about?' She turned to face him, still very much aware how close he was holding her. She could feel the firmness of his chest against her soft body despite the barrier of thick woollen clothes.

'Never had any trouble with his eye.'

'His eye?'

'Until he got an arrow shot into it.' Simon beamed an almost irresistible smile.

'You're mad, do you know that?' she said, fighting to control her feelings. She knew she had to hate him.

'Thank you.' His beam broadened. 'I was beginning to worry that I'd been cured.'

For a brief moment they stopped and stared at each other. She held her breath and then, suddenly coming to her senses, she said, 'No, it's I who should thank *you*.' She pushed away from him, wondering why he let her go so easily. 'I'll be on my way now.' Her manner was abrupt. She turned and began to walk away.

Simon went after her, caught hold of her elbow and turned her around angrily. 'Still not friends then? What's the matter with you?'

'Why were you following me?'

'I wasn't,' Simon insisted.

'Liar!' she yelled.

'Why were you having me followed then?' Simon countered.

'I wasn't'

'Liar!' he said, his voice rising triumphantly in the knowledge that he was right. They glared at each other for a moment, trying to read what was in each other's eyes. Eventually Simon broke the stalemate. 'Don't play games with me Rebecca. I'm serious.'

'Then go and be serious with some one else.' She pulled herself free, but he caught her with both hands on her shoulders.

'I wanted to let you know what it was like being investigated.'

'I really don't have any idea what you're talking about,' Rebecca insisted, not at all convincingly.

'I'm talking about being followed.'

'I don't see anybody following you,' she said sarcastically and glanced past his shoulder.

'Not now you don't because I stopped him.'

'Stopped him!' Rebecca's mind swung to Cowling. He must have been seen. 'Stopped who?' She still wasn't going to give anything away.

He shook her gently 'The man you are on your way to see,' he said quietly.

'What man's that?' asked Rebecca as she turned and walked on.

'Cowling,' Simon called after her.

Rebecca stopped in her tracks. Until now it had all been deniable. 'Cowling? Never heard of him,' she called back.

'That's funny. He knows you.'

'Can't think where we've met,' Rebecca lied.

Tiring of Rebecca's game, Simon walked up to her and took her arm in a grip that was clearly meant not to be broken. She didn't resist as he led her forward. 'We'll be there in a minute,' he stated, his grip still firm as they walked up the street together. He was taking no chances on her turning tail and scurrying away.

Despite Rebecca's contempt for her captor, she couldn't suppress the inner feeling she got from being so close to him. She stiffened to prevent it flowing through her whole body, and stared directly ahead as he propelled her towards the outer door to Cowling's office. 'Here we are,' he announced.

'Where exactly is that?'

'You really are getting to be a bore, do you know that?' Simon sighed. 'You can stop pretending now Rebecca. I really do know all about it.' He released his grip and she pulled away quickly.

'Go to Hell,' she snapped. 'You can do and say what you like, but just don't include me in any of your devious games.'

'Right, please yourself,' he said sourly. 'You play games as much as you like, but eventually,' he said, waving his finger at her, only inches from the tip of her nose, 'you'll realize you need me.'

'Need you!' Rebecca's temper rose. In the artificial light, Simon couldn't see the flush of pink in her cheeks and neither could he hear her heart pounding against the inside of her breast. He had touched a sore point and she lashed back like a whip. 'I need you like I need amputation!' she seethed. 'Damn you for your cheek!' She raised her hand to slap his face but Simon caught her wrist and held it.

'When you do,' Simon concluded, thrusting her away scornfully and dropping his hands to his side, 'you'll be lucky if I'm around.' Without saying another word, he spun on his heel and walked away.

Rebecca stared after him, breathing deeply to stop her exasperation boiling over. Simon turned the corner without as much as a glance back in her direction. For three whole minutes she stared, first watching him walk away and then, after that, blankly watching the street beyond. Gradually, as her heart beat slowed, and she began to breathe more evenly, she turned towards Cowling's office. As she approached the stairs, she began to think about what Simon had said, wondering what explanation the detective would give. By the time she had reached the second floor, her anger had begun to rise again. She approached the teak door, breathless with rage, her face flushed and her jaw clenched so firmly that the muscles in her face ached. She glanced at the sign on the door. 'Huh! *Discreet Enquiries*!' she said aloud.

The door opened almost as soon as she knocked. Cowling stepped back against the partition to let Rebecca step inside. She walked straight past him and stood facing the desk. 'Made it I see,' he said, closing the door behind her, and then circling to the corner of his desk.

'I think you owe me an explanation,' Rebecca stated flatly. 'Not to mention a certain fee!'

'All in good time, Miss Hampstead. All in good time,' he said holding up his hands submissively. 'Please, won't you take a seat?' He pointed to the cane chair.

'No thank you,' she said, standing her ground. 'The money will do fine, unless you didn't have the gall to cash my cheque.'

Cowling smiled. 'Please take a seat.' He held his hand out towards the chair again and waited until Rebecca had seen there would be no money, no explanation, until she had sat down. She dropped heavily onto the seat and folded her hands on her lap. She stared at the empty seat behind the desk. Cowling settled his own large frame into it and leaned forward on the desk to face her. 'Now, Miss Hampstead, let's just try and sort this out.'

'This *needs* sorting out!' she butted in angrily. 'There's no doubt about that!'

Cowling sighed and opened the top right hand drawer of his desk. He pulled out a thick green folder, which was held closed by two thick elastic bands, and handed it to Rebecca across the desk.

'What's that?' she asked, suddenly reluctant to take it.

'What you paid me for Miss Hampstead,' the detective announced dryly.

Rebecca shuffled in her seat awkwardly. 'What's in it?' she asked as casually as she could, and took it from Cowling's hand. It was heavy and its weight took her by surprise. She let it drop onto the corner of the desk.

'Open it and see.'

She glanced at it.

'Go on,' he urged.

Rebecca flipped off the rubber bands and opened the cover to reveal a thick wad of papers. The top one was marked with the words:

PRIVATE AND CONFIDENTIAL,

FOR THE EYES OF MISS REBECCA HAMPSTEAD ONLY.

Then, she flicked through the pile of newspaper clippings and sheets of typed paper that made up the bulky file. A couple of brown envelopes lay at the very end, but her curiosity was satisfied for the time being. She flipped the folder closed again, securing the elastic fasteners before speaking. 'Fine,' she said and stood up. 'I'll read it at my own leisure. I'll let you know if I am satisfied.'

'Miss Hampstead,' Cowling said in a raised voice to stop her leaving. 'Would you like to know where I got all that information?'

'Not particularly. All I want to know is, is it accurate and is it complete?'

'Oh yes. As far as I can establish within my own limited ability, I'd say it was just that,' Cowling replied haughtily.

'Then I'll let you get on with some other work. I'm sure you are quite busy.' She turned to the door and reached for the handle.

'Had you ever considered asking Simon Park for that information?' Cowling asked bluntly. Rebecca's hand hovered over the door handle. Cowling continued speaking when he saw he had regained her attention. 'He seems a reasonable enough chap.'

Rebecca swung around. 'You what!' she asked quietly, forcing herself to contain her temper. 'That's why you told him about this appointment, I suppose. Trying to be reasonable back to him no doubt?'

'I have spoken to him of course,' Cowling broke in superciliously.

'You had no right,' she shouted. 'You're supposed to be discreet. That means...'

'I had every right,' Cowling broke in. 'You wanted information about somebody. The easiest way is to confront them I've found. People are usually very cooperative, especially if they want to get you off their backs.'

'And you believe every word he told you I suppose?' Rebecca grated.

'I've drawn no conclusions, Miss Hampstead. I'll leave that to you. All I have done is supply you with the information you asked for, no more and no less.'

'What the hell gives you the right to insult your client by telling anyone about your contract, least of all the person you are paid to investigate?'

'There are no rules in this game. Information is just that. You wanted to know who he is and what he's up to. Well that is all in the folder. What I couldn't find out by sleuthing, I found out by plain old fashioned cheek. And what's more, if you do have an axe to grind with that man, then I suggest you bury it. Good night Miss Hampstead,' he finished, peremptorily.

Rebecca broke her icy glare and spun out of the door, leaving Cowling points ahead. He waited until he heard the street door slam closed and then picked up the telephone receiver and dialled a number. A hand lifted the receiver of a car cell phone at the other end of the line. 'She has it,' Cowling stated. The line clicked and went dead.

Rebecca paced out of the street door and strode off towards her car. She felt obliged to take the short cut just to spite Simon, and headed for the opening across the street, but swerved away from it and towards the pedestrian precinct at the last moment as she thought better of it. A welcome fresh wind was beginning to blow and by the time she reached the road where the car was parked she was already beginning to feel cooler and calmer. But the wind had preceded a storm, and already, large droplets of water were beginning to explode on the pavement as the cumulus clouds piled together above the town. She unlocked the car door and ducked inside, flinging the folder onto the passenger seat and slamming the door shut to escape from the torrents of rain that were already lashing at the windscreen. She leaned back in her seat, brushed her hair off her face, and exhaled heavily.

Several minutes passed before she looked at the folder that lay on the seat next to her. She stared at it whilst she reflected on the evening's events. She thought about Simon following her, about him holding her close to him when he rescued her from the hooligans in the alley and about what he had said to her. Things seemed even more confused now than they had been before she came into town. Just what was in the folder? She hardly dared to open it. She switched on the courtesy light, picked up the green bundle and laid it across her knees. She took a breath, removed the rubber bands once more, flipped it open, and began to read the first few pieces of paper but, eventually, realising the volume of material in her hands was too great to digest with a cursory glance, she began to thumb quickly through it. There were newspaper cuttings and photocopies of documents and articles. There were book reviews and critics' comments and a handful of other papers and envelopes. She would have to wade through them slowly at home, sifting out what she needed to know and putting the rest to one side. She slipped the elastic bands back around the folder and tossed it onto the back seat.

Rebecca took her time driving back to Pendle Court. She had much to contemplate and driving in the torrents of rain wasn't so easy. There was a good deal of traffic about on the main road and the heavy rain made every light reflect a dozen times on the windscreen as the droplets of rain impeded the view between every swipe of the wiper blades.

It was a relief to reach the country lanes and at last be away from on-coming headlights. The red tail lights of a car up ahead drew closer, despite Rebecca's lack of haste, but she followed the red dots, content for someone else to lead around the bends. The car seemed to be going slow as Rebecca closed up to it, dipping her headlights so as not to dazzle the driver, but it seemed to go even slower once she settled in behind it, easing around each bend as if the road was totally unfamiliar. There was no room to pass, so she leaned back in her seat and, for the first time that evening, began to relax.

Another car came up behind, its headlights on full beam, until its driver, too, dipped them and followed in procession. Not far to go now, Rebecca thought. She was looking forward to a meal and something hot to drink. She wondered if the driver of the car behind was eager to get home for his tea. He'd have to be patient. The car in front was going even slower now.

CHAPTER TWENTY ONE

That will be Rebecca now,' Andrew assured Dorothy, as a pair of headlight beams swung into the yard at Pendle Court.

'She gets later and later,' Dorothy grumbled. She got up from her arm chair and went through to the kitchen to put Rebecca's meal in the microwave oven. 'I just can't see her getting up tomorrow morning as early as she does normally,' she said to Andrew who had followed her through, still carrying his newspaper. 'Just look at the time!'

Andrew already knew what time it was. He'd been watching the clock in the lounge all evening. 'She's had a lot on her mind lately,' he pleaded on behalf of his niece.

'That's no reason for staying out this late without letting us know where she's gone,' she complained, and shuffled about busily.

The door knocker banged hard three times against the heavy door.

'Must have forgotten her key,' Andrew commented. 'I'll see to her.' He threw down the newspaper on the table and went out into the hallway.

'Now then young lady,' Dorothy said, turning towards the kitchen doorway as footsteps approached. 'What have you been..?' She stopped herself from finishing her question. The expression on her face changed instantly from one of scolding to that of contempt and disappointment when saw that it was Inspector Greythorpe standing in the doorway. She eyed the policeman as he stood there weighing up her reaction. His assessment wasn't wrong. He was used to such reactions from the people he met, not so much to what he said, but to his appearance. But, somehow, the solitude that his job and his mask had brought suited him well. The praise and approval of people with whom he came into contact during his investigations were neither wanted nor encouraged. He stood in the doorway in his heavy overcoat, holding his hat in one hand and a brown executive briefcase in the other.

'Good evening, Mrs. Hampstead,' he greeted from behind almost motionless lips.

'Oh, it's you is it?' Dorothy said awkwardly. 'God knows when she'll come home for this,' she grumbled, switching off the microwave oven and then bustling around the table to face the policeman. 'What do you want?' she asked rudely.

'I'd like a word with you both,' he replied politely, then paused a moment before saying, 'concerning your daughter.'

'Rebecca!' Dorothy exclaimed.

'That's right, Mrs. Hampstead.'

'You'd better come through to the sitting room,' Andrew said and stood aside for his sister and the inspector to go into the lounge. Dorothy waved to the armchair and Arthur Greythorpe nodded his thanks before sitting down and placing the briefcase on the carpet beside him. Dorothy sat on the sofa and Andrew stood next to her, with one hand on her shoulder to reassure her. Her whole body had gone tense.

'What about Rebecca?' Dorothy managed to ask.

The inspector waited for a moment, and then asked, 'Where is she?'

Before Dorothy could answer, Andrew spoke. 'Out,' he said abruptly.

'Quite. But where is she out, Mr. Hampstead?'

'We don't think to ask where she's going nowadays,' Dorothy retorted.

'So you have no idea where she is then?'

'No.' Dorothy said as she felt the weight of Andrew's reassuring hand. 'She's a grown girl now. It's really none of our business where she goes in her own time, or who she sees.'

'But it seems like it should be your business Mrs. Hampstead. Or should I say Mrs. Henson?'

'Huh! So he's eventually got around to telling you has he? I wondered what he was playing at.'

'Who?' Arthur asked naively.

'Your boss of course!'

'My boss?'

Dorothy decided that Arthur Greythorpe was being as obtuse as ever. 'I'm beginning to think you never talk to each other.'

'You've seen him then?'

'Of course I have. Came not long after you came the last time. Surely he mentioned it!' Dorothy said, a tone of sarcasm in her voice. 'Or is he out to get all the credit again?'

'Credit for what, Mrs. Hampstead?'

'Solving Creedy's...' Andrew's hand squeezed her shoulder tightly, causing her to take a sharp breath and break off what she was saying.

'Creedy's murder? Is that what you were going to say?' asked Arthur.

'No. I was going to say *disappearance.*'

'Just what do you know about that disappearance, Mrs. Hampstead?'

'She knows nothing,' Andrew butted in. 'Except what your boss told her.'

'Which was?'

'That he died in the fire down at Sunnybridge Farm,' Dorothy stated.

'Ah, of course! Yes, forgive me. I'm a little tired tonight. It tends to muddle one's thoughts, don't you think?'

'Looks like it,' Dorothy was quick to answer.

'I didn't make the connection right away,' Arthur admitted. I didn't realize actually, until tonight, that you were *the* Mrs. Henson of *the* Welsh Drugs Affair fame.'

'Tonight!' Dorothy exclaimed. 'You mean it took until tonight for him to tell you!'

'Not exactly, Mrs. Hampstead. You see, he didn't tell me.' He reached down for his briefcase and placed it on his knee. He clicked open the two catches and opened up the lid. 'I found out from this file your daughter has compiled.' He lifted out a thick green folder and held it in view above the lid of the briefcase. He closed the case and put it back on the floor, placed the file on his knees, and opened it.

'File? What are you talking about?' Andrew asked, agitated and becoming angry. 'Would you please get to the point?'

Arthur flashed his gaze at Andrew before levelling it back on Dorothy. She looked at the floor to avert the dreadful soul-searching stare. 'I discovered the connection between you both and the fire,' he stated. 'More important, I discovered the connection between you, Mrs. Hampstead, and the person who died in the fire. Until I read this, I really had no idea!'

'You still don't by the sound of it,' Dorothy replied irksomely, and shifted her eyes to the door jamb.

'Did you know that the farmhouse in Wales had been burgled recently?' Arthur asked casually.

'Burgled!' Dorothy said sharply, jerking her eyes to meet his. 'Burgled?' she repeated more calmly. 'Good heavens! What a terrible thing to happen to the new owners. And such nice people as well. From Scotland you know?'

'Terrible,' Arthur confirmed, still watching her.

'Much taken was there?' Andrew asked off-handedly.

'Ah!' Arthur uttered, lifting his hand and pointing at the ceiling. 'That's the strange part.'

'Strange?' asked Dorothy, more subdued now.

'Yes, Mrs. Hampstead. Very strange,' he repeated, his voice trailing off as he paused for a second. 'You see, nothing seems to have been taken, absolutely nothing. Not even the cash in the drawers that were rifled.'

'Now that *is* strange,' Andrew said with a hint of sarcasm.

Once again, Arthur's eyes shot from Dorothy to Andrew and back to Dorothy again.

'Very strange,' Dorothy confirmed with a deep frown.

'Quite. So why break in then?' asked Arthur.

'Vandals,' Dorothy proclaimed.

'There was nothing spoilt, Mrs. Hampstead,' Arthur stated, leaning back against the chair and trying his best to be patient.

'Have you caught the burglar yet?' Andrew asked.

'No. At least, I haven't been informed of any arrest yet.'

'Then you'll not be able to ask him what he was after, will you?' Arthur threw Andrew a strange glance. 'And it's no use asking us. We aren't clairvoyants,' Andrew continued

'Oh.' Arthur looked about the room. 'Surely a burglar would take something, anything?'

'Quite,' Dorothy agreed.

'Yet he took nothing.'

'Yes. So you said,' Dorothy confirmed.

'Unless...' Arthur paused as if in deep thought, but his eyes never left Dorothy's. He might just have seen a spark of fear in her eyes if Andrew hadn't spoken quickly.

'Unless, Andrew suggested, 'he was looking for something specific. Something that he thought was there but wasn't when he got inside.'

'Rubbish Andrew!' Dorothy scolded. 'What on earth was there that the new owners wouldn't know about?'

'I was hoping you'd be able to tell me, Mrs. Hampstead,' Arthur said, his eyes still probing her face. 'You see, whoever broke in probably didn't know that you had moved out.'

'I certainly have no idea.' She stood up beside Andrew. 'Now if you've finished.'

Arthur remained in his seat. 'The fact of the matter,' he said, 'is that I haven't finished, Mrs. Hampstead.'

Andrew put his hand on Dorothy's arm and settled on the arm of the sofa. 'We might as well hear him out,' he said, as he coaxed her to sit down again.

'No,' Dorothy said, shrugging off his hand. She had a determined look on her face, more determined than Andrew had seen in many long years. Her eyes were wide and alert, and her jaw protruded from her weary face with a set resolve. He could see now where Rebecca had got her looks from. Despite her age and her hard life, his sister still carried the remnants of the good looks he remembered she had possessed in her youth. 'I don't want to sit down. I want to know just what this man is getting at. And I want it plain and straight. I'm fed up with all his cat and mouse antics.' She turned her attention to Arthur Greythorpe. 'Now just what do you have to tell us?' she demanded. 'In words of one syllable if you don't mind.'

'Did you know your daughter had this folder?' he asked, prodding it with his finger, and then lifting it up with both hands, to let her see it more closely.'

'She has thousands of them in her office. And I don't know what's in any of them,' Dorothy boasted.

'This is a file containing information about several persons, Mrs. Hampstead.'

'I had no idea!' she replied cuttingly. Arthur took out a newspaper clipping and offered it to her. She stepped forward and took it from his hand, turned it around and read its headline out loud. '*Police Drugs Raid on Welsh Farmhouse.*' Dorothy stood on the spot for several seconds before turning to Andrew. 'Here,' she instructed and handed it to him. 'You read it for me. I haven't got my reading glasses with me.'

Andrew took it from her. It was marked in ink at the top. *'24/09/05.'* He read it out. '*Police drugs raid at Welsh Farmhouse,*' he announced. *'Following diligent enquiries by inspector Bernard Stubbs, three men were held in police custody last night. In a police raid carried out at Cil Cwm Farm by men of his force yesterday, William Henson, the owner of the farm, Alfred Creedy, a London nightclub owner, and John Prosser, one of Creedy's nightclub attendants, were arrested and charged with being in illegal possession of drugs. Further charges are expected later.'*

Andrew looked up at Dorothy. 'Go on,' she ordered.

'Detective Inspector Stubbs, in a statement to the press, announced that he had had the farm under surveillance for several months, and had successfully concluded his task by apprehending the three men together with five million pounds worth of heroin.'

'I suppose you believe all this,' Dorothy asked complacently. Arthur Greythorpe ignored the question. 'Carry on,' he said to Andrew.

Andrew glanced over the article to the place he had stopped reading, and then continued. *'A police spokesman has said the men will appear in the local magistrate's court tomorrow.'* He looked up at the inspector. 'I didn't know Rebecca had anything like this,' he stated.

'What do you make of that?' Arthur asked Dorothy.

'I've read it all before,' she stated blandly. 'All lies of course.'

'We'll come to that later. What I want is your thoughts on why your daughter should have compiled a file like this.'

'You said the file was about several people,' Andrew interrupted.

Arthur glanced down at the file and picked up another newspaper cutting. 'What about this?' he asked, and handed it to Dorothy. Dorothy handed it straight to Andrew without even glancing down at it.

'This cutting is also marked in ink. *27/09/05*, this time,' Andrew noted: '*Local farmer released on bail. Mr. William Henson, 55, of Cil Cwm Farm, was released on conditional bail. He has been charged with being in possession of and dealing in a Class A drug, namely heroin. Although counsel for the prosecution opposed bail, Mr. Henson's solicitor successfully argued that his client, a family man with a farm to look after, was unlikely to leave the country. He is to report to the local police station each day. The two men also arrested with Mr. Henson also applied for bail, but were remanded in custody pending further enquiries.*'

'Now this,' Arthur announced and handed another cutting across. 'This one is also dated the 24th. But it is from a national newspaper.'

Andrew stood up and reached for it, then, as with the others, he read it out aloud. '*Successful drugs raid on Welsh farmhouse*,' he began. '*After prolonged investigations by our own reporter, Simon Pears, into drugs dealing in the London underworld, his report to the local police, ended in a successful arrest of three men at a farmhouse in West Wales yesterday. Simon Pears confirmed that the farmhouse had been used each summer for the last three years for transactions involving drugs*'

'Huh,' Dorothy shrugged. 'So she is just finding out about that Pears fella. I told her about him, you know. I told her he was no good.'

'No good?' asked Arthur, sitting forward abruptly.

'I told her he was the one who killed her father.'

'Really? How do you know that, Mrs. Hampstead? Didn't he commit suicide?'

'No, he was murdered. I know. It's as simple as that.'

'But how do you know. How? What happened to make you know?'

'Because he came down to the farm after Billy got bail, all nice as pie and full of questions and advice. But no sooner had he left, than my Billy is hanged.'

'But the verdict was suicide, wasn't it?' Arthur emphasised again.

'Suicide my foot! He killed him I tell you. He killed him to keep him quiet. To stop him telling what he had seen.' Her lip began to tremble.

'And what had he seen?' Arthur prompted again rather more gently.

'It doesn't matter now.' Her voice shook with emotion. 'Nothing can bring him back.' Andrew put his hand on her arm to calm her.

'If it really was important, why didn't you tell the police?' Arthur persisted.

'Because Billy had already told Stubbs he hadn't told anyone else about it. Stubbs would have made Billy out to be a liar. And for what? All I would have done is give it away what Billy had seen, then I would have been the next to get bumped off. I had Rebecca to think about.'

'But the police reported no suspicious circumstances. And the coroner's verdict was that he took his own life,' Arthur still insisted.

'What do they know! That Stubbs fella couldn't run a fish and chip shop let alone a police force. God knows how he's got where he is today. I can't see how you haven't seen through him.'

'Dorothy!' Andrew urged her to be calm.

'Oh, well it's true. The stupid man was out to get all the credit and it didn't matter if he caught a few innocent people up in his net so long as he could feather his own nest. He hadn't the ability to be a proper detective. Detective!' she exclaimed waving her arms in exasperation, 'He never detected anything. He just saw a solution to getting credited with another case under his belt and took the easiest and simplest way out. Nobody could argue with him. He said Billy was involved. He wouldn't listen to any other explanation. It was he who said it was suicide. Nobody ever seemed to question his opinions. Rode roughshod over everybody at the inquest, he did. Thought he was somebody with his police raids. And he lied. I know that. That Simon Pears was nearer to the mark than he was.'

'How do you mean Mrs. Hampstead?'

'Well, Creedy did rent the farm each year as he said. That boss of yours reckoned he'd been watching the house for months. We were only away for two or three weeks each summer. Nothing went on when we were there, I know that much, so how could he have been watching the place for months?'

'Quite.'

'Quite!' She looked at him coldly. 'Is that all you can say? You act as if you agree or something!'

'I do, Mrs. Hampstead. I agree entirely.'

'Don't you patronize me,' Dorothy snarled. 'If you agree, then you'd know that Pears killed my husband.'

'No, Mrs. Hampstead, I don't know. Up to now you've told me nothing to persuade me that he was even remotely involved in the death of your husband. What I do know is that Mr. Pears, or Mr. Park as we know him now, was the one who tipped off the police in the first place. And I do know he was one of the last people to talk to your husband before his untimely death.'

'Untimely! Is there ever a good time to die?'

'I don't expect there is,' Arthur conceded with a submissive wave of his hand. 'Forgive me, what I meant, was untimely regarding the information he might have been able to give to the police.' He picked up another piece of paper from the folder. 'There are several more articles here. This one is a comment by inspector Stubbs that your husband's suicide did little to prove his innocence.'

'That man!' Dorothy hissed. 'I tell you, he's stupid. God knows how he's got as high up in the police force as he has now.' She shook her head in dismay. 'And God knows how many innocent people he has had convicted because he hadn't the ability to do a proper job.'

Arthur ignored her comments and pressed on. 'What did your husband tell Mr. Pears when he called?'

'He told him all about me suggesting he come back to Wales to see to the cattle. When he arrived home Creedy and his henchman Prosser were there, sitting about the house as if nothing unusual was going on. Then before Billy could turn around, the police were coming through the doorway.'

'Yes. What else?'

'I'm getting to that,' Dorothy said irritably. 'He told him he saw a car parked up on the top road, with one man in it and that there was another chap walking across the fields to it, with a bag in his hand, a duffle bag. Never thought anything of it after the police raid because he presumed it was one of the police cars to do with the raid. That's why he never mentioned it to Stubbs or anybody else in his statement.'

'Go on.'

'Well,' Dorothy continued, feeling that Greythorpe was beginning to be genuinely interested in what happened to her husband, 'Pears told Billy that it was important to tell Stubbs about the car, especially as he could remember the last part of the car's registration number. Then he ups and goes just as I came out of the kitchen with the tea and Welsh cakes. But before he left, Pears told Billy not to mention that he had told him about the car. But he didn't know I'd overheard everything.'

'Why would he tell your husband not to say he had told anyone else?' Arthur asked, frowning.

'Why indeed? He wanted time to plan how to silence him, of course, that's why,' Dorothy said raising her voice, 'I'd have thought that was obvious.'

'Hmm, I see.' The inspector contemplated what she had said while he thumbed through the folder. 'Quite comprehensive this file, you know. Here's an article about the trial of Creedy and Prosser. Eight years for Prosser, twelve for Creedy. Do you know they were out within weeks of each other?'

Dorothy shrugged her shoulders to indicate that she wasn't in the least bit interested.

'Prosser got no remission. Served his full sentence. Seems almost as if he didn't want to get out.'

'What point are you making now?' Andrew asked impatiently.

'Oh, I was just wondering if you'd ever met either of them, Mr. Hampstead, that's all'

'They had nothing to do with me. They were over in Wales.'

'What about Creedy? You never met him?'

'Don't even know what he looks like,' Andrew said, shaking his head.

'Hmm, I see,' Arthur said as he paged on through the folder. 'A good day's reading here,' he commented as he came to the brown envelopes at the bottom of the pile of papers. 'Your daughter had this file with her in her car earlier this evening,' he stated casually as he closed up the folder and snapped the elastic band around it.

'Rebecca? So where is she?' Dorothy asked. 'What have you done with her?'

'What have *I* done with her? I haven't done anything with her, Mrs. Hampstead. What I want to know is if you have seen her since she abandoned her car half a mile beyond Sunnybridge Farm.'

Andrew's his face became grave. 'Abandoned? What do you mean?'

'Her car ran off the road onto the soft verge,' Arthur explained. 'There was no sign of any attempt to drive it back onto the road, but it obviously skidded off it in the first place. The key was left in the ignition. I found this folder under the front passenger seat. It probably slid off the back seat when the car braked.'

Dorothy looked shaken. 'She's had an accident! Have you checked the hospitals?'

'Yes, Mrs. Hampstead, that's the first thing I did. Then I came here. I thought perhaps she'd walked home until I saw you preparing her meal.'

'And you've waited all this time to tell us!' Andrew exclaimed, furiously. 'My God! What sort of policeman are you?'

'The local police are making enquiries for me,' Arthur said calmly. 'There is nothing else we can do until we are sure she isn't calling on friends or something. After all, she might have been here at home.'

Andrew and Dorothy looked at each other in silence while Arthur Greythorpe replaced the file in his briefcase. He stood up, tucked it under his arm, and turned to the door. 'You will let me know if you think of any reason for the burglary at the farmhouse in Wales, won't you?' he asked as he let himself out. He didn't expect a reply, and was already unlatching the outside door. Dorothy and Andrew just followed him without saying a word.

'Good night,' said the inspector as he ducked into his car.

'Good night,' Andrew said with a cursory nod. Dorothy said nothing. Her mind was on Rebecca. She turned back into the house without waiting to see the policeman drive away. A few moments later, Andrew closed the door, and joined her in the kitchen.

'Oh Andrew!' she said, biting her lip to stop it trembling.

'What's happening? What are we going to do?'

Andrew put his arm around his sister's shoulders. 'We'll know soon,' he said and squeezed her reassuringly, 'I promise.'

CHAPTER TWENTY TWO

Any morning, seven o'clock was early for Simon to be knocked out of bed by the continuous thumping on his front door. But this morning he found it unbearable. He hadn't had much sleep. He had only arrived back at the house two hours ago, thrown off his shoes and jacket, and was dozing fitfully on top of the bedclothes, when he heard the noise. He groaned, swung his legs off the bed, and cradled his head. For a few seconds there was peace and quiet, and then, the loud knocking started again. He ran his fingers though his hair exhaled hard to drive the sleep from his tired body and stood up. A weary arm reached out and grabbed his dressing gown as he passed the bedroom door. He put his arms into it, wrapped it around his body and tied the belt as he walked down the narrow passageway towards the outer door.

A pair of deep sunken eyes stared at him out of the grey murky morning as the door opened. 'Oh, it's you,' Simon said with little enthusiasm.

'Hello Simon.' Arthur stood on the doorstep waiting for Simon to invite him in. 'Can I come in then?' he asked eventually to demolish the wall of silence.

'Huh, I suppose so, so long as you aren't going to make any more of your silly accusations.' Simon stood back from the door and turned to lead the way to the kitchen. Arthur closed the door, dropped his briefcase to the floor and followed him through to the kitchen. 'I seem to remember that you made a silly accusation, Simon,' he replied eventually.

Simon shrugged. 'All right, I'm sorry I accused you of having me followed, I was wrong.' he admitted without any further word of apology.

'Wouldn't mind a coffee, Simon,' he pleaded.

Simon went over to the worktop and began to fill the kettle. 'Right, coffee it is.' he sighed as he switched it on and then hunted in a cupboard for two mugs. Arthur seemed friendlier than he had been lately. Their solid friendship from years ago was gradually weathering the storm. Simon smiled inwardly to himself.

Arthur sat at the table. 'Got anything to eat?' he asked.

'You might as well join me for breakfast, if you like Arthur. What is it they say, two can eat as cheaply as one?' said Simon as he opened the refrigerator door and took out the bottle of milk.

'Could never reckon that one out personally,' replied Arthur in his usual droll voice.

Simon smiled. 'Cereals or fried?'

'Both?' Arthur suggested, intimating a plea of famine.

'Coming around I see,' Simon observed.

'You don't deserve a friend,' Arthur chided. 'You held back on me.'

'When?' asked Simon without turning around. He poured two mugs of steaming coffee as Arthur went on.

'You knew who Mrs. Hampstead really was, didn't you?'

Simon didn't answer. He set himself about the task of making breakfast. Arthur waited for an answer to his question but hit a wall of silence. 'What is it with you?' he said eventually. 'I don't think you realize just what a serious matter this is.'

'Me!' Simon exclaimed as he turned on the detective. '*I* don't?'

'That's what I said.'

'What a short memory you've got, Arthur,' Simon rebuked, shaking his head. 'It wasn't long ago that you were accusing me of murder.' He waved a spatula at Arthur, finding it hard to be angry with his long time friend. 'How much more serious can it get?'

Arthur fidgeted in his seat. 'That isn't exactly true. You know that.'

'Near as damn it.'

'I said,' Arthur explained, 'that you might have had good reason to do it. I didn't say you did.'

'Huh.' Simon turned back to the stove. 'It certainly didn't come across like that, Arthur, you know that.' He stabbed at the hot bacon, and sizzling tomatoes oblivious to the spitting, hot fat.

Arthur looked at Simon's back, and sighed. A deep frown cracked his mask as he spoke again. 'The truth isn't always the easiest to believe and you know that, Simon,' he stated in a conciliatory tone. He picked up his coffee and took a satisfying swig.

'So what changed your mind then?' Simon asked, his mood already softening noticeably. He cracked two eggs into a glass bowl and opened the refrigerator to search for more ingredients.

'As I said,' Arthur stated, 'the truth is sometimes hard to believe. I can hardly believe it myself in this case.

'Simon beat the eggs and then reached for four slices of bread from the bread bin. 'You mean everybody's here?' he asked as he cut the slices in half and dipped them in the egg.

Arthur watched him place them in the hot fat and then sniffed appreciatively. 'Everybody!' he said and nodded. 'It's as if all the actors in a play had appeared back on the stage more than eight years after the play had closed down, and carried on as if nothing had happened in between. Only, it's set in a different location.'

'All the actors?' asked Simon, turning to see Arthur's face.

'All the important ones at any rate.' Arthur stood up and started rummaging in the cupboards.

'Starting with me I suppose?' Simon asked and then added, 'Bottom left,' waiving the spatula at his kitchen units.

'No, starting with Prosser,' replied Arthur as he went to the far cupboard and opened it. 'It was he who re-catalysed the whole business. If it weren't for his death as soon as he left prison, I wouldn't have been here. It wasn't by coincidence that I was assigned to that case. I heard about his body being discovered by a man walking his dog. When there was a definite identification, I went to the Chief and asked if I might look into it. He contacted the police force in the area where the body had been found, and notified them that I would be investigating the killing from my own angle.' He took out two plates and placed them on the table and then continued his search.

'Which was?' Simon asked again, this time pointing to the third drawer from the end.

'Creedy.'

Simon placed the French fried bread on two plates and put the bacon and some fried tomatoes on top of them.

'And?'

'And I located Creedy,' said Arthur, placing cutlery next to the plates. 'He was at his old London nightclub. Seems like he was trying to gain control over the boys he had left in charge. They didn't particularly like him trying to take over the rackets they had run for themselves. He'd been away for eight years, remember, a long time in their business. New bosses and new partnerships had emerged.'

'But he still had his club?'

'On paper, he still had several. But they were being run by a man called Vickers.'

'Vickers?' Simon turned away from his chores again. 'You mean Martin Vickers?'

Arthur's face didn't move. 'That's the one. Surrounded by a stable of the hardest thugs you could wish to shovel out of a cesspit.'

Simon sucked in a whistle. 'I see,' he said and then turned and finished off cooking breakfast without saying another word. He placed them in the oven, then dished out the cereals and poured out more instant coffee.

Gradually, the corn flakes disappeared, the conversation resumed. 'Vickers was the one who supplied the heroin to Creedy,' Simon said through a mouthful of cornflakes. Arthur nodded, preferring not to speak with his mouth full. 'It was his car that Bill Henson saw.'

'You *think* it was his car, Simon. You only had half the number. The police never traced it to him.'

'Another coincidence then, his turning up and taking over from Creedy,' Simon quipped.

'Yes, that's what I thought. Right, how about that cooked breakfast?' Arthur asked as he put the cereal bowl to one side and picked up his coffee. Simon swivelled off his chair and opened the oven. He grabbed an oven cloth, took hold of the hot plates and put them on the table. Arthur had already demolished two half slices of French fried bread by the time Simon had closed the oven door, replaced the oven cloth on the hook beneath the worktop and re-seated himself. 'Well, anyway,' Arthur said between fork-fulls of breakfast, 'Creedy hadn't got his big guns anymore, and he hadn't much money to buy and set up his own stable.'

'So he came down here.'

'Went to Wales first,' Arthur corrected. 'He went to Cil Cwm Farm. I know because I followed him there. Now what did he want to go back there for?' Arthur asked as he waved his fork at Simon. 'What was the great attraction? Think about it Simon, he was short of money.' He waited for Simon to speak, but instead, he just looked back at Arthur patiently. He knew Arthur was going to tell him whether he knew the answer to his question or not. 'I'll tell you,' Arthur said, cutting into his last rasher of bacon. 'It wasn't the heroin that Prosser had told you had gone missing during the raid. Whoever took it, if there was as much as Prosser said there was, would have shifted the stuff long ago.

'Unless Creedy had hidden it.'

'In that case he would have found it and gone back to London,' Arthur said grinning triumphantly across the table.

'What if someone else found it and he came down here looking for it?'

'He came down here looking for something, that's for sure,' Arthur agreed. 'He squatted in that farmhouse down the road for four days in all, hardly going out as far as I saw. Couldn't watch him round the clock though. He made just the one visit during the day; that I do know.'

Simon looked up from his plate. 'One visit?'

'That's right. To Pendle Court Farm. He was there over an hour on the Thursday before the fire. Mind you, can't swear he saw anybody. Couldn't follow him far enough up the lane to see him actually call at the house or see him do anything else if it comes to that.'

Arthur finished off his breakfast and sat back in his chair, sipping at his coffee as he watched Simon finish his food. The silence seemed endless, broken only by the sound of Simon's knife and fork working on the plate, and a small carriage clock on the top of the cooker, monotonously ticking away the seconds of the early morning.

Eventually, Simon leaned back from his empty plate and picked up his mug of coffee. He drank it off. 'So where does that get us?'

'That gets Creedy on the stage,' Arthur answered. 'Then there's the fire. Until then, I hadn't connected anybody else with him.'

'But then you discovered that I was living practically next door.'

'Right. So what do we think? Creedy was on the stage. He dies in the fire, and I find you have been here all the time.'

Simon sighed. 'Meaning?'

'Meaning that puts you on the stage.' He watched for Simon's response. Simon just smiled.

'But, there's more.' Arthur continued. 'Gradually, and without any help from you...' Arthur's glare seemed to harden. 'I discover you are friendly with *Miss* Hampstead. But even more remarkably, *Mrs.* Hampstead then turns out to be none other than, guess who, Mrs. Henson!'

'That's three, not including Prosser,' Simon accounted before Arthur could state the same conclusion.

'Three, right.' He stared at Simon expectantly.

'That's all is it?'

'You tell me, Simon. Who else is down here? Who else was connected with that case eight years ago?'

'I thought you were telling this story,' Simon said evasively.

'Still not much help, I see,' Arthur said cuttingly. 'Well never mind, I'll tell you, since I don't think you know.'

Simon smiled confidently. 'Thought you might.'

'Andrew Hampstead.'

The name came out of the blue. It wasn't the one Simon had expected. 'Andrew Hampstead?' His face registered disbelief.

'The one and only.'

'How did he get into it?' exclaimed Simon.

'It just happens that it was he who introduced Creedy to William Henson in the first place.'

'He can't have,' Simon argued. 'Henson told me himself that they'd met in the pub.'

'By arrangement, courtesy of Andrew.' Arthur stated with a smug smile.

'If Creedy's dead, who told you that story? Certainly wouldn't be Andrew Hampstead.'

'An old farm worker called Earnest Henshaw. Got chatting to him in the lane the day I followed Creedy to Pendle Court.'

'Poor old sod, he probably thought you were being friendly!'

Arthur smiled a rare smile. 'I'm a friendly sort of person Simon, you know that! Anyway, I casually mentioned seeing someone drive past, someone I thought I recognized and he just told me he'd seen him meet Andrew Hampstead years ago. Got a good memory for strangers' faces these country folk, though it took him a minute or two to recall,' Arthur said casually. 'Now they *did* meet in a pub. It just happens it was in Earnest Henshaw's local.'

'Is that it then?'

'As far as it goes.'

Simon waited a moment. 'Not got all the players then yet?'

'Haven't I? You tell me, Simon.'

'You never met Stubbs, did you?' Simon asked in an aside manner.

'True. I got kicked back into touch before I could do much at all.'

'I'm grateful for what you did do,' Simon said with genuine affection.

'What are old friends for?' Arthur said raising his eyebrow.

'I sometimes wonder with you! But seeing you've levelled with me, I'm going to tell you that he is a fifth player on the stage.'

Not surprisingly, Arthur's face showed no sign of surprise. His answer gave more away. 'So I believe,' he said.

'You know then?'

'Seems like he's a chief inspector,' said Arthur derisively.

'I didn't know he was still in the force. I thought he said he was retiring and going private years ago.'

'So did I,' said Arthur. 'According to official records he left the police force. But that also happens when people go under cover. What I can't understand however is that he's parading himself as my superior officer by all accounts.'

'And isn't he?'

'Don't even know what he looks like, Simon, I never met him, remember?

Simon nodded

'I'll be sending off for a photograph of him when I reach the station. With that I'll have a chance at finding him. Then I'll find out just what he's playing at.'

Simon thought for a moment. 'He'll know your every move,' he stated eventually.

'Is that going to matter I wonder?' Arthur replied unperturbed.

'Depends what he's up to, doesn't it.'

'That's true,' Arthur nodded. He looked directly into Simon's eyes for a response to his next question. 'Do you know where Rebecca Hampstead is?'

For a moment Simon seemed perplexed. 'How do you mean?'

'Do you know where she is? It's a straight forward question.'

'Well, isn't she where she should be?'

'At the farm you mean?'

Simon nodded. 'Yes.'

'No,' Arthur replied. 'She disappeared from her car just a bit further down the road from Sunnybridge Farm. Drove her car onto the grass verge and left it there. A patrol car spotted it and notified me when they'd traced the number to her.'

'Didn't she walk home then?'

'Thought she might have called here, Simon,' Arthur suggested, watching for his young friend's reaction.

'Here! Heck no! She'd walk to hell and back first!'

'Oh, you've had a tiff then?'

'More of a difference of opinion, I'd say.'

'Are you going to expand on that?'

'Well if you really want to know,' Simon said awkwardly, 'It's just that she's got this crazy idea, nothing too serious mind, that I killed her father.'

'Hmm. I see.' Arthur's face gave nothing away. 'So she didn't go home, and she didn't come here.' He sighed and shook his head. 'It doesn't look too good,' he said and gazed at the table top.

'What are you saying Arthur?'

'It seems to me that somebody is still looking for something and it seems to me,' he said and watched Simon's response, 'that she would be a perfect lever, wouldn't you say?'

Simon scowled. 'Kidnapped? Is that what you're saying, she's been kidnapped?'

'Can't say for sure. She just might walk into Pendle Court this morning and say she stayed with friends.'

'Well haven't you checked them?'

'The local police will be doing that this morning. As I said, I only found out around midnight, that she hadn't gone home.'

'Bloody hell Arthur! You sit here while I make your breakfast, and then tell me this! We've got to start looking. Now!' Simon got up and went through to his bedroom. Arthur followed him and watched as Simon put on his shoes.

'No use rushing at it Simon. The local lads are doing all they can, I'm sure.'

'I tried to warn her,' Simon said, his voice shaking. 'I tried to warn her that she might be in danger. But she took no notice.' His face gave away much more in one second than words ever could.

'I see you like her,' the detective commented. He managed a slight smile. 'If I didn't know you better my boy, I'd say she'd hooked you!'

'Hell no Arthur! She's young and impressionable. I like her for that. But she's got one heck of a temper.' Simon shook his head and blew out his cheeks.

'A bit like you then,' Arthur sniped.

Simon put his hand on one hip and sighed. 'It never ceases to astonish me just how little you know me Arthur, do you know that?'

Arthur ignored the remark. 'She's a thinker as well,' he said.

'Thinker?'

'Can use her head.'

'Oh, she's very clever,' Simon confirmed. 'She practically runs Pendle Court Farm now,' he said as he took a sweater out of a drawer.

'You'd know all about that, wouldn't you,' Arthur said and picked up his case from where he'd dropped it. He walked through to the kitchen and Simon followed. 'I'm getting to know you better by the day,' he said as he lifted a thick green folder onto the table.

'So I see,' Simon replied with a scowl. 'Where did you get that?' he couldn't help himself asking.

'So you recognise it then?'

Simon nodded. 'Yes, I compiled it for somebody.'

'I found it in her car. It looked to me as if it had slid off the back seat and underneath the front passenger seat when she pulled up on the grass verge. If she was kidnapped, that file could easily have gone unnoticed. Quite a biography on you isn't it?'

'That's one of the things she wanted.'

'And what else did she want?'

'Information about the death of her father more than anything, Arthur. You know,' he said sarcastically, 'she thought I killed him, remember?'

'And you supplied that information?'

Simon gave Arthur an uneasy smile. 'It seems like I was wrong about your having me followed. It turned out to be a P.I.'

'I told you, but you refused to believe me Simon!' Arthur said, raising his voice triumphantly.

'Well, do you blame me?' Simon shrugged to evade the admonition.

'I suppose you cornered him then?'

Simon nodded. 'Seemed quite cooperative. In fact, I got the feeling he wanted me to stop him.'

'Oh? How's that exactly?'

'He told me outright what he wanted to know.'

'And you told him of course?'

'Well, eventually. After a little bargaining. After all,' Simon said raising his arms in resignation, 'when I'd established it was Rebecca who wanted the information, I realized he could accomplish what I had failed to do over the last few weeks.'

'Which was?'

Simon's brow creased. 'Which was to try and explain what really did happen all those years ago, when Rebecca was only a child. She wouldn't listen to me. Every time I thought I had just broken down her barrier so that I could talk to her, I found we were no longer on talking terms!'

'Beginning to lose your touch then?' Arthur commented. 'I seem to recall...'

'Rubbish!' Simon broke in. 'You've never hung around me long enough to recall anything!'

'Not in your adult life, perhaps. But I saw you had a way with the girls even at school. I remember coming to visit you one weekend and you practically had a roster for them.'

'You just happened to call at a busy time, that's all Arthur. I'd been ill and had a lot of notes to copy up. You really mustn't read into things.'

'It'd be a devil if I didn't in my job!'

'I've told you about that as well.' His frown deepened and his face became deadly serious. 'What about Rebecca, Arthur?'

'As I've said, the local lads will let us know if they have located her. Give them a chance, heh?' Arthur stood up to leave, but then turned to face Simon once more. 'Tell me Simon,' he asked, 'can you recall how William Henson remembered the car on the road above the farm?'

'Easy. I asked him.'

'Why?'

'Because the police raid involved several cars, all of which would have had to be stationed within radio contact of each other. One would have had to be on the top road to watch what was going on at the farmhouse. The others would have had to be in the same valley to get good reception. It would have been tried and tested well in advance. It wasn't just an ad hoc swoop, according to Stubbs; it was a planned and organised raid. I told him long before the Hensons went away on holiday. He should have caught the supplier as well.'

Arthur nodded.

'Right,' Simon continued, 'so why weren't the police cars there? If Henson had seen a police car, plain or otherwise, then the supplier would have been arrested as well. So obviously they were nowhere around until the supplier had been and gone. I knew that had been the case, so I asked Henson if he'd seen any cars as he drove to the farm to establish for sure that the police hadn't acted on my information until it was almost too late. He'd only seen the one, and that wasn't a police car! All they had done is go straight from the station, drive to the farm, go into the yard, and knock at the door. The one person I had expected to be caught got away Scott free, money and all!'

'Vickers?'

Simon nodded. 'As soon as Henson told me, I knew it was Vickers' car Henson had seen. When he described it I realized that Stubbs had fudged the whole thing from start to finish, and then, to cover his tracks, he denied getting any information from me!'

'But you told Henson to tell Stubbs about the car, didn't you?'

'Yes. It was a last resort to try and get Vickers nailed.'

'It would have helped clear Henson as well,' Arthur added.

'Right.'

'So why did you tell Henson not to mention the fact that he had discussed this with you? You told him to say he'd just remembered the car.'

'Because I wanted to see what Stubbs did about it. The fact that there were no police cars there made me sure Stubbs would have to tell the truth about my tip off, but I wanted to see if he would, without his thinking I'd put Henson up to it. How was I to know Henson would get killed?'

'You don't think he killed himself then?'

'To be quite honest, I have no idea. He was depressed by the whole affair, but he didn't seem suicidal, especially when I told him that if he mentioned the car to Stubbs it might clear him of any involvement in the case.'

Arthur sighed. 'I see,' he stated flatly, pausing a moment before continuing. 'Mrs. Henson is convinced her husband was murdered.'

'You don't have to tell me that! She thinks I did it!'

'If he was murdered, then I can only presume Vickers knew Henson had seen him in the car. It could have been providential that you told him not to mention speaking to you.'

'Providential?'

'If he was killed because of what he saw it might just have saved your neck as well.'

Simon shrugged. 'I'd thought that myself. Involving Vickers though would take a lot of proving Arthur. You'd need a confession.'

'Not if he's the latest actor in our little play,' Arthur said and turned to the door. Then he turned back and faced Simon. 'What put you onto the deal in Wales to start with, Simon?'

'A tip off the year before, Arthur. You know how these things happen. A woman who worked behind the bar at one of Creedy's night clubs. It went on from there. It seemed obvious he was up to something when he went on holiday without either his wife *or* his mistress. Just his bouncer, Prosser, for company! But when he was there, he carried on the semblance of being on holiday, fishing in the river and walking during the day, and talking to the locals in the pub in the evenings.'

'And did he have any visitors' Arthur asked.

'Oh yes, he had visitors all right.'

Arthur grunted and turned to the door once again. 'Hmm.' he said, and then, 'There's something we don't know fully yet, something about those other visitors. Who were they, what did they want? Have you any idea?'

'All I know is what Prosser told me when I saw him in jail. Some sort of deals, but not drugs. Creedy never let him sit in on them like he did with the deliveries of heroin; that's when he needed a body guard.'

With little else to discuss Arthur nodded his appreciation and unlatched the door.

Simon smiled as he watched Arthur leave and then, when the car was well out of sight, he turned quickly to go inside. He had much to do and just hoped he wasn't running out of time.

CHAPTER TWENTY THREE

Dorothy had neither slept nor eaten anything in the last two days. Try as she may to believe that Rebecca would return safely, the words of Inspector Greythorpe kept coming back into her mind. Two local police officers had been stationed at the farm to record any incoming phone calls and Arthur had instructed them to contact him if anybody rang with a message about Rebecca. But apart from a short call from his superior, Stubbs, nobody had called about her. All he had done was ask the same questions as Greythorpe, and she had told him exactly the same; she didn't know what Creedy had been looking for. Apart from that one call, the telephone had been strangely quiet.

It was almost noon when the sudden noise of the door knocker hammered through the quiet lonely house. Somehow, the banging had come as a relief, breaking through her anxiety and injecting a glimmer of hope into her weary mind. 'Good morning Mrs. Hen...er, Hampstead.'

'Oh,' she said despondently. 'It's you again is it?'

'Yes,' Arthur confirmed in a not too serious voice. 'It's me again.' He waited for Dorothy to ask him in, but she just stood and waited for him to say something. 'I've called about your daughter.'

'You have?' Her voice rose excitedly. 'You've found her?'

Arthur shook his head. 'Not yet, I'm afraid'.

'Is Mr. Hampstead about?' he asked.

'Yes,' came Andrew's voice from the office.

'So what's on your mind?' Dorothy asked, eager to move things along. She waved him through to the kitchen.

'Mrs. Hampstead,' Arthur began 'I need to go over the events that led to your husband's death again.'

Once again Dorothy slowly narrated the story for Arthur. 'If only I hadn't persuaded him to go back to the farm that day,' she stated sadly, shaking her head. 'But he was so worried about his stock. It seemed like the best thing to do.' She paused and reflected on what she had done. 'And if we hadn't rented out the cottage to Creedy in the first place.'

'And if you hadn't arranged for Billy to meet Mr. Creedy in a pub by accident as it were,' Arthur added. 'After all, you didn't know Creedy was a crook, did you?'

Dorothy scowled. 'No,' she said firmly. 'I didn't. You're a very devious man, Inspector Greythorpe. I suppose you're expecting me to break down with a confession or something. God knows how you found out about that, but it's too remote for you to blame me for what Creedy did. And even more remote for me to be blamed for what that Pears man did. Oh,' she said, leaning over the table and waving her finger in front of the deep sunken eyes, 'don't think I don't regret it. I do. Now I do. After everything that's happened, I do. But not before that. It was the best thing we ever did as far as we were concerned. An ailing farm, a chance for us all to get away and have a holiday each year, a windfall from renting the house, and wages for Billy into the bargain while he worked on this farm. It was the best thing we ever did and if he hadn't been framed and then murdered we would have lived and not regretted it one bit of it.'

'Hmm. So you don't deny that you knew Creedy before he met your husband?'

'You are on the wrong track, Inspector. It was you who suggested that I had arranged for Billy to be in the right place at the right time. I didn't say I knew Creedy.'

'Then who did? Mr. Hampstead was it?'

'Does it make all that much difference that it was Andrew who had introduced him?'

'I'm not sure.' He thought for a moment. 'So Andrew met Creedy first,' he concluded. 'Then what? Did Andrew contact you?'

'Andrew needed a reliable worker during the combining season. He knew we were struggling to make ends meet. He told me he knew somebody who was willing to rent a remote holiday cottage for three weeks every year, and he knew how much the man was willing to pay.'

'So why go all around the houses? Why didn't you just deal with Creedy direct?'

'Because Billy was a proud man. The harder he worked, the less he seemed to have to show for it. So we arranged it so that he could take the credit for renting the house. There's nothing like a bit of success to build a man's confidence you know.'

'That's true,' Arthur nodded

'So you see it makes no difference who met Creedy first. Nobody knew he was a crook.'

'Not then perhaps, Mrs. Hampstead. But what about now? What if Creedy was at Sunnybridge farm at the invitation of your brother? You both knew he was a crook when he came here.'

'He wasn't invited,' came a voice from the kitchen doorway. 'He's the last man I would want back into my life.'

Arthur swivelled around to see Andrew standing behind him.

'Ah, Mr. Hampstead, if you knew he was there,' Arthur ploughed straight in, 'that would mean you could have killed him.'

'I said I didn't tell him he could stay there. You aren't listening are you Inspector?' Andrew's tone was more adversarial than angry.

'Did you ever meet Prosser?'

'Never.'

'Hmm. I thought you'd say that,' said Arthur. 'It strikes me that you haven't been totally open about all this.'

'The whole matter was closed until you and that Pears chap came along, that's why,' Dorothy stated. 'No amount of re-hashing the facts will bring Billy back.'

'But it might save your daughter,' Arthur said and waited for a reaction.

'You mean you know where she is?'

'No, Mrs. Hampstead, I don't. But I do think that somebody has taken her against her will.'

'Oh no!' Dorothy uttered shakily. 'Then she *has* been kidnapped.'

'It looks very much that way. We'll know better as time passes of course, but I'd say that's about the strength of it.'

'So what can we do?' asked Andrew.

'We have to know why. Up to now, all I have come up with is a load of people who were involved in some way with the drugs raid on your farmhouse in Wales eight years ago. Somehow, they have ended up all together again only instead of in Wales, it's here. You knew Creedy all those years ago and I know you met him again here before the fire.'

'He called here the day before. I didn't know where he was staying. He called and then went. Simple as that.'

Arthur turned to Dorothy. 'What did he call for?'

Andrew looked at Dorothy. She wrung her hands and then clasped them together in front of her on the table. Arthur waited patiently for her to answer the question. 'What has this to do with finding my daughter?' she said evasively.

'Mrs. Hampstead,' Arthur said reassuringly. 'There are already several people who have been murdered, and all for the same reason. For all I know your husband might have been the first. What I do know for certain, however, is that both Prosser and Creedy have been murdered, Prosser probably for what he knew, and Creedy for what he was after. Creedy was definitely looking for something. He went all the way to Wales and then came here and squatted in Sunnybridge Farm in an attempt to find whatever it was. Now your daughter is missing and I have absolutely no doubt that the murderer has got her, and it isn't for what she knows. So it must be to get you to talk.' He grasped Dorothy's hands across the table. 'You must know what he was after. If you didn't know before he called, you must know now. He was a desperate man. He needed money. So what did he come here looking for? Tell me Mrs. Hampstead. You must tell me. Whoever has Rebecca will want to know. If I know what your answer will be I'll know where to be when that person goes looking.

'I...I...'

'Go on, tell me.'

'Perhaps...' Dorothy stuttered.

The telephone rang in the hallway. Her head swivelled, breaking Arthur's hypnotic gaze as her eyes unlocked themselves from his.

'Perhaps,' Andrew interrupted. 'Perhaps nothing has happened to Rebecca. She's a grown woman. We don't keep tabs on her all the time.'

'Mrs. Hampstead!' Arthur shouted after Dorothy as she stood up and rushed to the telephone. He grabbed her sleeve. 'Wait! What did Creedy want?' he shouted after her but it was too late, the moment had passed. She shrugged him off and ran into the hallway as fast as her legs could carry her.

'Hello,' she shouted desperately. 'Rebecca, is that you?'

'Could I speak to Inspector Greythorpe please?' a man's voice asked at the other end of the line.

'Oh.' Her heart sank. 'Hold on,' she said and put the receiver on the hall table. She walked unsteadily through to the kitchen. Arthur had already moved towards the door. 'It's for you,' she said despondently and brushed past his shoulder.

Without another word, he walked through to the hall to take his call. Dorothy stared at Andrew.

'Be careful,' he warned. 'That man is as slippery as bath soap.'

'But what about Rebecca?' she pleaded. 'He's trying to help.'

Andrew stood up and looked past her to the hall. He could still hear the policeman talking on the telephone. 'Rebecca will be all right,' he stated firmly. 'Believe me.' He took hold of Dorothy's shoulders and squeezed them. 'One thing I do know,' he said softly, 'is that dealing with that policeman won't find where she is. We'll find out soon enough.'

Dorothy shook her head in confusion. 'It's got to be that man down the road. He must have my daughter. He's doing this to me!'

'No, no,' Andrew whispered. 'Don't get it blown up out of proportion.'

Dorothy looked up into Andrew's determined face, her eyes filling with tears. 'You don't think it could be that man Creedy do you? Perhaps he isn't dead. Supposing...'

'Believe me,' Andrew said and squeezed her even harder. 'Believe me Dorothy, Creedy is dead. He died in the fire. Remember?'

'Did he though?' she implored, 'Did he die in the fire?' She sobbed into the palms of her hands. 'I should have told Creedy what he wanted to know when he came here. I should have, I know it.'

Andrew sat her at the table and patted her shoulder. 'Shh,' he said. 'Come on, be strong.'

'She needs to be strong,' Arthur's voice came from the doorway. Andrew was sure he'd not been there long. 'All I needed was a bit of cooperation.' He glared at Andrew. 'Now it's too late.'

'Rebecca!' Dorothy screamed. 'You've heard haven't you? Tell me!'

'Yes, I've heard, Mrs. Hampstead.' His voice was angry. 'Up to now, you've insisted on obstructing me in my investigation.' He looked them both in the eyes in turn. 'Both of you,' he growled. 'Well from now on, you are on your own. I won't wish you luck. You've had your share for today.'

'What have you heard?' Andrew demanded.

Arthur looked at Dorothy. 'Your daughter is going to be all right. She's on her way to the General hospital.' He swivelled on his heel and was gone before the others could reply.

CHAPTER TWENTY FOUR

It was another terrible dream in which her whole body ached, the blood pounded in her ears and the cold numbed her limbs. Rebecca didn't want to open her eyes for fear that she was still in that dream, because each time she woke she found that the dream became a nightmare. She wanted to sleep on.

The first time she woke, she had a splitting headache and every joint in her body ached with cold. A damp, foisty smell filled her nostrils as she took a conscious breath and prized open her eyelids to stare up at a dimly lit and unfamiliar ceiling. As her eyes focussed, she could see the flakes of old time-greyed whitewash hanging down on damp and ancient cobwebs. The cold seemed to bite even harder at her body as she moved her eyes from one bare wall to the other. Her back ached with the pressure of her bound hands beneath her spine, hands with no feeling, but which she knew were there from the position of her arms. A sharp pain shot through her throat when she tried to hoist her body off the damp mattress, forcing her to remain in the same painful position.

'My God! What's happened?' she croaked as a thin wire cut into her neck. Her head throbbed and unbearable pain racked every part of her body as she tried to remember, but her thoughts were muddled and nothing made sense. Two cars kept filling her mind. They were hemming her in and crushing her. She realized that she was fading back into unconsciousness and jerked her eyes open as wide as she could force them. They scanned the bare empty room but there was nothing there to see except a paint-flaked door facing the foot of the old bed, and a dirty window that let in a dim grey light.

It seemed like endless hours before a splash of mid-morning sunlight washed across her legs, restoring a little of the heat her body had lost. She was thankful now that she had put on her overcoat and her leg warmers before she had set out on her journey. The journey! She was remembering now. She remembered setting out to see the private detective. She remembered Simon appearing from nowhere and walking her to the offices after the trouble in the dark alley way.

As the sunlight began to flood into every corner of the room, she felt the chill leaving her body and even managed to move her hands beneath her enough to rest her back against the mattress, letting the blood circulate to her fingers. She hardly felt the pins and needles in her hands as her mind struggled to recall what had happened.

Gradually it all began to come back to her. She recalled the folder and the heavy rain, then the long slow drive home. Only she hadn't arrived home. Again, her memory faded. She struggled again to remember but the effort was sapping her strength and gradually, no longer able to hold back the tide of sleep, her eyelids closed and she gladly let unconsciousness wash over her again.

She awoke with a start. Something was on her neck, a hand, checking the tightness of the wire. As her eyes flashed open the strong sunlight blinded her. She hadn't slept long. The sun had hardly moved across the window. Or was it another time, another day? She wasn't sure. Her eyes still hurt from the sudden light. Perhaps she hadn't been awake before. Perhaps she wasn't awake now. It all seemed so unreal. It *was* unreal. As she regained her sight, she realized that two eyes were looking at her from behind a black and red woollen ski mask, not evil eyes, but an evil disguise. 'Who are you?' she rasped through dry lips.

The figure didn't reply but turned and walked out of the open door. Rebecca watched and waited and a few seconds later the figure returned holding a small syringe. Terrified, now she remembered the two cars, one in front driving slower and slower, one behind getting closer and closer. Then, the car in front stopped suddenly. She remembered twisting hard on the steering wheel. Her car swerved off the hard road onto the grass verge where, with her foot hard on the brake, it slid to a halt. Before she could unfasten her seat belt the car door had opened and an unfamiliar face peered inside. A hand with a syringe hovered near her. She screamed and tried to grab the hand but it had gone, plunging the needle downwards and into her thigh. A sharp prick and then all she could remember after that was a tranquil euphoric feeling gradually working its way through her whole body. Her scream echoed in her head as she closed her eyes and the soft floating sensation flooded over her once again. In the shallow and fitful sleep that followed she could hear distant sounds but she couldn't move her body, nor could she lift her eyelids to allow her eyes to look for what was making them.

Suddenly she was conscious once more and the sounds had disappeared. Despite the sleep she felt much weaker. She struggled feebly with the plastic chord around her wrists, desperately tugging at the knot with her finger nails but nothing came free. She groaned desperately as the same faceless head appeared and disappeared before her eyes, and then she felt she was alone again. She shouted at the top of her voice, but no sound came from her dry throat. She pleaded, but nobody heard her plight. She tried to roll over to get off the bed, but the chord tightened again around her neck. The last thing she heard before passing out was the sound of men's voices shouting and then a loud crack that echoed through an old and empty building.

The room seemed to be moving. If only Simon had been here, she dreamed, he would have saved her from this nightmare the same way he saved her from the thugs in the alley. She saw his face through closed eyes, and heard his gentle soothing voice as he caressed her cheek with his fingers. He came and went with her delirium. Was it hours or seconds between each touch, each gentle word? She had no way of knowing. It was impossible to tell. One minute it was dark, the next it was light. Her body was cold but felt strangely warm. 'Rebecca,' a familiar voice coaxed. 'Rebecca, you are safe now,' she heard him say before passing out again.

The two tone siren barely broke through the blanket of sleep. A firm hand closed on hers and another gently stroked her brow as she drifted in and out of consciousness. The room was moving.

'You're all right now. You're safe,' she heard a voice say but it wasn't Simon's. She opened her eyes. It took a moment or two for them to focus, but gradually she could make out the pale pink features of a smiling, young ambulance man. He placed an oxygen mask to her face but she pushed it away with a heavy arm.

'No,' she croaked. 'Where's Simon?'

He smiled down at her. 'Who?' he asked.

'Simon,' she whispered, desperately. 'Where is he?'

The young man smiled comfortingly. 'I'm sure he'll be along soon,' he said and squeezed her hand to reassure her she was no longer dreaming.

CHAPTER TWENTY FIVE

Two squad cars were already parked outside the row of derelict houses when Arthur Greythorpe arrived. He pulled in behind them and brought his car to a halt. A uniformed police officer opened his door for him and he stepped out onto a crumbling pavement. 'Where is it?' he asked flatly.

'The one with the green door,' the officer replied and pointed beyond the two squad cars. Arthur walked to the building without a further word. He pushed the unlatched door back against the jamb.

'Ah, Inspector,' a plain clothed police officer greeted. He waved Arthur forward. 'It's through here.'

Arthur followed him through an open doorway into an old scullery. A photographer with a large camera stood up straight from a stooping position and stepped back for the inspector to see. 'You got all you want?' Arthur asked as he looked down at the corpse that lay in a sitting position against the back door. The dead man's eyes stared at the wall beside the scullery door and a red dash of blood that oozed from a hole in his forehead, had left a trail down the side of his nose, and dripped from a protruding bottom lip onto the collar of a white open-necked shirt.

'Just about, Sir.'

'Any idea who he is?'

'No Sir,' the officer was about to reply when a voice came from behind.'

An accomplice,' Simon stated.

Arthur swung around. Simon, unshaven, and weary-looking, stood at the door. 'Ah! It's so good of you to stay and explain! Where the hell have you been?'

'Had to see somebody off in an ambulance,' Simon smiled, his white teeth gleaming against the dark shadowy stubble that covered his face.

'Oh. How is she?'

'She's fine as far as I could tell. In the land of nod. Seems like she'd been given some sedatives.'

'Why didn't you tell me where you were?' Arthur demanded crossly.

Simon shrugged. 'I didn't know where I'd be going, not until I knew for sure that it was him.'

'Him?' Arthur's eyebrow asked the question.

'Stubbs.'

'Oh, and you just happened to know where to look, I suppose? Out of all the places where a person could hide, you logically thought, Ah, this is the most likely spot!' His sarcasm made his voice raise an octave.

'I knew he'd come to this area about the same time that you did Arthur.' Simon said, unperturbed by Arthur's mood. 'That was logical. But the rest was just coincidence.'

'You use that word a lot, I notice,' Arthur commented, rather sourly, Simon thought.

'Where was the best place for you to stay in order to keep an eye on what was happening, Arthur?' he asked pointedly.

Arthur grunted. He knew now what Simon's answer was going to be. 'The Windsurfer!' he said with a nod of acknowledgement.

Simon smiled. 'There were plenty of other hotel registers to check of course, but that seemed like the best place to start. You didn't know what he looked like...'

'They're faxing his picture to me this afternoon,' Arthur explained.

'But *I* did,' Simon continued. 'I knew somebody who might fit his description had booked in at the Windsurfer the same day as you arrived.'

'And how did you know this?'

'Mary Blandford,' Simon replied with a smile. 'She runs the hotel.'

'An old friend of yours, I suppose?'

'Well not so old actually,' Simon said, smiling.

Arthur just shook his head. 'And you discovered what?'

'I discovered that a man who fitted Stubbs' description had booked in. Stenton was his name.'

'Huh,' Arthur grunted.

'So after you left yesterday I went to the Windsurfer and asked if he was still booked in there.'

'And?'

'And I found out that he was, but that he came and went a lot during the day. He wasn't in his room, and his car wasn't in the park, so I just waited in my car and he turned up late in the evening. He eventually emerged after a late breakfast the following morning and I followed him here.' He paused and looked at Arthur, but Arthur just stared back at him waiting for him to finish his story. 'Well,' Simon continued, shrugging his shoulders, 'he entered the house and then left after about ten minutes.'

'So you came inside to have a look?'

'Well, no,' Simon said, fidgeting uncomfortably.

Arthur sighed.

'As he left, I saw there was another man in the doorway of the house, so I wasn't sure what to do then.'

'Call me, that's what you should have done,' Arthur reprimanded.

Simon shrugged again and continued his story, ignoring Arthur's stony glare. 'Well anyway, I waited for another hour or so, then, just as I was about to call you...' He looked into Arthur's deep eyes as the inspector grunted and gave a loud *tut.* 'Stubbs drove back up to the door,' Simon finished saying.

'But why didn't you call me? You had a telephone in your car.'

'I had to make sure I was right, Arthur,' Simon pleaded in mitigation. 'Anyway, things started to happen fast after that.'

'Really. You surprise me!'

'Yes,' Simon stated, ignoring the sarcasm in Arthur's voice. 'Stubbs went into the house, and I was just about to follow him in, when I heard a gun shot. That's when I decided to ring the station.'

'Not before time!'

'But then, Stubbs came out of the house and drove away.'

Arthur sighed. 'So did you ring the station then, or didn't you?' he asked, totally exasperated.

'I thought I'd better go in and have a look first.' Arthur shook his head incredulously and Simon continued his version of what had happened. 'I felt pretty sure it was Stubbs who had fired the gun, so I wasn't too worried about being shot at.'

'Obviously not!'

'But I was worried in case Rebecca was in there and he had been shooting at her.' He looked for approval in Arthur's eyes. There wasn't any. 'But I couldn't follow Stubbs and go into the house at the same time though, you understand?'

'Oh, I understand.' Arthur's tone was flat. 'So you chose the house, right?

'Right,' smiled Simon. 'And there this chap was.' He pointed past Arthur's shoulder to the corpse that sat watching them.

'And then what?' Arthur snorted in disgust.

'Then I had a good look around. I found Rebecca tied to the bed upstairs, so I released her and then called the police and you.'

'Hmm. I see.' Arthur rubbed his eyebrow. 'You've given the boys Stubbs' car number I suppose?'

'Yes.'

Arthur took a cursory look around the scullery and then walked past Simon. 'We'll need a statement. Are you coming?'

'Yes,' Simon answered obediently and followed him outside.

'Then, when we've sorted you out, we'll go see if Miss Hampstead can say anything about it.'

CHAPTER TWENTY SIX

When she awoke again, Rebecca felt warm and relaxed. Her left arm was stiff and bound in bandages but apart from that, the feel of crisp clean sheets was totally refreshing. The air smelt clean and antiseptic. A hand lifted her wrist and felt her pulse. Gradually, she opened her eyes. A young girl in a pink, starched nurse's uniform, smiled and glanced at the watch on her lapel. 'Good evening,' she said, and placed Rebecca's hand gently by her side.

Rebecca opened her mouth to speak, but her throat was dry. She whispered, 'Hello,' and then filled her lungs with air. 'Where am I?' she asked.

'Hospital,' the nurse replied. 'You've had a bit of an ordeal.' She gave her a sip of water from a spouted cup. 'There, I think that'll be a bit better.'

Rebecca tried to push herself up into a sitting position, but her left arm wouldn't move. She turned her head and saw that her arm was strapped to a board, and a drip feed, hanging from a frame, was connected to a cannula in the binding by a clear plastic tube.

'We'll be able to take that off for you now you've woke up,' the nurse explained cheerily as she proceeded to take Rebecca's blood pressure. She released the pressure and watched the mercury fall before speaking again. 'We'll soon have you up and about,' she stated. 'Everything seems to be back to normal now.' She jotted something down on the chart that hung at the foot of the bed and then asked, 'Is there anything you'd like?'

Rebecca thought for a moment. She couldn't help thinking how peaceful and quiet the place was. 'How about a cup of tea?' she said eventually.

The nurse smiled again. 'I'll see what the doctor says,' she said and walked away from the bed. It was then that Rebecca realized that she was in a room on her own. She looked to the window. It was dark outside. 'Nurse,' she called as best her voice would allow. 'Nurse!'

The nurse turned to face her patient. 'Yes?'

'What time is it?'

'Eight thirty,' the young girl said, glancing to her lapel.

'How long have I been here?'

'You came in yesterday dinner time according to your admission sheet. I wasn't on duty then.'

Rebecca nodded. 'Sunday today then?' she said to make sure just how long she'd been unconscious.

'No, Monday,' the nurse corrected.

'I see. Has anybody..?'

'Your mother and father have been to see you, but you were fast asleep. They only left a while ago. They'll probably be back soon.'

'Uncle,' Rebecca corrected. 'It would be my uncle.'

'Oh, sorry, I just presumed...' She shrugged her shoulders.

'Has anybody else been?'

'I'm not sure. I can ask if you like.'

'No, that won't be necessary. My mother will tell me when she comes.'

'Right, I'll see what we can do for you as far as tea goes,' the nurse said and floated out of the room. As the door closed, she thought she caught a glimpse of the shoulder of a policeman sitting outside in the corridor.

Within five minutes the nurse had returned with a doctor. Rebecca had already pushed herself into a sitting position. The doctor, a short man with dark hair, a dark sun tan and a tiny splash of a moustache, asked how she felt while he looked at the chart.

'I feel fine doctor,' Rebecca said with a grateful smile.

'Good.' The doctor smiled back pleasantly. He turned to the nurse. 'You can bring her some tea and a little something to eat if she wants.'

'Doctor,' Rebecca said suddenly. 'I've changed my mind.'

'Very well,' he said as he hooked the chart on the bed rail. But if you want anything...'

'No, I mean I want to go,' Rebecca stated firmly. The doctor looked at her quizzically. 'My dear,' he said in a concerned voice. 'You have just come round from a very heavy dose of tranquilizer. Even now, we have not had the tests back from the lab to tell us just what it was. We have a rough idea, and gave you stimulants to counter the effect, but you are best resting until your system is totally clear of it.'

'I'm fine. I just want to go home.'

'Miss Hampstead, we cannot advise that.' He shook his head. 'But we cannot force you to stay. If you are determined to leave, however, then we would ask you to sign a document exempting us from liability.'

'That's all right. Can I use the phone?'

The doctor turned to the nurse. 'Have a telephone brought in will you. And tell Sister to get a discharge form.' He turned back to Rebecca. 'Just when do you intend leaving?'

'When I get some clothes.'

'Very well, I'll come and see you shortly.' He turned and left the room, leaving Rebecca staring after him. 'Get in touch with your superior officer,' he instructed the policeman outside the room. 'Tell them she is going to discharge herself.'

No sooner had Rebecca put down the telephone than Dorothy came bustling through the doorway. 'Good heavens!' she gasped. 'You've woke up!'

Rebecca grinned. 'I know, you thought you'd pop out and do some shopping!'

'I wouldn't have gone out at all, only they said you'd not wake up till morning. Doctors!' She put her arms around Rebecca and hugged her. 'Still, they won't get me out of here again so easily.'

'I hope so mum. I've just called Uncle Andrew for my clothes.'

'You what? You young monkey! Don't you think you are pushing your luck a bit too far? You're lucky to be alive, do you know that? If it hadn't been for...' She stuttered to a halt.

'For what mother?'

'For...For that man.' She looked away awkwardly.

'What man mother? Who are you talking about?'

'That...that man. You know!' She pointed her thumb over her shoulder as if it explained everything.'

You mean Inspector Greythorpe?'

'Heh?' Dorothy said, looking back at her daughter. 'Oh, yes, him as well I suppose.'

'Then who did you mean mum? What's the matter, can't you remember?'

'Of course I can remember,' Dorothy said crossly. 'That Park man, you know.'

'Park man? You mean Simon Park?'

Dorothy scowled. 'Well who else do you think I mean, the man who cuts the grass on the municipal playing fields?' She shook her head. 'One of him's enough isn't it?'

Rebecca didn't answer. She didn't know the answer to that question any more. There had been a time when her mother would have been right. One Simon Park would have been just enough. Now, well she didn't want to say that. She couldn't bring herself to say it was one too many. She didn't really feel that any more, but she didn't really know why either.

'It's just that he…' Dorothy paused.

'What about him mother?' Rebecca asked, fearing that somehow he'd had something to do with what had happened to her.

'He went and found you, didn't he?' Dorothy said as if anybody else in the world would have been better than Simon Park for accomplishing that task.

'Found me? You mean...'

'I mean he found you. That's what I said and that's what I mean,' Dorothy said reproachfully.

Rebecca's serious face cracked into a grin. 'It *was* him!' she whispered. 'I knew it!'

'Knew what?'

'Oh, I just vaguely remember seeing him. I thought I'd been dreaming.'

'Well it seems like you weren't. I've just been talking to that Inspector Greythorpe feller and he told me it was him that found you and called for an ambulance.'

'How? How did he find me?'

'Oh don't ask me. That's all I could get out of the policeman. I had a feeling he was gloating. Horrible man!'

'Oh mother! He can't be that bad.'

'No. That's what I've been thinking about that Park chap.'

'Simon mother. His name's Simon. You really do make him sound like a community gardener or something.'

'It might have been better if he had been. Wouldn't have turned up in our lives again then would he?'

'But you don't still think he had anything to do with dad's death do you?'

Dorothy took hold of Rebecca's hand and squeezed it. She settled on a chair at the side of the bed. 'Well,' she said awkwardly. 'I must admit, that I was beginning to have my doubts anyway. You see, I always had a feeling right at the back of my mind that your dad did go and see that inspector.'

'Inspector? You mean...'

'Stubbs,' came a voice from the doorway. Arthur had come through the door and was waiting for an opportune moment to break up the reunion. 'Seems obvious now, doesn't it? Especially since he was the man Simon followed to where you were being held prisoner.'

Rebecca leaned back against her pillows. 'The man in the mask,' she said and stared at the opposite wall. 'The man in the mask; of course!'

'That's what I need to talk to you about Miss Hampstead,' Arthur said as he pulled up a chair and sat beside Dorothy. I need to know for sure who your kidnappers were, and how they abducted you.'

Rebecca shook her head. 'I can't tell you. He wore a ski mask.' Rebecca thought for a moment. 'It was black with a red band around the face.'

Arthur put his hand in his pocket and took out a Polaroid photograph. 'Did you see this man?' he asked and handed it to Rebecca.

Rebecca looked at it. Nothing was hidden. The face was that of a dead man with blood running down the side of his nose. She took a sharp breath when she saw it, looked away, and handed it back to the inspector. 'Yes, that was the man who grabbed me out of my car.'

Methodically, Rebecca related what had happened from the moment she had began her journey home that night. Arthur sat and listened without any look of acknowledgement. Dorothy sat spellbound; unable to utter anything except for the odd interjection. When Rebecca had finished her account of what had happened, Arthur stood up. 'Fine, that will do for now. I believe you are going home tonight?' he said in an appreciative manner.

'Yes.'

'Then I'd be obliged if I could collect you in a day or so and take you down to the station to get this all in writing.'

'OK.' Rebecca smiled. She felt almost light headed. Recalling the story had got it off her mind. Now all she had to do was go home and be with her family. Somehow, she knew she'd be seeing Simon again as well. That, alone, was making her light headed.

CHAPTER TWENTY SEVEN

The doctor had been right. The effect of the drugs had not worn off fully and Rebecca was near exhaustion by the time she arrived home. Dorothy made her some hot tomato soup, but after a few mouthfuls, Rebecca had had enough. Andrew helped to her bedroom and by the time Dorothy had helped her to undress, the world was spinning uncontrollably around her. Her heavy eyelids closed out the jumbled scene as she let her mother ease her gently into bed, and by the time Dorothy had pulled the covers up to her daughter's chin, Rebecca was fast asleep.

When she did eventually open her eyes, the mid day sun was streaming into the bedroom through the open window. The air was cool and refreshing and a gentle breeze stirred the curtains. Gingerly, Rebecca eased herself out of bed and went to the shower. The prickly hot water soon washed away the remainder of sleep left in her body, and feeling much refreshed, she dressed in fresh clothes, and went down stairs.

'Good morning!' Dorothy said as she looked up from the worktop. 'You've managed to sleep it off then?' She gave her daughter a fond smile.

'It seems like it,' Rebecca shrugged and blew out her cheeks. 'I'll not be getting much work done today,' she said, still regaining her strength.

'Well you're just in time for lunch,' her mother said softly and then, 'I do hope you've got your appetite back.'

'I think I'll eat Uncle Andrew's as well,' Rebecca whispered as her mother came over and gave her a big hug.

'Well, you sound a bit more cheerful this morning!' Dorothy exclaimed. 'That lie in has certainly done you good.'

'Apart from the bruising, I feel great,' replied Rebecca, rubbing her wrists. She stood up and went over to the worktop, pinched a piece of raw carrot out of her mother's bowl and munched it.

There's been a couple of phone calls for you while you've been sleeping,' said Dorothy.

'Who from?'

'One from Greythorpe. He asked if you'd ring him. He left a number for when you woke up. It's a mobile, but he said you should be able to get through to him so long as he isn't anywhere near this black spot.'

'I see,' Rebecca said pensively as she raised the saucepan lid and sniffed at the contents that bubbled appetizingly beneath it. 'Mobiles are a bit useless around here, aren't they?' She paused and then said, 'And who else?'

Dorothy didn't answer straight away. 'Simon rang to ask how you were,' she announced eventually. 'He said he'd rung the hospital but you'd left.'

'Simon? You mean that park man?' Rebecca taunted.

'I'm not going to be able to live it down now, I can see that.'

'What did he say when you answered the phone?'

'He was a bit offish.' Dorothy shrugged. 'Can't blame him I suppose. But he was polite and asked me if I'd pass on his best wishes.' She paused again. 'I said I would.'

Rebecca smiled. 'Does that mean I'm not banned from seeing him?' she asked dryly as she dropped the lid back on the saucepan.

'Could I have stopped you,' Dorothy asked seriously.

Rebecca just smiled. 'One thing I do know,' she said, 'I'm glad all this mess is sorted out now.'

'Well, let's hope it is, heh? Perhaps we can all get back to being happy again.'

An hour and a half later Rebecca dialled Simon's number and waited. 'Thatch Cottage,' she heard his voice announce.

'It's Rebecca here,' she said awkwardly.

'Hello!' he replied in an unexpectedly friendly voice. 'Are you all right now?'

'Fine thanks.'

'I suppose your mother told you I rang.'

'Yes.'

'Just thought I'd call and see how you were. I'd heard you'd left the hospital.'

'Yes.'

There was a long silence while each picked their words. 'Well then...' Simon began just as Rebecca spoke.

'Look,' she said and then, 'What?' as Simon began to speak.

'What were you going to say?'

'I was just going to say I'm sorry for the way I treated you. I realize I was wrong.'

'Oh, that's all right.'

'No it isn't. I've been beastly.'

'Yes, I thought so,' Simon said with a chuckle, 'but that's all right, I'm getting used to it!' His mirth triggered the same response in Rebecca.

'You know, my mother actually called you by your first name when she told me you'd called.'

'She's coming round a bit, then, is she?'

'A bit.'

'Then she'll not mind my calling to pick you up tonight then?'

'I shouldn't think so.'

'How about you?'

'I shouldn't think so.'

They both giggled.

'Right, let's try seven o'clock then. See if we can break a new record and remain on speaking terms for a whole evening.'

'Right, I'm willing to give it a go. Just don't be late!'

'Right,' he said obediently. She heard him chuckle as he hung up.

CHAPTER TWENTY EIGHT

'Come on through, Miss Hampstead,' Arthur Greythorpe said from the door of his temporary office. Rebecca went past him and waited until he had closed the door. 'Please, take a seat.'

'Thank you.'

'As you see,' Arthur explained and pointed to the paper on his desk, 'I need to get your statement down in writing.'

Rebecca nodded. 'Of course,' she said and gave him a smile.

Arthur sat behind his desk and took out a ball point pen. 'Now I know we've been over it once, but what I'll do this time is write down what you say, and then, when you've finished, you can read it and sign it. OK?'

'Fine.'

'Now what I need is for you to start by telling me where you'd been on the evening you were kidnapped.' He watched for Rebecca's response. When he saw her hesitate, he spoke again. 'We did find this in your car, Miss Hampstead,' he said and lifted a thick green folder out of the right hand drawer of the steel desk. He placed it down beside the pile of blank statement sheets.

'I see.'

'I might explain that we are fairly sure where you'd been, but I don't wish to lead you by asking questions. Your statement is more likely to vary from the actual facts if I put suggestions into your mind. Understand?'

'Yes.'

'And Mr. Cowling has confirmed that he compiled the file for you.'

Rebecca nodded. 'But I don't see how this has any bearing on what happened later,' she argued.

'I don't think it has Miss Hampstead. But I need a clear picture of where you'd been, what made you go there, and with what results. That way I can perhaps see how the two cars and their occupants that were involved in your abduction happened to know where you were and when you'd be there.

'I see.' Rebecca hadn't considered the fact that her kidnapping had been planned. Somehow, it unnerved her to think that Stubbs had been watching her. 'Well, I went to see John Cowling,' she began. 'I had an appointment for six forty five.'

'And you went straight to his office?'

Rebecca hesitated. 'Well yes.'

'You parked near his office?'

'Well not very near. His office is in one of the streets that make up the pedestrian precinct.'

'So where did you park?'

'Just off the dual carriage way. Fenton Road I think it's called.'

'Ah! So you walked from there, across the precinct and then up Maudling Street to Cowling's office?'

'Well no, I cut across the back street actually.'

'Ah, right.' He scribbled down several lines of writing and lifted his head. 'Now, did you see anything or anybody acting suspiciously?'

'Well, no, not really.' She blushed a bright pink.

'You mean you did or you didn't? This is important, Miss Hampstead.'

'I... I did bump into some young hooligans,' she confessed.

'Oh! And what happened?'

'Well nothing,' Rebecca replied, seeming a little flustered.

'Then what makes you call them hooligans Miss Hampstead? They must have done something to make them seem different to ordinary young folk.'

'They surrounded me and...and one grabbed my chin.'

'And you fought them off?'

'Well no,' she said, trying not to look as awkward as she felt. 'A friend came along and escorted me to Maudling Street.'

'A friend?' asked Arthur, beginning to get interested.

'Yes,' she replied hesitantly, 'it was…it was…Simon Park.' She couldn't understand why it was so hard to say his name.

Arthur leaned back in his seat. He didn't speak for a full half a minute, and then he leaned forward and scribbled more writing on the statement sheet. When he'd finished, he looked up at Rebecca. 'I thought you two weren't on very friendly terms,' he said casually.

'We weren't,' Rebecca said frankly. 'In fact it was I who was being unfriendly. You see...' She stopped and tried to pick her words carefully.

'Your mother didn't like him,' Arthur prompted.

'Oh, you know!' She was surprised at just how much the inspector had found out. 'Well, I didn't know what to believe. I was confused.

Mother kept saying he'd been involved with the death of my father, so that's why I asked Cowling to find out about him.'

'I understand,' said Arthur. He wrote some more. 'So you accepted his safe passage and then what?'

'I said thank you and told him I still wasn't interested in being friends.'

'Tell me,' Arthur asked and looked her straight in the eye. 'Do you know what Mr. Park was doing in the alley way? How did he happen to be there?'

'I've no idea,' Rebecca said with a shake of her head. 'I expect he just happened to be passing.'

'Well stranger things have happened,' Arthur said seriously. 'You don't think he could have been following you, do you?' Arthur asked, still keeping his eyes locked onto Rebecca's.

Rebecca frowned and then shrugged her shoulders. 'He knew about Cowling. Apparently Cowling had followed Simon and he'd caught him at it. I think perhaps Simon was a bit angry.'

'Why do you say that?'

'He said he wanted me to know what it was like to be followed and investigated.'

'Hmm. I see. Anything else?'

'Well he thought I was foolish walking up dark back alleys.'

'Told you that did he?'

Rebecca nodded. 'Damned fool thing to do, he said.'

'I agree,' Arthur said as he turned to a new sheet of paper. He looked up again. 'How did you find out that he'd cornered Cowling?'

'Simon told me.'

'And what did Cowling have to say about that?'

'He didn't. He presented me with that file and said it was what I wanted, and that's what he'd got for me.'

'And then what did you do?'

'Then I took the file, walked back to my car and drove home.'

'I see. So you don't know what's in this folder then?' Arthur asked as he patted it lightly.

'I glanced through it when I reached my car, but then I decided to take it home to study. There seemed too much to wade through on the spur of the moment.'

'So you set off for Pendle Court. You didn't reach home though, did you?'

'No, a car appeared in front of me and then, a little while later, one came up behind.'

'What kind of cars were they?'

'I don't know. I wasn't really thinking about them. My mind was on other matters.' She thought for a moment. 'Just red rear lights in front and bright headlights behind.'

'Yes, of course,' Arthur nodded, 'I understand.' He looked at the green folder and then, turning his eyes to the statement sheet, began writing once more.

'When did you realize things weren't as they should be?' he asked eventually.

'Well the car in front of me kept going slower and slower. I suppose I did think it a bit strange, but it was too late to do anything. The car behind was almost on my back bumper. Then suddenly the one in front braked, I swerved to try and go around but ended up off the road, and before I knew it the door had opened, a man jabbed a needle in my leg, and that was that.' She gave a little shudder as she recalled what happened.

Again, Arthur wrote for several minutes before speaking. 'Now,' he said and lifted his head, 'when do you remember regaining consciousness?'

'I'm not sure. I felt to be asleep even though I was awake, if you see what I mean.'

'I think I do,' Arthur consoled. 'Let me try putting it this way; is there anything you remember about the place or the people there that might help us with our enquiries?'

Rebecca thought hard. 'Well, the man in the photograph that you showed me was the one who opened the car door and injected me, I know that much. I…I can't be sure he was the same man who wore the mask.'

'Did you recognise anything about him? His voice perhaps?'

'No. I don't remember him speaking.' Rebecca rubbed her head. 'I remember asking him what was happening, but he never replied.'

'His clothes then, what was he wearing?' Arthur tried again.

'A sweater I think. Yes, a polo-necked sweater.' She shook her head as she tried to picture him in her mind.

'What colour was the sweater?'

'Er.. bottle-green, I think. I'm not sure. It might have been some other dark colour. Things weren't too clear.'

'Did you notice the man's eyes? Cruel eyes were they?'

'No, they seemed…' She pictured the masked face hovering over her, 'concerned.'

'And their colour?'

Again, Rebecca rubbed her forehead. 'I...I can't remember.'

'Try Miss Hampstead. It could mean the difference between proving and not proving our case.'

'They were dark eyes.'

'Dark you say? Would that be dark blue?'

Rebecca shook her head. 'No, not blue.'

'Brown then?'

'Brown,' Rebecca said pensively. 'Yes, possibly.'

'Or dark grey, perhaps?'

She shook her head. 'I really can't remember. I can't.' She cradled her aching head in her hands as she desperately tried to remember what colour Stubbs' eyes had been the day he had called at Pendle Court.

'Never mind,' Arthur soothed. 'We have the man in custody. I just would have liked to have more evidence. You don't remember anything else?'

Rebecca shook her head. 'No,' she said. 'That's all I remember, apart from some shouting and a loud bang.'

'How many voices did you hear?'

'Two,' Rebecca answered immediately.

'Two? Are you sure?'

'Yes, at least two.'

Eventually he lifted his head and thanked her as he brought the interview to an end. Rebecca was relieved. Finally, Arthur asked her to read what he had written and sign at the bottom of each sheet, close up to the writing. 'I'm so glad this is all over,' she said with a faint sigh.

Arthur Greythorpe grunted. He tidied away his papers, and then he escorted her to the Range Rover and watched as she drove away. He pushed his hands deep into his trouser pockets and turned back to the police station door. 'Over?' he said aloud to himself, and shook his head tiredly. He exhaled hard turned and puffed out his cheeks. 'Over my foot!'

Stubbs was scheduled to come before the magistrates in the morning. With the statements and witnesses Greythorpe had, he'd be lucky not to have to drop the charges.

CHAPTER TWENTY NINE

Rebecca was already waiting when Simon drove into the yard at Pendle Court at two minutes to seven that same evening. She watched from her bedroom window as Simon got out of his car and walked towards the front door. He gave a short wave and a smile as he caught a glimpse of Rebecca at the bedroom window, and then, springing up the steps two at a time, he gave three loud raps with the brass knocker. The door opened and Dorothy stood before him. 'Hello,' he said with a smile.

'You'd better come in young man,' she replied and stepped away from the door. 'No telling how long she'll be.'

Simon stepped inside. 'You'll have a cup of coffee will you?' she asked, knowing full well that Rebecca would be exactly five minutes before she emerged. It had been pre-arranged. Dorothy was to have five minutes in which to make her peace with Simon, and not a second more. She knew Rebecca would be timing her and would be there on the dot to let him whisk her off into the dark evening.

'That would be nice,' Simon grinned.

'Well I thought you'd want to hear what I have to say,' Dorothy said, taking the bull by the horns. 'Rebecca and I have discussed the matter and we have both decided that I owe you an apology. You see I thought...'

'Oh that's all right, Mrs. Hampstead,' Simon interrupted. 'So long as things are sorted out now, that's all that matters.' He grinned again, and accepted a cup of coffee from her hand.

Dorothy beamed. It had been less painful than she'd thought.

'Well, you sit yourself down, and I'll call that daughter of mine,' she said and shuffled out of the kitchen.

When Dorothy returned, Rebecca was at her shoulder. Simon stood up and smiled. For a moment, he just stood and stared. He'd always thought Rebecca was attractive, but, he'd quite forgotten what a spell she cast. She wore a yellow, silk wrap over a long sleeved evening dress. Her only Jewellery was a thin gold necklet which only partly covered a bruise around her neck and a matching bracelet which rested on the top of her right hand beneath the sleeve of her dress. Her hair rolled off the fair skin of her shoulders like waves off chalk rocks and, as she smiled, a sparkle in her deep blue eyes matched the glint of light on her moist lips.

'I hope you're not taking me ice skating,' she said to break the spell.

Simon laughed. 'That was my first choice. It seems like I'll have to take you to a concert after all!'

'Do you want a hot chocolate before I take you home?' Simon asked as they drove nearer to Thatch Cottage.

Rebecca looked at his face as he concentrated on driving along the country road. She felt tired but didn't want the evening to end. For the first time, she felt that their real feelings were coming to the surface, and regretted that she had ever let anything in their past sink her natural propensity in some deep trench.

'I'd love one she said softly.'

Simon swung the car into the small yard and stopped the engine. 'Considering what happened the other day, I think you should let your mum know where you are.'

Rebecca looked at her watch. It was nearly midnight. She sighed. The evening had disappeared, leaving so much unsaid and so much to do. Now she had him to herself, she didn't want to let him out of her sight, but she knew he'd be there tomorrow and the day after that. At that particular moment she wanted it to be for ever. 'I'll give her a ring.' She took out her mobile phone from her small evening bag and opened the flap. 'No signal here,' she said a moment later with a shrug.

'No, there never is. I've got used to it now. Don't even bother getting mine out when I'm at home,' he explained. 'But, never mind, you can ring on my land line,' Simon said and waved his hand to signal that Rebecca should proceed to the cottage.

She smiled. 'Good, it will give me chance to look at your office.'

'It's a bit untidy in there at the moment,' Simon excused. 'I've been quite busy really. Perhaps it would be best to see it later. There's an extension phone in the far room at the end of the passageway.'

'You promised to show me your place of work,' Rebecca insisted, 'and I'm going to. I want to see where all your novels are created.'

'I wasn't here when I wrote the ones that I've already had published,' Simon explained.

'Then I want to see where all the future novels will be created,' she protested.

Simon smiled. 'Come on then,' he said, taking her hand and walking her to the front door. As they stopped outside the door, she slipped her arm around his waist and he wrapped his around her shoulders. They pulled each other close.

'It's been a lovely evening,' Rebecca said and looked up into Simon's face. She could feel his strong heart beat against her breast.

'I'm glad you like music,' Simon said softly. 'Concerts can be fun if you like what the orchestra is playing.'

'I'd have told you if I hadn't liked it.'

Simon grinned and nodded. 'Yes, I think you would.'

Rebecca smiled back at him. For a moment, their eyes locked. It wasn't the first time their eyes had spoken that evening, but it was the first time they had been totally alone. Rebecca moistened her lips, and slowly Simon lowered his mouth onto hers. It was a long close kiss, their lips and their bodies pressing hard together in an embrace that neither wanted to break. His taste; his smell; the feel of his face against hers made her legs so weak that if Simon hadn't been holding her tightly she would have melted into heap at his feet. Slowly, the pressure between their two bodies subsided and she regained her balance.

'You smell good,' Simon said in a soft low voice. He held her shoulders and looked her in the eyes. Rebecca didn't speak. Her eyes spoke for her. She knew deep in her soul she wanted him as much as he wanted her.

'Let's go inside,' she said eventually.

Simon took a key from his pocket and placed it in the lock. It turned easily and he unlatched the door and pushed it open. He switched on the light in the narrow passage. 'Better phone your mum,' he said and led her through to his office. The door was already open.

Rebecca thought she saw him scowl, but the light wasn't good, and when he looked at her, all she saw was his inimitable smile. 'The phone's on the desk,' he said, and switched on a small light.

Rebecca watched as he stepped over to the corner where he lifted some papers off the top of a CD player.

'I work well to music,' he stated, putting in a CD and then closing the lid. Rebecca sat on the corner of his leather topped desk and watched his every move. 'Albinoni,' he announced, and walked through to the kitchen. 'You'll like that,' he shouted as he heard the music begin to play.

She looked around. The leather topped desk was piled high with books and papers. Beneath them she could just see the lid of a laptop computer and next to it a printer and a box full of pencils. To the right was a small side table on which stood a telephone and a bronze ornament of an Arab horse. She walked over to it and inspected it closely. The flying main and dished face reminded her of Simon's horse the day they had first met. 'Looks just like your Hassan,' she shouted to him and ran her finger along its back.

'Yes. I think that's why I bought it,' Simon replied proudly. He knew it would be the first thing she saw. 'I have some photos of him running free in the back paddock. If you'd seen them you'd think the sculpture was of him.'

'I'd love to see them.'

'I'll have to look for them. It shouldn't take a minute,' he said.

'That's all right. I'll browse around in here while you get them.'

'Feel free,' Simon said. 'I'll be with you in a jiffy.' Rebecca smiled at his leaving her to minutely examine his place of work. 'By the way,' he said and popped his head around the door, 'There's something of yours in the top drawer of the desk.'

She slid out the drawer and looked inside. She smiled as his head disappeared again. 'I knew you'd keep it safe for me,' she called, and picked out a silver and black-spotted package from beside a ball of parcel twine, and placed it next to the bronze horse so that she wouldn't forget it.

Next, she tidied the books off the top of the laptop and read a half page of a manuscript that was lying on the tray of the printer beside it. She hummed her approval and let her eyes wander away. She noticed that the waste paper basket hadn't been emptied for some time. It was so full that several sheets of screwed up paper had toppled onto the floor. She picked them up, balanced them on top of the full basket, and then, began to look further afield. An old mantelpiece caught her attention next. There were a couple of small china ornaments and an oriental ginger jar on the ledge. She picked each up in turn and examined them. The ornaments were marked Royal Worcester, but there was no name on the jar, just some Chinese characters on its base. As she turned it upside down, she heard something solid rattle inside it. She turned it upright, lifted the lid and peered inside. For a moment she found it hard to see what the contents were, but eventually her eyes made out what looked like a small bottle and a syringe. Slowly she tipped up the jar and let them slide out into the palm of her hand. She scowled. What was Simon doing with a syringe and a fifty millilitre bottle of straw coloured liquid? There was no label on it. Probably for his horse, she thought and replaced them in their container.

She put her fingers to her temple; it had started to throb. A thought seemed to be developing at the back of her mind and it was giving her a splitting headache. Or was it just the wine she had had with the meal. It had been a lovely evening. Five or so hours with a man of whom she had begun to grow very fond, a concert of chamber music by Mozart, and a light evening meal in a secluded corner of a top-class restaurant. It had been the happiest night of her life and she wanted it to last for ever. But the doctor had advised her to keep off alcohol because of the affect it might have if combined with the sedatives she had been given. Now she was paying for having indulged in two glasses of wine.

'Don't know where I've put them,' Simon said as he walked through the open door.

Rebecca swivelled around. 'What? Oh, the photographs!'

Simon saw the change in Rebecca's mood. 'Is something the matter?' he asked.

'No, why should there be?'

'You seem a bit unsettled.'

'Nonsense!' Rebecca said with a soft smile. 'I'm just a little tired.' She rubbed the side of her temple. 'Perhaps I'd better have that drink of chocolate and be on my way.'

'If that's what you want,' Simon said soothingly.

Rebecca smiled. 'I'm never the best of company when I'm tired.'

Simon nodded. 'I understand,' he said and went into the kitchen again.

Rebecca sat in the chair behind the desk and slipped off her shoes. She leaned forward and rested her head on the back of her arms. The music was soothing. She couldn't help feeling that she shouldn't have had the wine to drink. She closed her eyes and let the music wash over her.

'Here you are,' she heard Simon announce as he tapped her on the shoulder. She opened her eyes and he was holding out a mug of hot drinking chocolate.

'That didn't take long,' she said as the record player clicked off.

'I've been sitting next to you for the last fifteen minutes. It would seem like you are still not recovered from your ordeal.

'Rubbish!' Rebecca protested. 'I was just enjoying the music.' She looked at her watch. It was nearly one o'clock. 'Huh,' she exclaimed. 'You can tell I'm not used to late nights.'

Simon stood up. 'Come on, I'll run you home.'

'Haven't brought my trainers,' Rebecca chuckled as the alcohol in her bloodstream lightened her mood.

'We don't want your mother thinking you've been kidnapped again, do we?'

'Kidnapped?' Rebecca stood up a little unsteadily. 'Ooh, I'd forgotten about that. I never rang mother either. Forgot again,' she chuckled. She stepped toward Simon and realized she'd forgotten her shoes. 'Oops, hold on,' she said and bent down behind the desk. Her shoes were in the knee-hole alcove, next to the waste paper basket, where she had slipped them off. She bent down and reached for them, and pulled them towards her so that she could slip her feet back into them. She emitted a tired groan when her elbow unbalanced the waste paper basket and tipped out more than half the balls of paper it had originally contained.

'Oh just leave it,' Simon said in an effort to distract her from the mess. 'I'll have to get around to tidying up anyway.'

'No trouble, I'll come over in the morning and tidy up for you if you like,' she said, stuffing some of the paper back on top of what seemed to be an old woollen scarf. She glanced at the container again and chuckled at his one foible she had uncovered.

'I'd love you to come over,' Simon smiled. 'but not to do my housework for me. And anyway, I've promised to meet Arthur in the morning. Court hearing you know.'

'Well I'll see you after lunch. Don't you dare touch a thing.' Rebecca wagged her finger threateningly. 'If you don't promise to leave it, I shan't come. I'll enjoy it enormously. It's surprising what you can find out about a person by examining their rubbish you know.'

Simon shrugged. 'Can't argue with that,' he said, careful not to make any promises. He put his arm round her shoulder, and at the same time resolved to get down to clearing up first thing in the morning before setting off to meet Arthur.

Rebecca leaned on him and slipped on her shoes. 'Right, now we've got that sorted out...' she said and picked her parcel up off the table as she walked out close to his side.

Their final kiss of the evening, on the front step of Pendle Court, seemed all too brief. Simon's body felt hot and hard against hers. As their lips closed on each other's and as Rebecca felt the moist warmth of Simon's tongue their embrace became almost too strong to break. A powerful force of nature had taken over and was unmistakably calling upon them. After what seemed like no time at all but was in fact several minutes, they both sighed deeply and let the passion subside. Simon held one of Rebecca's hands in his and moved the other to her face. 'Goodnight,' he said, gently caressing her cheek.

'See you tomorrow then,' she whispered giving him a final kiss on the lips as she pushed herself reluctantly away from him, leaving their finger tips softly stroking past each other as they broke the last magnetic touch of the evening.

CHAPTER THIRTY

At first, Rebecca had slept well. The sheer enjoyment of the evening had sapped what reserves of energy she had been able to store during the previous twenty four hours. The after effects of the sleeping drugs, combined initially with her lack of food and later with two glasses of wine, had taken a telling affect on her stamina. She fell asleep as soon as her head touched the starched white linen of her pillow. It was a deep flawless sleep which gradually, after several hours, lessened in intensity as it neared the shallows of her dream filled subconscious. Though she knew not that she would forget the dreams as she beached on the shores of consciousness, they were reality themselves, filled with everything that had befallen her in those last few days. And although only dreams, they were no less horrific. At first she smiled and cuddled her pillow; it was just Simon, wrapping his arm around her and escorting her to safety from the clutches of some faceless gang of hoodlums, but then her head lashed violently from side to side as the blackness of the drug induced stupor trod the stage of her imagination. Tight chords cut into her wrists and chilled blades of ice cut into her body. Suddenly, the blackness was broken by the face of the man who had first entered her car, a cruel hard face with shifty eyes. She tried to scream and the sea of blackness returned. Only a voice broke through to the surface, a voice she recognized, a voice of someone who had come into her life at some time. As her head swung from one side of her pillow to the other, the face belonging to that voice drew out of the darkness. She panted desperately as her mind struggled to form the face's features. Suddenly, she thought she saw it clearly. For an infinitely immeasurable fraction of a second, the face smiled down at her, its eyes filled with regret at what would have to be done. 'There's a time to let live and a time to kill,' the voice behind the mask said; but then it was gone faster than the speed of light, only to be replaced by a muted and hideous mask. But despite the knitted helmet, she knew the eyes behind it. She shook her head, in a desperate attempt to shake herself awake. A loud crack and then strong fearless arms replaced the chords that bound her; a warm affectionate body replaced the pangs of cold. Now, Simon's voice soothed her, and the vision faded, giving way to the tranquillity of a spellbound trance. All she could see now was Simon sitting in his office and rapidly typing page after page of a manuscript on his laptop and then printing them off and placing the sheets of paper in a neat pile on his desk. There was a strange look in his eyes, a look of fear perhaps, as she saw him stand up, take each sheet in turn, and screw it up into a ball, before piling it in the waste paper basket. But then the image subsided once again, and this time, she saw him walking on a vast open beach of silver sand, and holding hands with a woman, a woman who looked into his eyes and laughed and played, a woman overtaken by love. She knew that woman. She recognised herself. Now, at last, the worst was over. She could sleep soundly again.

Rebecca's pillow was soaked with perspiration when she awoke, though she didn't know why. She felt fresh and more alive than she had done for weeks. She sat up and looked at her clock. It was eleven thirty. She smiled. She felt good, relaxed and refreshed.

'Did your night go as well as I think it did? Dorothy asked her as she made Rebecca a light breakfast.

Rebecca just beamed.

'What are you doing today?' Dorothy pushed on raising her eyebrow inquisitively.

'Construction work mum,' Rebecca stated lightly.

'What on earth... You're not working, surely?'

'I'm going to spend a little time mending bridges,' she chuckled.

CHAPTER THIRTY ONE

Bernard Stubbs smiled at Arthur and Simon as he left the court room. 'I can't believe it, Arthur,' Simon exclaimed. Stubbs was striding away released on unconditional bail.

'Unless we get more evidence, he's is going to walk,' Arthur stated coldly. The police search of his hotel room and his car had come up with nothing. The house in London that had been his home for the last six years had been searched. Again, there was nothing to incriminate him. The forensic laboratory had failed to find anything to link him with the old house in which Rebecca had been kept prisoner for thirty six hours. On top of that Bernard Stubbs had been a senior police officer, and since his retirement from the force, he had been a model citizen, running his own successful investigations firm. Simon, the one man upon whose evidence the prosecution hung by a thread, had been named by Stubbs as the person whom he was investigating, and himself had been accused not only of making up the story about Stubbs' involvement in the kidnapping, but also of being the actual kidnapper. The magistrates had no choice but to adjourn the case for two weeks pending further investigations, and they instructed Inspector Greythorpe to drop the charges if they could collect no more evidence to support his case.

Simon couldn't tell what Arthur was thinking. His face gave nothing away. He neither acknowledged nor reacted to the smile. He just watched as the one time inspector of police got into a black police car to be taken back to the police station to collect the personal belongings.

Arthur was deep in thought as he followed Simon towards his car. 'Somehow, Simon,' Arthur said, leaning through the open window, 'you're getting the dirty end of the stick again from Stubbs. Once again, without any corroborative evidence, he's trying to discredit you.'

Simon seemed distracted. 'What? Oh well, I'm glad you don't suspect me any more, Arthur.' I'll see you later.' Without another word he drove off leaving Arthur staring after him. Simon was wishing he hadn't gone to the court. He had only one thing on his mind now, one thing that overrode any other thing that was happening; he had to get back and tidy up his cottage before Rebecca arrived.

The first thing Simon did when he reached home was to have a hot shower. But he had much to do and it was already after noon. Rebecca could be here any time and he was determined to straighten up the place before she arrived. He took less that five minutes to freshen up and was just about to step out of the shower when he heard a faint tapping on his front door.

'Coming!' he shouted and reached for his dressing gown. He managed to pull it over his arms and fasten the belt as he walked up the passage way.

Rebecca beamed at him radiantly as he opened the door. He smiled back at her and held out his hand. 'Come in,' he said as she put her hand in his. He led her into the passage and stopped by the kitchen door. She looked up at his face and moved close to him as he turned to face her. Even in her shirt and denims she was as attractive as ever. Throughout the previous evening he had struggled to prevent himself from staring at her. Today it was going to be impossible. Rebecca felt her cheeks pink as he continued to study her face.

'Well then,' she said to break the spell. 'What are we doing today?'

Simon pulled her up close to him. Rebecca put a hand on his shoulder as he moved his head forward and pressed his lips firmly down on her mouth. She responded with her tongue. It was what she wanted, what she needed. His body felt like iron against hers, moulding into every feminine curve of her own soft torso. It was a long excitingly close embrace that neither wanted to break. As their passion mounted, Rebecca pressed her hand firmly against his shoulder. Simon lifted his lips away from hers, lightly kissed her on her forehead, and leaned back his shoulders while he studied her face once more. 'I think we'll celebrate,' he said.

Rebecca watched the sparkle in his eyes as they crinkled into a fond smile. 'Sounds good to me,' she replied and put her finger in the cleft of his chin. 'What are we celebrating?'

'How about our discovering each other?'

'I discovered you long ago,' Rebecca confessed. 'Though I'm not sure I knew it.'

'Yes, I feel the same about you.'

'How about rediscovering then?'

'Can't fault that. Shall we start with some coffee?'

'Right,' Rebecca said and moved away from him. It was hard to pull herself away. All her instincts wanted her, required her to let it engulf her, and she knew Simon knew it and wanted to do the same. But she was scared; not of Simon but of her own feelings. She needed to take things more slowly; give herself time to clear her head. 'I'll make it while you get dressed,' she panted, her breast heaving and her face flushed. Her resistance was weak and their emotions were accelerating to warp speed. A flimsy silk dressing gown did nothing to reinforce her will. Despite her body telling her differently, it seemed like the best move she could make to put some extra distance between them, be it only the thickness of a layer of clothes.

Simon grinned broadly. 'I'll be with you in a few minutes,' he said, and turned back along the passage way to his bedroom. He looked around and realized that over the last few days he'd been slipping. Even the bedroom looked untidy. It wasn't like him at all. The telephone was on the floor by the side of the bed, there were clothes strewn over a wicker chair and, despite hardly moving in his sleep, his bedclothes were more than just awry. Quickly, he straightened the bed, picked the telephone off the floor and put it on the little oak side table where it belonged, and then got dressed in a sweater and slacks. The rest of the clothes that were about the room, he collected in his arms and carried them through to the bathroom, where he bundled them into a large, white, wicker laundry bin.

By comparison, the kitchen was remarkably neat and tidy. 'I'll make you something to eat as well,' she called to him, her metabolism settling down to a simmer.

'Sounds good,' she heard Simon reply.

She hunted through all the cupboards until she found the things she needed, and then set about making Simon a breakfast while the coffee brewed. From the contents of the cupboards, she estimated accurately that he had corn flakes for breakfast most days, since it was the only cereal in sight. She looked in the refrigerator; eggs, milk, tomatoes, everything she needed was there. She hadn't had a guinea pig for her cooking for a long time. Simon was going to get the works!

As Simon emerged from the bathroom, the smell of frying bacon, and the sound of crackling of hot fat on raw eggs, began to make his mouth water. He was glad Rebecca had started in the kitchen. He peeped in as he walked past the open door. Rebecca didn't see him. She was busy with the frying pan. He opened the office door quietly, let himself in, and closed it behind him. He sighed. The waste paper had taken over the whole room. It wasn't normally so untidy. Hell, what a mess, he thought. He looked at the desk. Papers were everywhere. And the waste paper basket was overflowing. It didn't usually get as untidy as that! He shook his head in disbelief; he was taking work too seriously if, by working on auto pilot, he couldn't even remember getting the place in such a state.

'Breakfast is being served,' Rebecca shouted.

'All right, coming!' he called back. If he acted quickly, he'd just have time to clear this lot up. As fast as he could, he collected the odd fallen pieces of paper, pressed them into the top of the waste paper basket the best he could and carried it to the fire place.

'Are you coming?' Rebecca called.

'I'll be right with you,' he replied and tipped the bin upside down. The paper was wedged tight and refused to be shaken loose. Determined more than ever now to present Rebecca with a *fait accompli*, he scooped the compressed balls of paper out of the top with his hand and scattered them in the grate. A box of matches lay in the corner of the hearth. He picked up the box, opened it and took out a match. A couple of strikes and the paper was well alight. He put his hand in the basket and scooped out more of the paper. The fire drew furiously. As he raked out the remainder of the contents into the hearth, ready to pile them onto the fire when it had settled, his hand felt something soft and woollen in the bottom of the basket. He pulled it out as he turned the basket up to face him. For a moment he stared at what he had in his hand, trying to make out what it was and what it was doing there. With a feeling of foreboding, he put the container to one side and unfolded the knitted, red and black cloth. He stared at it in horror when he realized what he was holding; it was the ski mask! With a sharp breath drawn in through clenched jaws, he fought to suppress his anger. He pulled the mask tight between both hands, stood up and looked around the office once again. He was right; it had never been so untidy. He stopped in the middle of what he was thinking as he heard a faint gasp behind him. His eyes turned to the door. It was open and Rebecca was standing there, transfixed, her eyes wide like a frightened deer caught in the headlights of an oncoming car. 'Rebecca!' he exclaimed.

Rebecca didn't answer. She couldn't, her voice had gone; her throat was dry. Her adrenalin was preparing her for what she had to do. She turned and ran.

'Rebecca!' Simon shouted after her. 'Wait, Rebecca!' he called in vain. It was no use. She had fled. Her car spun out of the small yard, missing his leg by less than an inch. He banged on the side window with his fist but she was speeding away and was gone in seconds. 'Rebecca!' he called again and again. He looked at the mask that now hung loosely from his left hand, and flung it to the ground. He spun on his heel, ran back to the house and dashed into his bedroom.

Rebecca drove as hard and as fast as she could. She wiped away the tears that were clouding her eyes and drove regardless of any vehicles that might be coming in the opposite direction. She sobbed deep insuppressible sobs that welled up from deep inside her. How could she have been so blind? It had seemed all too plain when she saw him kneeling in front of the fire place with the mask in his hands. It had become crystal clear. He'd been going to burn it. But she was confused. Why did he not throw it to the back of the flames? Why did he stand up with it stretched tight between his fists? Why was his face contorted with anger? What was he going to do? She groaned and put her hand on her forehead. It hurt to think. Suddenly her life had flipped back into a nightmare, and all she could concentrate on now was putting as much distance between herself and Simon.

CHAPTER THIRTY TWO

As Simon rummaged in his suit pocket for his car keys, he began to organize his thoughts. He knew what Rebecca must have been thinking. But I wouldn't have hurt her, he thought. How could she think that? I didn't know the mask was in the bin. It shouldn't have been there.

His fingers fell on the keys and he pulled them out of the pocket, dropping the suit jacket to the floor as he turned and ran to the passage way. Suddenly he stopped; he realized he was panicking. It was no use following Rebecca. He knew what he had to do. He went to the open door and looked around; then he stepped out and began to search. He had to get rid of the mask. He had thrown it down and run inside. He stopped and thought for a moment to let his head clear. It had to be somewhere near the house. He tried to remember where he'd thrown it but wherever he looked it wasn't to be seen. 'Where the hell is it!' he exclaimed, as sweat beaded his forehead and began to tumble down his face.

'Looking for this?' The voice came from behind him. He spun his head and there, under the pergola, stood Bernard Stubbs. He held up the ski mask in his left hand. His teeth glinted as his face cracked into a broad grin. Simon stood speechless. 'Tut tut,' said Stubbs, shaking his head. 'You are falling apart at the seams.'

'You!' Simon shouted. 'You put it there! I knew it had to be you.'

Stubbs nodded. 'Your reasoning overpowers me sometimes,' he said sarcastically. He laughed again. 'You're a fool, an incompetent fool. You thought you could get me. Me!' he chortled. 'You, a tin pot snivelling little journalist! You should have kept your nose out. But you couldn't. You had to stir things up.'

'What the hell are you talking about? I didn't ask Creedy to come creeping around.' He moved forward towards Stubbs.

'That is just far enough,' Stubbs said threateningly. He pulled his right hand out of his pocket and pointed a revolver at Simon's chest. Simon stood perfectly still. While he was talking, he still had a chance, but he knew that once the discourse stopped, Stubbs would have to kill him.

'Hid that here as well?' Simon asked sarcastically. Stubbs just smiled.

'You really don't know when to shut up do you?' he grated. 'All this would never have happened if it weren't for your big mouth.'

'*My* big mouth!'

'Yes, your big mouth.'

'What have *I* said?' Simon protested. 'Creedy was dead before I came into this?'

'Wrong. You came into *this* eight years ago. I had a nice little arrangement going until you pushed your nose in.'

'Like taking a rake off from Vickers,' Simon said confidently.

'Oh, you guessed that much then?' Stubbs said, raising his eyebrows.

'I knew you were behind it all. You had to be. I knew that when Henson told me he had seen Vickers' car.'

The look of surprise on Stubbs' face was only momentary. 'He told *you*?' Simon didn't answer. Stubbs shrugged his shoulders. 'Oh well, you're right of course.' He sneered and shook his head. 'But it doesn't matter now what you knew. It's what other people know that matters, and what they'll know, is what I tell them or what I leave for them to find.'

'You're insane!' Simon said between clenched teeth. 'You don't really think you can pull the wool over everybody's eyes. Some people, perhaps, but not everybody.'

'Everybody that matters,' Stubbs smiled confidently. It was a crooked smile. He tilted his head on one side and observed the look of disgust on Simon's face. 'What's the matter?' he chortled. 'Beginning to regret being a busy body after all are we?'

'I did what I had to do,' Simon answered calmly. 'I told the police what I knew about the smuggling. Spoilt things for you though, didn't I?' he chided. 'You had to raid the place or I would find out you were in on it. That's right isn't it?'

'Oh yes, that's right,' Stubbs growled. 'You couldn't leave it alone could you? But I knew you'd tell everybody I bungled it. You'd have to tell them you'd told me so far in advance that I should have caught Vickers as well.'

Simon shrugged. 'How was I to know you were bent?'

Stubbs just shook his head. 'Well now you know why I had to discredit you. You had to be stopped somehow.'

'Why didn't you just shoot me?'

It wasn't my style. I didn't intend killing anybody.'

'Until?'

'Until Henson remembered Vickers' car. I knew then, that if Vickers was nailed, he'd spill the beans on everything.'

'So you hanged Henson? Hardly your style either, I'd have thought,' Simon scoffed.

Stubbs shook his head. 'It's so good to see you getting it all wrong for a change.'

'Oh no?' Simon scathed. 'I know he was murdered.'

'But I didn't kill him. All I did was meet him with Vickers. He recognised Vickers straight away. 'Hey, that's the man in the BM,' he said, when he saw him sitting behind me in the back seat of my car. 'Don't worry,' I said, 'I wanted to let you know he was working with me,' Stubbs chuckled and shook his head again. 'Poor sod. He'd have blown the lid off the whole business.'

'So what made you come here and start killing after all this time? Don't tell me you became a vigilante, getting rid of all the bad guys!'

Stubbs waved his gun. 'Come on, I think we've done enough talking. Turn around slowly and walk inside.'

Simon did as he was told and turned towards the cottage door. 'I talked to Prosser before you had the squeeze put on him,' Simon said casually as he entered the passageway. Stubbs' eyes burned into his back. 'He told me about another deal that was going down that day in Wales.'

'Did he now?' Stubbs grunted and pushed him forward to the open office door.

'Didn't tell me what it was though.'

'He didn't know.'

'He knew that half of the heroin didn't come out of that house.'

Stubbs burst into a fit of laughter. 'God you're a fool,' he said and pushed Simon inside the office. 'Of course it left the house! A team of top detectives wouldn't have missed that. And I couldn't have had them in on the deal. I couldn't have trusted a single one of them to be bent and mean it!'

'I know there was more than they found,' Simon insisted and turned to face him.'

Of course there was. So I sent them out with the prisoners. Three detectives; three prisoners. Easy!'

'You bastard! You knew Henson was innocent all the time! And I thought it was your alter ego and the desire for promotion at all costs!'

'But how else could I get three conscientious detectives out of the house for long enough to pocket the heroin? If I hadn't arrested Henson, he and one of the detectives would have still been in the house.'

'Your pockets!'

Stubbs shrugged almost apologetically. 'Simple really. Nobody would search me. I just filled my pockets, stuffed the rest down my shirt and closed my Jacket. I followed them out a minute or so later with the case.'

He pointed to the chair behind the desk. 'Pull it to the middle of the room,' he ordered.

Simon pulled it out and sat in it. 'Good boy,' Stubbs grinned. 'Glad to see you are being reasonable about this.'

'You killed Prosser when you found out he didn't know what that deal was, did you?' Simon probed.

Stubbs grabbed the telephone and yanked it off the wire. He looked at the cable and then tossed it to one side. It wasn't right for his purpose. 'I didn't kill him. It was Vickers' men again!' he chuckled as he searched through the desk drawers. Two love to me,' he laughed.

'Well I can understand that,' Simon conceded. 'Prosser was a loyal old dog and Vickers had taken over the nightclubs of his boss. Best out of the way I suppose.'

'Put your hands on the chair arms,' Stubbs said and pointed the gun at Simon's temple. He had found what he wanted, a ball of parcel string. Simon realized he was running out of time, but he knew Stubbs would shoot him if he had to.'

'I know you killed Creedy though,' Simon stated confidently. 'He died the same way as I'm to go didn't he?'

'Three love,' Stubbs grunted and bound Simon's hands to the arms of the chair. This time he didn't laugh at his victory. 'I knew he wanted money to get a crack at Vickers so I followed him. But somebody else got to him first.'

'It left you with a bit of a problem though. How to find what he'd mislaid.'

'It wasn't a problem really. He'd got within a mile of it. It had to be with Mrs. Hampstead.' He began to bind Simon's feet to the legs of the desk.'

So you kidnapped her daughter.'

'She was an obstinate old crow. She'd have died before telling me what I wanted to know. Her weakness was that beautiful girl of hers.' He sighed. 'It seemed such a waste to have to kill her.'

'That's why you wore the mask?'

'I suppose I still hoped I wouldn't have to do it. I must be getting soft in my old age. The old girl might tell me what I wanted to know before things got out of hand.'

'Out of hand!' Simon said incredulously. 'You don't think things had already got out of hand? On top of kidnapping, you shot a man in the head!'

'Had to kill Barnes. He wanted to kill her before I'd got what I wanted. She'd seen his face. I told him to be patient, but he kept asking why I was wearing the mask.' Stubbs sighed and leaned on the corner of the desk. 'Eventually he realized I wasn't going to do it, and I realized he had to go or he would eventually tie me in with the whole thing.' Suddenly his voice changed. 'She'd have been all right if you hadn't interfered. You always interfere,' he grated.

Simon's blood ran cold. Rebecca *was* all right. 'What do you mean?' he demanded.

Stubbs smiled and stood up. 'I shan't be caught, not if I do what I have to do.'

Simon glared at him. 'Just what have you got in mind?'

'Dear chap, you know too much for a start. I'm a murderer, an accessory to murder, a kidnapper, a thief. If I did time now, I'd be dead before I left prison. And if I didn't die of old age, I'd be killed. They don't like ex-coppers in those places you know.'

Simon just scowled.

'But,' Stubbs said cheerily. 'Apart from you, who else knows? As I have said, people will only know what I tell them. When I saw you going into the house and discovering where I had taken the girl, I knew I had to discredit you once again.'

'You saw me!'

'Yes, I saw you as I left.' Stubbs nodded reproachfully. 'I knew then what I had to do. It was the only way and it has worked. I came and planted the mask and the drugs that I used on the girl in the house. It has your hair inside it; I took a sample from your comb. I even planted this gun in your garden. I had hoped the police would search your cottage, but it doesn't matter now. My one witness will put the blame on you and at the same time, clear my name. She'll be calling the police about now,' he said and glanced at his watch. 'Too late to help you though,' he grinned.

'Rebecca!' Simon whispered to himself and frowned. So Stubbs had seen it all!

'It's just a pity that the killing has to go on,' Stubbs said and stood up. 'I can't say I'll be sorry to see the back of you though. You've been a thorn in my side long enough.' He gathered a pile of papers off the desk and began to screw them up and place them around Simon's feet. He set about the task busily, like a mouse preparing a nest. Simon watched as the pile of kindling grew. He watched Stubbs' face and wondered at the complete concentration in the man's eyes, a kind of manic obsession for perfection, as he positioned each piece precisely. Simon watched in silence. There seemed little else to say. He hoped Rebecca had already called the police, but somehow knew she wouldn't have. However much she was afraid of him, she still felt about him the way he felt about her. That sort of feeling is impossible to kill all together. He knew she was at Pendle Court and when she realized he wasn't following her she'd come out of her panic and think. She was a thinker, Arthur had said as much. She'd take her time and try and think a way out of her dilemma. By that time, the paper stacked around his legs would have burned him to death, and the thatched roof of the cottage would have done its job of obliterating any traces of his having been bound to the chair.

Finally, Stubbs scurried out to the kitchen. The breakfast that Rebecca had cooked was still warm. The frying pan was set to one side of a still glowing hot plate. He placed the pan on the ring and then shuffled through the cupboards until he found a bottle of cooking oil. He filled the pan, placed the half full bottle near the edge of the worktop, and opened the cupboards above it. Then he opened the window slightly, turned the heat of the hob up to full, and walked back to the office. 'Just this to bury,' he said holding up the ski mask. He walked up the passage and opened all the doors wide, glancing in and around each room as he did so.

'Well, I have to go before the police get here,' he called.

'Go to hell,' Simon shouted as Stubbs put his head around the door for the last time. The face disappeared, and he heard the outside door close. He knew he was alone and he had only minutes in which to escape with his life. He struggled to pull himself free of the binding that anchored him to the chair. He pulled and twisted until the string drew blood and his body was soaked with perspiration but the strings had hardly stretched or moved. He could hear the oil beginning to bubble; he could smell it begin to smoke. In a few more minutes the whole place would be an inferno. He slumped back in his seat and thought. First, he thought of his sister, whose picture hung on the wall of the lounge. Very soon he would be joining her, he felt sure. Then he thought of Arthur. Arthur had been close to him. It saddened him to think that his old friend would never know the truth about him. He felt sad because he knew Arthur would be sad. His mind turned to Rebecca. Somehow, he knew she would never truly believe he was the man in the mask. He knew it, he believed it. It was the only thing that gave him comfort as the flames began to fill the kitchen, and a blanket of black toxic smoke swept along the ceiling.

CHAPTER THIRTY THREE

'What's the matter with her?' Andrew said to Dorothy. From the kitchen window they saw Rebecca's car skid to a halt in the yard and dash to the front door.

'Goodness knows,' she replied and shuffled as fast as she could to meet her.

Rebecca burst into the hallway and headed straight for the stairs. Her face was streaked with tears; her tousled hair clung to her cheeks. She didn't stop to acknowledge her mother.

'Rebecca!' she called as her daughter mounted the stairs. 'What on earth's the matter?

'Rebecca didn't look around. 'I don't know,' she said in a broken voice and ran on out of sight. She dashed into her bedroom locked the door, pushed the hair from her face and flopped onto her bed. Everywhere she looked she could see the face behind a mask. She shut her eyes tightly but the face was still there, the eyes still looked at her through the woollen hood. She held her head in her hands and groaned. 'No. No,' she called as mixed feelings churned over in her mind. She couldn't decide if she hated Simon more than she was in love with him. She loved him for what he was. She loved him for his cool calm manner, his demeanour when they first met. She loved him for his patience in gaining her affection despite of herself. She loved him for his self confident smile, his hard magnetic body, his bronzed face, his gleaming white teeth, his laughing eyes. 'No,' she groaned and hung her head in her hands. She hated him. It *was* hatred, it had to be. She didn't trust him, she was afraid of him. There was nothing left to be in love with. There was no reason at all why she shouldn't call the police and tell them what sort of man he was.

She looked at the door. A few short strides and she'd be there. But she couldn't move. Something held her back. The telephone was at the bottom of the stairs and she couldn't even get as far as her door! 'Damn him!' she grated and tossed her head back with a final resolve. 'I hate him!' She pushed herself up off the bed only to find herself walking towards the window. She looked down at the yard. The car stood alone where she had left it. Minutes must have passed already. More time passed as she waited and watched. Nothing, nobody came or went. Gradually she began to feel a little safer, and slowly, the tension in her body subsided. Her heart slowed and her breathing relaxed. She didn't know how long she had watched and waited before she turned from the window and looked at the door once again, it seemed a long time, but gradually her resolve gathered strength and she went over and unlocked it. A few short steps and she was at the top of the stairs looking down at Andrew and Dorothy. They were standing at the bottom of the staircase looking up. For five or more minutes they had debated whether to follow Rebecca and find out what was the matter. She looked down at the two faces. Her mother smiled. 'Are you all right love?' she asked softly. Rebecca nodded.

'Are you coming down to talk about it?' Andrew asked her. She looked at his face. It was his usual confidence inspiring look. He smiled reassuringly. Rebecca looked into his dark blue eyes as they crinkled at the edges. 'I'm all right now,' she said and managed a weak smile. 'I just have a phone call to make. 'Andrew noticed a quizzical look on Rebecca's face as his eyes left hers. He put his arm around Dorothy. 'Come on, I think she wants to be alone.'

Rebecca stood on the stairs and watched as they turned and began to walk back to the kitchen. She scowled. There was something at the back of her mind, something she should have said. It troubled her. She wasn't normally absent minded. She wasn't usually forgetful in any way. The thought began to germinate when he was facing her, but it had died when he turned away. 'Uncle Andrew!' she called. 'Don't go!'

'What's the matter, Becki?' he asked, his voice coaxing her gently. 'What's wrong?'

Rebecca stared at him hard, grappling to recall that seed of thought that seemed to be eluding her.

'What's the matter?' he asked again as he came closer. Still Rebecca's gaze was fixed on his face. She could feel the thought. It was there again, tickling and contriving at the back of her mind. She walked down the stairs until she reached the second step. It brought her face level with his. He gently gripped her shoulders and coaxed her again. 'What's the matter, Becki?' he asked as he tried to break through her bemused stare.

'Your eyes are a deep blue,' she said as if she had never noticed them before.

Andrew smiled. 'I thought you knew that,' he replied. 'They're the same colour as your own and your mother's.

'Yes, I know.'

Andrew began to be concerned. It wasn't like his niece to be so transparent, so vague. 'Your phone call,' he asked. 'Who is it to?'

She hesitated before she answered. She was going to say the police, but something had changed. 'To Simon,' she said and noticeably regained her composure. 'He has brown eyes.'

'Come, I think you need to sit down and tell me all about it,' he said and moved to guide her to the lounge.

'No!' she said, raising her voice indignantly. 'You don't understand.'

Andrew didn't give way. 'You need to sit down and rest,' he said firmly. 'You aren't your normal self today. A good rest and a drink is what you need my girl.'

'No!' Rebecca shouted and struggled to pull herself away. 'No, you don't understand. I have to ring Simon, tell him I know it wasn't him.'

'She's not making sense,' Dorothy said and took hold of Rebecca's arm to assist Andrew. 'Come on, you come and sit yourself down in here my love,' she said nodding towards the lounge.

'No! I mean it.' Rebecca's voice was firm but her eyes pleaded with them to let her go. 'His eyes are brown, don't you see. I thought it was him but it wasn't.'

'It wasn't what?' her mother asked, impatiently. In her mind she knew Rebecca was having some sort of breakdown. It wasn't surprising after what had happened to her over the last week or so. The sooner she tackled the problem, the sooner she could get it sorted out.

'It wasn't his face behind the mask. It was Stubbs, don't you see?'

'I'm not sure I do,' Andrew said and released the pressure on her arms. 'I thought we already knew that.'

'Simon is in danger, I know he's in danger,' Rebecca insisted. 'I found the ski mask in his office.' She shook her head. 'No, I mean *he* found it in his office.' She ran her fingers through her hair as she compiled her thoughts. 'He found it,' she explained again. 'And I saw him find it. It was in the waste paper basket. It had been there all the time. I'd seen it last night, but I didn't realize what it was.'

'What are you saying, Becki?' Andrew asked. 'Are you saying somebody else put it there?'

'He must have. He must have, because it was Stubbs who wore the mask. I remember he had dark grey eyes. I saw them when he came to visit mother here. But I panicked when I saw Simon with the mask. I thought it was Simon, and I ran out and came straight here.'

Andrew picked up the receiver of the telephone and handed it to Rebecca. Without a word, Rebecca took it and dialled. She tapped her fingers on the table impatiently while she waited for it to connect. 'He...he's not answering!' she groaned and held it for Andrew to listen to the continuous ringing tone. 'And these bloody mobile phones are useless round here,' she blasted as she took hers our of her pocket and put it next the land-line phone.

'Well don't worry, Stubbs has been arrested, anyway,' he consoled. 'Simon can't be in any immediate danger.'

'He can, I know it. There's something wrong! I've got to get back to him!' She made a dash for the door and Andrew grabbed her arm.

'Wait! I'll come with you.'

Together they both went to the door, leaving Dorothy staring after them with her hand over her mouth. She felt helpless. 'But what can we do?' she asked as the door opened.

'What indeed, Mrs. Hampstead?' came Stubbs' voice as his face appeared in the open doorway. 'What indeed!'

CHAPTER THIRTY FOUR

Andrew and Rebecca stared in bewilderment. While they had been working out the facts, Stubbs had cruised into the yard in his Jaguar, without anyone hearing.

'What are you doing here?' Dorothy gasped.

Stubbs grinned. His face contorted like she had never seen it before. 'Let's say that justice is taking its course shall we. I'm out on bail while the police look into your daughter's kidnapping a little further. It seems like they'd got the wrong person.'

Rebecca looked at his eyes. They seemed to lack the compassion they had held when they looked through the mask, but they were the same eyes, she knew that now, there was absolutely no doubt in her mind.

'No they hadn't,' she said as he stepped forward. Andrew stepped between them and blocked his way.

'Don't come any further,' he commanded.

'Or else?' Stubbs asked, still grinning like a Cheshire cat.

'Or I'll break you in half,' he growled.

'Like you did Creedy?' The confident grin still covered his face.

Rebecca spun her head and looked at her uncle.

'You don't know what you are talking about,' Andrew said unexpectedly, with the confidence of someone who did. 'You obviously weren't a very good copper.'

The grin on Stubbs' face vanished as it transformed into an angry sneer. His eyes narrowed as he pulled his Smith and Wesson revolver from his overcoat pocket. 'I'd like you to move inside if you don't mind,' he menaced, pointing the gun past him at Rebecca's head.

Andrew stepped back and took hold of Rebecca by the arm. 'Come on, Becki, we'd better do as he says for now,' he stated solemnly. 'Let's find out what he wants shall we?'

Rebecca nodded her agreement, and together, they backed along the hallway.

'Into the kitchen,' Stubbs ordered and waved the revolver at them. 'Let's all sit around the table and have a little talk, shall we?'

'If you say so,' Andrew replied casually. 'Although I doubt if we can talk down to your level.'

Stubbs winced as if he had been physically struck. 'It will give me great pleasure...' he said and left the statement hanging in mid air. The tone of his voice sent a shiver down Rebecca's spine.

One by one, they seated themselves at the table, first, Rebecca, then Dorothy. Andrew took his time and sat at the end of the table to their right. Stubbs sat down at the opposite end of the table on the left of Rebecca. 'Now,' he said and held the gun over the table, 'I want you to answer my questions. If I think you are being the slightest bit awkward or uncooperative, I shall start and blow pieces off this fine looking girl.' He glanced at Rebecca and pointed to her with the barrel of his pistol. 'Do you understand?'

Dorothy nodded. Her face had turned a very pale grey. Andrew waited a moment and then replied, 'Yes.'

'Good. Now first of all, taking into account your daughter's revelation at the front door, do I gather she didn't call the police?'

'No,' Andrew answered.

'Did she call anybody?'

'No,' he replied again.

'Has anybody rung anybody, in or out, since she returned?'

'He wasn't in,' Dorothy blurted. 'We...we rang Mr. Park for her. He didn't reply.'

Stubbs smiled. 'Good. I like to, see people cooperate. That would be the case, Mrs. Hampstead.'

'What have you done to him?' Rebecca demanded. 'Why didn't he answer?'

'Now, now, calm yourself. All I did was disconnect his telephone, that's all.' He waited and watched the faces around the table. 'So, nobody rang the police?' he asked to confirm their answer.

'Why should they?' Andrew asked. 'We thought they had you in jail.'

'Ah, well it doesn't matter now,' he said, and looked directly at Rebecca. 'I had hoped you would think that Mr. Park, as we know him now, had been the one who kidnapped you. That would have let me off the hook.'

'And let him onto it,' she replied between pursed lips. 'You're despicable.'

'You know,' he said proudly, 'I can't disagree with that!'

'Obviously you are going to kill us all now, anyway,' Andrew stated. 'Why don't you get on with it?'

'Oh? And what makes you so sure of that, Mr. Hampstead?'

'The fact that you can't make her tell the police that Simon Park did it. If she'd believed it, then we might have had a chance, but you can't make her say what you want. Not without standing with a gun to her head forever.'

Stubbs nodded. He wasn't smiling any longer. 'You are a big man, Mr. Hampstead. You have to hope that I will give you the chance to stop me. As long as that hope remains, and as long as you think you can break me in half as you wished to demonstrate a few minutes ago, then you can hope that you will all escape. *Dum spiro spero.* While there's life there's hope.'

'You'll not give us that chance,' Andrew said and moved to get up.

'You are foolish, Mr. Hampstead,' Stubbs shouted and pointed the gun at Rebecca's temple. 'Sit down!'

Andrew resumed his seat. 'So what now?' he asked.

'Now I finish asking my questions.' He looked at Dorothy. 'I shall ask you this once, and only once. If you don't answer the way I want you to, then I'll shoot your daughter. I won't shoot to kill, but I shall disfigure her beyond repair. It won't be a very pretty sight, I warn you.'

Dorothy's bottom lip trembled as Rebecca gripped her hand tightly under the table. 'I've no doubt he'll do it mum,' she said softly. 'But he'll kill us anyway. He has to. Don't give him what he wants before he does it.'

Stubbs ignored what Rebecca had said as if she hadn't spoken. His eyes didn't move from Dorothy. 'Now, Mrs. Hampstead, what was Creedy looking for?'

Dorothy looked at Rebecca, her whole body shaking like a leaf. 'I'm sorry love,' she began to sob. 'I can't let him hurt you.'

Rebecca stared ahead and pushed out her jaw. Beneath the table, she held firmly onto her mother's hand. She knew her mother would give into the man's threats. She also knew it meant certain death as soon as she had told him.

Dorothy knew Stubbs needed her more than Andrew or her daughter. Andrew was a threat, and Rebecca knew none of the answers to his questions. She and only she knew what he wanted to know. But it wouldn't keep Rebecca alive to withhold what she had long tried to forget. She pulled her hand away from Rebecca's and pushed her chair back from the table. Slowly, she stood up while Stubbs' eyes followed her, and she walked towards the window. Over the tops of the trees, she could see a pall of black smoke rising high into the clear mid-day sky, carrying with it a galaxy of burning orange sparks. It was the sort of debris-filled smoke that rises from a burning haystack. She knew it had to be Thatch Cottage. She turned around and faced the table again. She didn't want to cause Rebecca any more pain. Rebecca hadn't seen the smoke; her seat was just a fraction too far to the left of the window. She mustn't see it. Please God, she thought, let it be painless for us all.

'Well?' Stubbs asked impatiently. He was running out of time. The fire at Thatch Cottage would soon be reported.

'Diamonds,' Dorothy said in a controlled voice. Her emotions had passed beyond fear. She was resigned to her fate.

'Yes,' Stubbs said and nodded. 'High value, low bulk, easy to hide.'

'Goodness knows what they were doing there,' Dorothy went on.

'He needed them to raise the cash to buy another supply of heroin. Probably the proceeds from the Matlock jewel theft. It was in all the papers you know.'

'Was it?' Dorothy asked calmly. Her fear had left her now, and in its place was a cool and determined courage.

'The stones were never found,' Stubbs stated. 'It was just the sort of caper that Creedy was starting to move into. A very ambitious man, Creedy.'

'I didn't know,' Dorothy said with a resigned shrug.

'Well why should you know?' Stubbs said as if to comfort her.

'I didn't know they were Creedy's,' she explained. 'When I found them, I didn't think he had anything to do with them.'

'Where were they?'

'In a well beneath the fire range.'

'The fire, of course! It was lit when we raided the house. I thought he'd been trying to heat the water.'

'I didn't know Creedy knew about it. Billy didn't discover it until we'd been living there for five years, and then it was only by accident. There was a stone flag at the base of the ash pit. If he hadn't spilt his tea when he was cleaning it out, he'd have never found it. The tea just disappeared down a crack.'

'So Creedy discovered it as well?'

'I didn't know that. A week or so after Billy died, I noticed that the mortar around the flag had been scraped away, so I prized it out and looked inside. When I found the diamonds, I couldn't believe my eyes. I began to believe that Billy really had been connected with Creedy after all.'

'And now. Where are they now?'

Dorothy hesitated. She had to give him an answer. 'I'm coming to that,' she snapped. 'I'm telling you this so that you'll know why I did what I did.'

'Well please continue,' Stubbs answered sarcastically.

'I was so ashamed of him, I didn't want anything to do with what had been going on.' She stopped and looked at the face of her certain executioner.

'Come on woman!' Stubbs shouted. His patience was wearing thin.

'So I buried them.'

'You buried them! Good! Now all you have to tell me is where.'

'In the one place I would never go again, the place where he was killed.'

'You mean the garage?'

'Beneath the very spot that I found him hanging. That was the last time I ever went in there. It was the last time I ever wanted to be reminded of the whole damned business.'

Stubbs squinted an askew glance at Dorothy's face. 'You're lying,' he said confidently.

'No!' Dorothy protested. 'It's the truth.'

'I remember clearly that there was a concrete floor on the garage, and an inspection pit in the centre.'

'That's right. I buried them at the bottom of the inspection pit. If you look, you'll find a new layer of cement in the bottom with no oil or grease or anything on it. That's because it was never used after I did it. You'll see.'

'Didn't you ever think of using them?'

'What for? I didn't know how to go about selling them. There were times when I seriously considered it, but I never got up the courage. They're still there.'

'Well, well. It seems like I'll have to believe you.'

'I'll take you and show you if you like,' Dorothy offered.

Stubbs grinned through his curled lips. 'That won't be necessary,' he said and stood up.

CHAPTER THIRTY FIVE

Simon regretted not tackling Stubbs before he'd bound him. While he was talking, he thought he'd had a chance, but now he realized that he'd have been as well rushing him and chancing being shot, despite the fact that the policeman had been trained in the use of firearms, and was a highly skilled marksman. Barnes had argued with him and with one single shot was dead. Now the choice had been made. If he couldn't get out of the cottage, he'd be dead anyway.

The smell of burning cooking oil filled his nostrils as he leaned forward over the desk, tilting it backwards and spilling his type script, printer and laptop onto the floor. His own feet and the feet of the desk were clear of the floor for only a second before rocking back into their original position. He pushed again, harder this time, knowing that he could end up on his back under the heavy desk. But he had nothing to lose now. He'd be overcome by the dense, black smoke in a matter of a few more seconds. Smoke usually kills fire victims well before the flames reach them; usually scalding hot smoke, breathed in, scorching the lungs. Not a pleasant death, but preferable to the flames.

The desk fell backwards, crushing the laptop and the printer, and leaving Simon spread-eagled across the knee-hole. The captain's chair that was still firmly anchored to his forearms helped him balance backwards again and, driving with all the strength he could muster, he contracted his muscles to bend his legs. Gradually, he pivoted back onto the chair so that his ankles prized against the knob feet that tethered them. He felt no pain as he kicked and struggled to free his feet, there was no time left. The first whiffs of smoke were reaching his lungs and would soon be starving them of oxygen. Then the scalding hot smoke would follow, probably whilst he was unconscious. His eyes streamed as they tried in vain to clear away the darkening blanket. He began to choke and kicked again and again, until he thought he would surely break both ankles before breaking the string around them. He had no strength left as less and less air reached his heaving lungs. His head began to spin and he fell sideways. The chair still held him tight, but the air was a little clearer near the floor as he felt the pressure of his twisted left leg snap the foot off the desk, and drop freely to the floor. The flames were billowing into the passage now. Desperately, he kicked out with his free leg at the desk again. Somehow the other foot began to come free. He coughed and choked as, it too, became detached from the carcase of the desk. The flames were roaring, stretching with burning, licking fingers to reach the open office door. The heat from them was unbearable as they began scorching his face. He could hear the explosions as the kitchen windows cracked with the flames. The fire roared more fiercely than ever as it drew in more air from outside. There was no air left in the room now. The black smoke was down to the floor. He knelt up and staggered away from the flames in the doorway, barely conscious. With no time left to reach the window as he heard it shatter.

Then, suddenly, barely conscious, Simon felt fingers touching his arm. They grabbed a hold of his sleeve and dragged him towards the dull light of the window.

No longer able to hold his breath, and still clutching at Simon's sleeve, Arthur dived at the window and gasped for air as a strong hand reached inside and grabbed him, pulling him clear. 'Get Simon,' he coughed and pointed to the head and shoulders that were just visible through the billowing smoke. A moment later, Earnest Henshaw had yanked Simon and the chair clear. As they landed on the hard concrete path, Earnest looked back inside. The whole floor was breaking into flames. As the paper ignited the dense smoke, there was a roar and a dull thud. He dived to the floor for cover as smoke and flames shot out of the opening above his head.

Arthur was already with Simon, pulling him clear of the building, when Earnest scrambled away. As he coughed, and heaved to get his breath, he picked up a piece of broken glass to begin to cut the strings that held Simon to the chair, but he wasn't as quick as the old farmer. He had his penknife out and had freed Simon before Arthur's streaming eyes could blink or focus properly on the bonds. The next thing he knew, Earnest had turned Simon on his back and was pressing rhythmically on his breastbone. He tilted Simon's head back, prized open his jaw and breathed into his mouth before resuming the pounding action on his chest. Arthur just sat up, rubbed his smarting eyes and watched. For a whole minute he looked on as the old farm worker bounced his weight on Simon's chest. Once again he breathed into Simon's mouth making the lifeless chest rise as he breathed into it a mixture of oxygen and carbon dioxide, and then watched it fall with the natural pressure of his own chest cage. 'There's a weak pulse,' Earnest said between breaths. 'But I can't seem t' get him t' breathe.'

'Then keep going, for God's sake!' Arthur said and scrambled to Simon's car. He pulled open the door, grabbed the cell phone and dialled 999. What a bloody mess,' he coughed. 'No damned signal round here at all.' He tossed it back on the seat. 'They'll be ages unless someone sees the fire and reports it.' He looked at Simon. 'He needs oxygen. By the time...' He stopped and listened. As Simon's chest fell, it had contracted and coughed out a dry gasp of air. Earnest was ready to breath for Simon again. He bent over him once more and was about to blow into his lungs again when, suddenly, spasmodically, Simon sucked in air and his chest rose on its own.

'Done it!' Earnest mumbled, turning Simon on his side. He sat back on his heels and for a minute or so, they both just watched as Simon breathed, coughed and spluttered, oblivious to anything or anybody.

'Done that before have you?' Arthur asked Earnest, his own lungs still stinging.

'Only wi'new born calves,' he said with a grin. 'Surprising what we'll do t' save a life, isn't it?'

'Bit of a shock to the system when they open their eyes though,' Arthur said and actually laughed. Earnest Henshaw looked at him and studied his face. With a smile on it, Arthur's whole personality seemed to radiate outwards.

'Y'know, y'could be right about that.'

They both laughed. They were both happy. They had just saved a life. But nobody was happier than Arthur.

CHAPTER THIRTY SIX

'You've left me no choice,' Stubbs said, and pointed his gun at Andrew. 'I can't leave you alive. You do understand, don't you?'

Andrew nodded. 'We understand,' he said and then, 'that you are forced to be caught. Who are you going to blame for our murders?'

'Murders? Who said anything about murder?' Stubbs's face contorted into a hideous smile. 'Just another accident!'

'Not another fire!' Dorothy said sarcastically. 'Hardly fits in with your explanation that Simon Park did it,' she stated.

'As I have said, you have left me no choice. When your daughter didn't ring the police then I knew my plan had floundered.' He pointed to the corner. 'Pass me that clothes line,' he ordered.

Dorothy shuffled slowly over to the worktop where a plastic laundry basket stood empty except for a coil of thin rope and a few dozen pegs.

'You're mad,' Rebecca said and stood up. 'Don't you realize?'

'Shut your mouth,' Stubbs snarled and swiped her across the face with his revolver.

Rebecca gave out a small scream and fell backwards away from her chair. Stunned, she knelt up and held her head with one hand while she steadied herself with the other. 'It's called pyromania,' she gasped as the pain of the blow began to bite.

'I'm not mad!' Stubbs shouted at the top of his voice. 'I am saner than you are. A sane person would keep their mouth shut when faced with a gun.'

'Mad as a hatter,' Dorothy said flatly.

Stubbs spun around and hovered over her with the butt of the gun. 'You'll die slowly for that,' he said and turned on Andrew who had stepped closer. 'You'll all die like that man,' he said and waved his gun at the window.

For the first time, Rebecca saw the smoke rising above Thatch Cottage. 'What have you done to him?' she screamed and struggled towards the window.

Dorothy helped her up and put her arm around her. 'He'll be all right, don't you worry,' she said trying to be positive.

'He's dead,' Stubbs gloated, a wild leer beginning to engulf his whole face. 'By now he'll be roasted like a chicken.' He burst out laughing. 'I made sure the mask didn't get too near the fire,' he said after he'd caught his breath. You'll see he'll still get the blame. They won't be able to prove I did anything.' He snatched the rope out of Dorothy's hand and grabbed hold of Rebecca. 'Now you get on the floor,' he said, waving his gun at Andrew. 'And you,' he said to Dorothy.

Slowly, they knelt down on the kitchen floor. 'On your bellies,' he commanded. 'Hands behind your backs. And be quick about it, I don't have all day.' He glanced out at the column of smoke beyond the trees. He'd cut it fine. He had to be on his way before the fire brigade or the police got word of the fire. He tied Andrew's hands first. Then he tied the rope to the heavy kitchen table. Finally, he tied Dorothy in the same manner before turning his attention to Rebecca. 'You're coming with me,' he said.

Arthur knelt beside Simon when he saw him coming around. 'How do you feel?' he asked and helped him sit up.

'Just great!' he replied in a whisper, when he saw who was asking. His throat and his lungs were raw. 'I think I'm going to be sick!' he said and lay back down again.

'Take deep breaths. It'll soon pass.'

Simon did as Arthur suggested. It helped a little, but his chest burned with each breath. He relaxed and tried to recall where he was and what had happened. Earnest had brought him a bottle of water from his jeep and, helped by the old farmer to sit up, Simon took a swig. It cooled his throat but tasted really bad. He took another swig and spit it out to wash the taste of smoke out of his mouth, and then drank some more before offering it to Arthur. 'Hell!' he gasped as he remembered what had happened. He rolled over onto his hands and knees.

'Just relax,' Ernest said calmly, 'we can't do anything about the fire now.'

Simon glanced at the blazing cottage. 'Have you called the fire brigade?

'What with?' Arthur gesticulated with his hands. 'Mobiles don't work around here!'

'Too damned late either way,' Simon coughed looking at the ravaging fire.

'The house might not be saved, but you need medical care,' Arthur stated after reaching for the bottle and taking a gulp of the water.

'I agree wi'that, young man,' Earnest said from the corner of the yard. 'You wa'damn near dead a couple a minutes ago!'

Simon shook his head. 'No, we've no time. Stubbs did this. He's trying to frame me.' He stopped talking and panted to get some more air into his lungs and then carried on in a whisper, 'He expects Rebecca to have rung you and told you I was her kidnapper.'

'That doesn't make sense, Simon,' said Arthur shaking his head.

Simon explained as best he could. 'He planted the mask in the house for you to find. The gun he used on the man called Barnes is in the garden. Rebecca saw the mask first and went off in a flap - as usual,' he added, 'Stubbs saw what happened and was expecting she'd tell you it was me who abducted her.'

'Not heard a thing!'

'Either way, he's likely to kill her. I think he's gone a bit mad!'

Arthur looked at the cottage. 'I think I agree with you. At one time he was one step ahead of us. Now that we've caught up to him, he seems to be on a self destruct routine. It gets a lot of criminals that way. They carry on as if they were still miles ahead of you. The trouble is...' Arthur paused, not wanting to agitate Simon in his condition.

'Is what Arthur? Spit it out.'

'It usually runs to a confrontation because they don't know when to run to ground.' He looked in the direction of Pendle Court. 'If he's there now, he's got hostages.'

'Not if he thinks he's still ahead of us,' Simon said and used Arthur's sleeve to pull himself up.

'I reckon he's going to kill them when he finds out what he wants from Mrs. Hampstead,' Arthur argued, 'That's how I came to find you here having a barbecue; I was on my way to the Hampstead's. It's the only place Stubbs can go.' He handed the bottle of water back to Simon. 'And my guess is he'll get what he wants by threatening to kill one of the others. Once he gets what he's been looking for, none of them are safe.'

'Well then, we have to get over there now!' croaked Simon as he staggered to his car.

'Better go in mine,' Arthur said and helped him into the passenger seat of the Mondeo. He turned to Earnest 'Have you got a mobile phone?'

'Back at t' house,' Earnest said with a shrug.

Arthur pointed to Simon's car. 'Can you drive that to a signal and then use that car phone and call the station. Tell them where we are going, and that Stubbs is armed and dangerous. They'll know what to do.' Without waiting for an answer, he ducked into his seat, started the engine and spun the wheels wildly as he reversed out onto the road.

CHAPTER THIRTY SEVEN

'Get me the cooking oil,' Stubbs ordered.

Rebecca stood absolutely still. 'Get it yourself,' she said between clenched teeth and waited for another blow from the handle of the revolver. It didn't come. Stubbs was going to take her with him. He needed her face in one piece if he was to drive past anyone without arousing suspicions. He had plenty of time to sort her out later. 'What's the matter? Getting soft are you?' she asked as he began to open every cupboard door.

He didn't seem to hear, but just carried on his search. When he located the right cupboard, he took out the cooking oil and four packs of sugar. 'Come on,' he said and dragged her by the arm. He went into the lounge and pushed her into the corner. 'Stay there,' he said, and started pouring the oil over the settee. He threw the empty bottle on the arm chair, poured the sugar all around it and then took the papers from the Canterbury. It took him less than a few seconds to screw them up and pile them on the seats before taking out a lighter to set a flame to them.

It was then that Rebecca saw her only chance. She knew she had to keep out of direct line of fire if she was running away. Whatever his intentions for her, he would shoot her before let her escape. While he concentrated on putting the flame to the papers, she would move along the wall. She hoped he would be distracted by her running away, enough to fail to light them, but not before she had got ten yards start. Her heart thumped as he flicked the lighter into action. In a split second she was out of the door, and heading for the stairs. She daren't look around.

She just kept going, swerving up the stairs and running as hard as she could.

Stubbs saw her disappearing out of the doorway. He looked up and growled to himself. When she ran across the yard, he would drop her like a rabbit. He looked down and completed his task, only lighting the one pile of paper on the settee before storming after her. He looked straight ahead. The hall door was still closed. Then he heard her footsteps as she pounded as fast as she could up the stairs. It took him less than a second to reach the bottom step, and less than that to turn and fire his gun.

Rebecca had left her door open when she came out of her room, so she knew she wouldn't have to stop to open it. It was that that saved her life. But it didn't stop the bullet smashing into her shoulder as she swung around the door frame to the sanctuary afforded by the thick stone wall. She yelled and fell forward against her bed. With her head spinning and her heart pounding in her ears, she couldn't hear her pursuer, but she knew he was coming, she knew he'd make her pay. She pulled herself up and waited.

Stubbs bared his teeth in anger. He was going to make her pay for this. He walked up the stairs with a determined stride and burst into the room. 'Hoomph,' he groaned as a bronze Shetland pony hit him in the eye and sent him reeling backwards. He'd underestimated Rebecca. The strength she had gained from working on the farm was well out of proportion to her size. She'd put all her weight and strength behind her arm. She was no longer afraid of him. It was fight or die; and since she knew she had no chance of beating him, she'd already settled for both.

The gun went off as Stubbs somersaulted backwards down the stairs. The door jamb splintered beside Rebecca as she followed him out. It wouldn't take him long to pick himself up and come after her again, and she realized that she'd not get the same chance again. She was trapped in her bedroom and wounded in the left shoulder. Her only hope was to get past Stubbs. Andrew's gun cabinet in the office was locked, and Andrew had the key. There was no chance of arming herself. The door on the old back staircase would probably be locked and she didn't want to be trapped in a corridor when Stubbs came back after her. She had to take her only chance and try and get past him to get outside.

Her reasoning took no time to formulate. It seemed to be in her mind already. As Stubbs tumbled backwards she was following as fast as she could. He came to rest on the bottom step with his legs splayed up the stairs as his head struck against the newel post. He was stunned, but the gun was still in his hand. Rebecca leapt over his legs and lunged again at his face. Instantly, blood spurted from his face as the momentum of the heavy bronze ornament sank it into the bridge of his nose. Stubbs growled like a wounded bear. Before she could withdraw her weapon for another blow, the reflex of his left arm swept his fist round and landed it under her armpit. Rebecca felt her ribs buckle as the force of the blow sent her sprawling sideways, over his right hand, and landed her on top of the revolver. Stubbs, half by reflex again, and half in sheer desperation to rid himself of this tigress that threatened to delay him too long for him to make his escape, franticly squeezed the trigger again and again.

The short journey to Pendle Court seemed to take for ever. Simon sat on the edge of his seat, his fingers gripping the dashboard in exasperation. As Arthur slammed on his brakes and skidded on the gravel to a halt in the centre of the yard, they could both see the fire in the lounge was already licking hungrily at the hall window opposite the open door. 'My God, he's done it again!' Simon shouted and jumped out of the car. His legs felt weak, but from somewhere, his body found new reserves of energy as he bounded towards the front door. Suddenly, he heard the muffled sound of gunfire. Once, twice, and then again. 'He's killing them!' he screamed, and ran up the steps and pushed against the door. It didn't move. Stubbs had dropped the latch. It was a heavy door, and it had a good lock. Simon knew he'd never break his way in through it. 'We'll not get in here,' he shouted.

'We'll have to find another way in then,' he heard Arthur shout. He turned around and surveyed the front of the house desperately. Arthur was already on his way along the front wall to the far side of the house, past the hall window. The kitchen was still free of flames and he was heading there. Simon followed.

'There's somebody in there,' Arthur shouted as Simon caught up with him.

Simon looked through the window. Already, the smoke was beginning to seep under the door and fill the kitchen, but he could see Andrew sitting against the table, and dragging it towards them with his feet.

'I'll get him,' Simon shouted, and smashed the window with his elbow. The large pane of glass shattered and fell inwards, and before it had landed on the kitchen floor, Simon had already dived through the gap and rolled against the table. A sharp pain in his back told him he hadn't got inside without drawing blood.

'Get a knife,' Andrew coughed, and nodded at a drawer beneath the kitchen worktop. Simon got up and snatched the drawer clean out onto the floor, spilling carving knives and cutlery all around him. He picked a likely looking knife and set to cutting Andrew free. As Andrew pulled his hands away from the cord, he took the knife from Simon and turned to the other side of the table. 'I'll see to Dorothy,' he choked. 'Find Becki!'

Once outside again Simon looked around for Arthur. 'Arthur!' he shouted. He was nowhere to be seen. He must have gone to look for Rebecca around the other side of the house. Andrew was already helping Dorothy out of the window. Without another word, Simon ran as fast as his legs would carry him, along the front of the house. He stopped and tried the front door once again. It was still locked and didn't budge when he ran his shoulder against it. Already, they were running out of time. Another loud crack resounded through the right wing of the house. 'He's shooting again!' Simon exclaimed.

'The back door!' shouted Andrew. He had already sprinted ahead.

Rebecca had grabbed the arm that lay beneath her with her right hand as it twisted at the wrist to turn the gun on her. She'd clung on with every ounce of strength, desperately trying to hold it away from her body. Her left hand was useless; she could hardly move it as she rolled over onto her left shoulder. She felt a hot dull ache in her side as the recoil of the gun carried the arm out of her reach, and suddenly, all her strength sapped from her body. Strangely she heard only the first shot. Everything after that lapsed into a haze of fading consciousness as two more .38 calibre bullets exploded from the barrel of the gun.

Stubbs rolled on his side and pushed the lifeless body off his twisted arm. He knelt over Rebecca for a brief moment, and for an even briefer instant, a look of regret passed across his eyes. In his life he had seen a lot of death. But though there always came a time when someone had to be killed, he couldn't ever really get used to it. It was just necessary sometimes.

He stood up and wiped the blood from his eyes as he turned to the door. There was no choice but to run for it now; the police would find the body and the bullets. They would match the bullets to the one that killed Barnes. Simon was dead, or at least, so he thought. He couldn't pin this killing on him. His hand was reaching for the door latch, when he heard the sound of a man's voice. 'We'll not get in here,' he heard him shout.

Stubbs flinched. He thought he recognized the voice, but it couldn't be that one! Simon Park was dead. He'd seen the smoke of Thatch Cottage billowing into the sky. 'No!' he muttered. 'No! He's dead, he's dead!' He spun his head in the direction of the kitchen. He needed a hostage. 'Damn you!' he cursed and looked down at Rebecca's body. He kicked it. 'You bitch!' he hissed. She'd spoilt everything. He couldn't get through to the kitchen now. The flames from the lounge were already billowing out of the open door, into the hallway, and cutting off his access. His eyes suddenly took on a wild and desperate look. He glanced around again and checked his revolver. One round left! Without a hostage, he'd not get far if he was seen. With the panic of a trapped animal, he ran along the passage to the right in search of a back way out. He had a feeling that there was more than one door to the old farmhouse, and he hadn't seen it at the kitchen end. He went through the door at the end of the passage. He was right. This was what had once been the old servants' quarters in the time when the house belonged to the owner of the original estate. The rooms were used for storage now, and had a disused look about them, but not unkempt. The first room was dark and windowless, and only the light from the passage enabled him to see where he was going. When he entered the second room, he went straight to the window. It had bars and shutters on the outside, obviously an old kitchen and cold room. Both rooms now had a variety of antique tables and chairs, cupboards and ornaments scattered over the floors, and various old oil paintings adorning the walls. In the furthest corner, by the door of the last room were stacked tea chests full of books and papers, but apart from those containers, everything else was free standing. Stubbs didn't stop to take a lot of notice what was in the rooms, but the tea chests caught his eye as his shoulder brushed past them. The door at the back of that room would undoubtedly lead to the old servants' entrance, now the back door. Quickly, he ruffled up some of the old papers, took out his lighter, and set light to them. He emerged from the room into a small hallway. To the left a staircase ran up to the one time servants' bedrooms. As he had guessed, directly ahead of him was the back door of the house through which he could make his escape. He ran towards it and then stopped in his tracks.

Arthur had disappeared around the back of the house. He ran past the orchard, along a gravel path, to the pavement that led to the back door. He gripped the handle of the door and tried to open it. It too, like the front door, was locked. He looked at the windows, but the house had been built on a slope and floor level was three feet from the ground. The windows were too high to reach. A small shed stood near the corner of the orchard. He went to it, hoping to find something on which to stand. He unlatched the door and looked inside. It was a tool shed. There wasn't even an orange box that would give him extra height. He glanced around until his eyes fell on a sledge hammer. He grabbed it, and was just about to turn and leave when he saw a sickle. He grabbed that with the other hand and ran to the door. He threw down the reaping hook, and standing to one side of the jamb, began to swing the big hammer with as much force as he could at the door.

Stubbs stared at the old back door. A loud banging echoed through the small vestibule. The sound was definitely coming from the door. He could see it move each time something heavy banged against it. His eyes stretched wide and took on a wild, angry glare. He was trapped. Somebody was hitting the door with a heavy hammer. There must be more men round here, he thought. His head swung from side to side as despair began to grow inside him. He lifted his revolver and fired. The shot resounded through the whole house as the door splintered. He squeezed the trigger again, but the hammer just clicked on an empty chamber. He tossed the gun to one side and went to the door. The banging had stopped, he'd hit whoever it was that had been trying to get in, he was sure of it. Now he had to take his chance and run. He slid the bolt and pulled the door open. Arthur Greythorpe's face glared back at him like some terrible reflection in a fairground mirror. Somehow, Stubbs had missed.

Arthur was almost as shocked. Stubbs looked as if he'd shot himself in the face. His right eye and the bridge of his nose were just one mass of oozing blood. 'Up to your usual tricks,' Arthur said almost casually.

'Well try this one,' Stubbs grated and lunged forward.

Arthur knew all along that he was no match, armed or unarmed against Stubbs. He was well trained in self defence, but he knew from Stubbs' records that Stubbs had taught unarmed combat to new recruits in his early years in the force. And now, despite his age, he looked as fit and as capable as he ever had, as he gathered speed towards Arthur. He lifted the sickle and swung it towards Stubbs. I knew I never had a chance! he thought, as his wrist suddenly stopped and the sickle was expertly removed from his hand. He swung his free fist hard at his assailant's face. It landed against Stubbs' forearm and was driven down faster than he'd thrown it. A blow from somewhere hit him on the side of the head, and then another in his chest. He felt weak at the knees and, although he'd already decided to lie down and let Stubbs past, he had no choice as his legs were swept from under him.

Two seconds after swinging the sickle, Arthur lay on his back with Stubbs standing victoriously over him. The big ex-policeman was enjoying his easy victory. He wasn't ready to run past Arthur yet. He hated the spindly little detective. He wanted to make him suffer, but hadn't the time. Instead, he would make him pay with a single twist of his neck. He bent over Arthur, grabbed hold of his hair, and sat him up. Maintaining his hold, he placed his other hand on Arthur's chin and was about to carry out the neat execution when something solid hit him and sent him hurtling sideways.

Andrew knew when he saw what was happening, exactly what Stubbs was going to do. He knew a professional when he saw one. He'd been one himself in the marines. Stubbs was revelling in his easy contest and Andrew knew he only had seconds to get to them. No time for organized combat, he just had to stop him before he killed the detective. The only thing he could do to reach Stubbs in time was to take off from his sprint and dive at him. It worked. His shoulder hit Stubbs squarely against his arm. Stubbs fell sideways and Andrew, in a descending trajectory, fell half on Arthur's head, and half on the legs of the policeman's would-be executioner.

Stubbs was first back on his feet, but then, he was ten years younger than Andrew, and those ten years had taken the spring out of Andrew's legs. Andrew balanced on his knees. He knew Stubbs wouldn't run. He was going to fight, and he was right. Stubbs' foot came forward to connect with his temple, but Andrew was ready. He blocked the kick and used the momentum of Stubbs' body to pull his leg forward and from under him. Stubbs fell awkwardly in front of Andrew. A blow landed on Stubbs' throat, making his eyes roll in their sockets and his tongue loll from the corner of his mouth grotesquely. Stubbs was weakened now but he twisted and rolled away, and he too, was then balancing on his knees. The blow to his throat had damaged his larynx and his chest heaved to help him gain his breath.

Andrew was soon standing and ready for the next attack. He was unsure of his ability to counter anything Stubbs threw at him, but he knew that any attacker is always the most vulnerable and open to attack when they are coming forward. If he attacked Stubbs, then he would himself be exposed.

Stubbs grinned through a crooked mouth. The farmer was afraid to come at him even though his opponent was on his knees. Stubbs took his time, pushed himself up into an offensive position and then went at Andrew with a rain of body-wrecking blows.

Simon wasn't far behind Andrew, but things happened so fast that Andrew was already standing when he caught up to him. He watched the awesome attack that Stubbs made and realized that he would never have been able to overpower the man back at Thatch Cottage. He watched as Andrew was pushed back one step and then two. He picked up the sickle, ready to use it when Andrew's defences failed, and stepped back to give himself more room to swing it. He waited, ready to thrust forward with his weapon, but Andrew's reflexes were better than he could have ever imagined. Slowly, Andrew was demoralizing his opponent, fending every blow, and then, suddenly and without warning, he stepped forward instead of back. Simon watched as somehow Andrew, with a single thrust of his hand, stalled the onslaught of his determined attacker. Stubbs jerked to a halt, his arms first recoiled to his face and then flopped down loosely as his knees gave way and he fell forward. There was a dull thud as his head hit the square flags that lined the path.

'I'll watch him. Get after that policeman!' Andrew shouted as if Simon had been wasting his time.

CHAPTER THIRTY EIGHT

Arthur had vanished from beneath their feet. Rebecca was still in the house somewhere and he knew he wasn't going to be any use outside. He ran through the rooms towards the front door. He knew the shots had been fired at the front of the house, and they had sounded to be downstairs. The tinder dry papers and books in the tea chests were already blazing furiously, and scorching a nearby Buhl inlaid cabinet. He knew he had little time to find Rebecca and get her out the way he had entered. He looked around each room rapidly, before going to the next one. His eyes searched the floors and the walls as if he could, by accident, miss what he was looking for. At the front of the house the fire was belching flames and thick smoke into the hallway. He could hardly see the front door as he groped his way along the floor beneath the thickest of the black smoke which was hanging malevolently against the ceiling. Just ahead, he could see Rebecca's body, lying across the bottom step of the staircase. He noticed how frail and small her body seemed as it lay close to the flames. He didn't see the trail of blood as he grabbed her feet and dragged her back the way he'd come. He stopped momentarily to try and open the front door, but the flames and the smoke were coming at him faster and he was running out of air. If he didn't get out of the hallway now he would surely die the death he narrowly missed at Thatch Cottage. Still crouching down, he pulled Rebecca along the hall until he was well clear of the flames, and then he took a deep breath of the only air there was from near the floor, picked her up, stood up straight, and made for the back door.

———

Simon stopped at the bottom of the old staircase. He didn't know which way Arthur had gone. He, too, believed that the shots had been near the front of the house and probably down stairs. One of the stacked up tea chests had already fallen across the doorway and blazed out of control. He considered dashing through the flames, but there was no telling how deep into the room they went or what obstacles stood in his way. He turned back to the outer door. 'Is there any other way through?' he shouted to Andrew above the noise of the drawing flames.

'Only up the back stairs,' Andrew shouted back.

Simon turned and bounded up the old staircase. It led onto landings from which doors led to several rooms. He went past them all to the door at the end of the passage. It was locked. Simon kicked at it a couple of times and as it began to burst he gave it one last thrust with his shoulder and staggered forward as the door gave way and swung open. He turned right onto another landing. It led onto the main bedrooms.

He ran along the passage to the front staircase but already flames and dense smoke were advancing up the steps and blocking his way. He glanced inside the open door on his right. It was Rebecca's bedroom; he knew that. *The Lace Maker* stood on the side table next to her bed. The pink and white patchwork quilt and the decor of the room were just as he'd imagined it would be. Some part of Rebecca was in that room. He could feel her, he could almost see her. The deep feeling of love for her that had grown since the day he'd met her, and which he'd nurtured inside him without ever saying it in words, suddenly filled his whole being. He had to find her before she was lost to him forever. He knew she was in the house but she was nowhere to be found. Arthur was in there looking for her. 'God help them,' he groaned as the realization that they were both trapped by the fire, finally hit him.

He turned around slowly and wandered, dazed with shock, despair and sheer fatigue, back the way he had come. He opened the door of each room that he passed, and glanced almost casually inside. He knew Rebecca wasn't there. Arthur would have found her. He got through the right way. Good old Arthur. Poor Arthur. He'd gone to his death to save Rebecca. There was no way out for him if he had found her. He rubbed his fingers though his hair and trod heavily down the steps of the back staircase. Thick smoke was pouring up them now, but it didn't matter any more. He just kept walking down into the blackness.

'Get out of there man!' Andrew's voice rang in Simon's ears as a hand grabbed his sweater and yanked him out of the black void. Andrew had followed Simon when he saw the flames begin to spread to the stairs. The thick black smoke was already sweeping upwards when he saw Simon stumbling dazed, from the bottom step, and heading towards the fire instead of turning back to the open door. The flames were almost up against him and he'd felt nothing. Andrew threw him to the floor and ripped off his smouldering sweater. Simon had something in his hand, but he wouldn't let go of it. 'Come on,' he said and put his arm under Simon's. 'Let's get you out of here.' He supported Simon as they walked around to the yard.

CHAPTER THIRTY NINE

Already, two police cars, an ambulance and a fire engine had arrived from Thatch cottage. That place was practically burned out when they arrived, and Earnest Henshaw had simply explained, and redirected them to their next and more urgent job of the day. The police were scurrying about the grounds, the fire engine was beginning to pump water through the broken window opposite the lounge, and Stubbs was being loaded into an ambulance ready to be transported to the hospital.

'Where's the police guard for Stubbs?' Simon coughed, knowing that he was a man who would use his condition to his advantage if there was any hope of escape.

'Not necessary,' the ambulance man stated with a straight face that reminded him of Arthur's. 'It's the mortuary for him I'm afraid.'

Simon looked at Andrew in astonishment. He didn't say anything. He'd seen how the two men had fought their lethal fight with their own lethal weapons. No comment was necessary.

'I think you'd better go along there too,' Andrew said to avert Simon's gaze. 'You have a few bad blisters coming out on your face and arm already.'

'I'll wait,' Simon answered emphatically. 'Until I know where my two friends are, I'm going nowhere.'

As they stood back and watched the fire consume the house, and the firemen fight in vain to stop the flames from completely engulfing it, Simon's spirits fell even lower. He sank down on his haunches and sat on his heels as another and yet another fire engine came and more and more water was pumped from the river into the building. Nobody came out. A scurrying of men and a shout of 'Look out!' managed only to turn his eyes as the roof collapsed and fell in on all that remained of his hope. He stared vacantly ahead when a kind ambulance man put a blanket around him and asked if he was cold. He felt like crying but his eyes were dry. All he could do was sit and watch.

A fireman came over to them and shook his head sadly. 'Sorry,' he said as if he was personally to blame. 'It was too hot to get anyone in. There is nobody alive in there now.' He tossed his head in the direction of the ambulance. Andrew knew what he meant. It was time to get Simon to hospital. Carefully, so that they didn't break the stupor, they lifted Simon to his feet. Andrew put Simon's arm over his shoulder and walked him to the doors of an ambulance.

'No!' Simon shouted and pushed himself away with new found energy. 'The ambulance might be needed for Rebecca and Arthur. We've got to wait.'

'It's no use,' Andrew said, and held him firmly by his arm.

'He's right,' Dorothy said as she came over to them. Simon looked at her face. She looked tired, tired of struggling, tired of life. He knew how she felt. He'd lost Rebecca too. And he'd lost his best friend. He knew exactly how she felt. But he couldn't accept it as easily as that. Something was still keeping the spark of hope alight in his heart. Something, somehow, he felt Arthur needed him; he needed his help.

He turned to Andrew. Andrew looked at Simon's blistered face. His stupefied, glazed stare had vanished. 'There's another way out. Where is it?' he demanded.

Andrew shook his head. 'Simon,' he said and put his hand on his shoulder, 'let's go.'

Simon shook it off and pushed himself forward towards the house. In his mind was an idea, just a thought, perhaps more of a hope than logic, but it was there. He knew Arthur. He wouldn't give his life in vain if he could help it. He was the most logical man he had ever known. 'There must be somewhere that they could go. Arthur wouldn't go in knowing that he couldn't get out,' he stated and ran towards the nearest fireman. 'Are there any bodies in there near the front door?' he asked.

'We haven't come across any. The fire is coming under control at the front now. We'll be able to see better in a minute or two.'

Simon turned and stared at the ground as he thought. Still, he could swear Arthur needed help. He couldn't be in the house, not and be alive. He must be...'The cellar!' Simon shouted. 'Where is the cellar?'

For a moment, Andrew stared back at him. The cellar, he thought. 'The cellar!' he shouted and ran. Simon ran after him, along the front of the house, and then beside the walls of the old servants' wing. Andrew was scraping at the grass when Simon caught up.

'Is anybody up there?' he could hear the distant voice of Arthur calling.

'We're here!' Simon shouted back, sobbing, and began to help to clear away the years of grass above the circular plate that covered the old coal chute. 'We're here, Arthur. Hang on!'

A minute later, with the help of the sickle, they prized the iron plate out of its ring and saw Arthur's blackened face gazing up at them. 'Thought you were trying to drown us,' Arthur said and offered up Rebecca's limp and lifeless body. 'Here,' he said. 'Get her to hospital. She's barely alive.'

Andrew and Simon gently hoisted the blood soaked body out of Arthur's weary arms.

'I'm all right,' Arthur said to prevent them delaying getting her to the ambulance. If the water rises any more, I'll be able to swim out, he thought as the water slopped around his waist.

Rebecca was given plasma to help replace her lost blood, as she and Simon travelled together in the same vehicle to the General Hospital. Simon stroked her forehead, held her hand and whispered, 'You're going to be all right Rebecca. Simon's here.' He said it time and again, until the doctors whisked her away to theatre. Once and only once did she seem to hear. The first time he spoke, he thought he felt her squeeze his hand. He thought it was a squeeze. It was barely noticeable. He believed it was a squeeze and not a muscular spasm brought about through loss of blood.

Simon was admitted to a small surgery where he was cleaned up, his burns were dressed and several splinters of glass were removed from a gash in his back before being stitched. He was injected with something to help reduce the shock he had suffered and then taken on his way to a small observation ward. He felt sleepy as the porter wheeled him in a chair along the corridors. The sedative was working.

'Stop!' he said, and held up his arm. The porter did as he was told. 'Take me to the operating theatres. I have to be there!'

'But my orders are to get you to the ward,' the porter objected.

'I have to know how Rebecca is. I'm not going anywhere, until I know.' He pushed himself out of the chair and stood up unsteadily.

'All right!' the porter said and put his hand on Simon's shoulder. 'Sit down, and I'll take you there.'

Simon sat back down in the wheelchair and the porter turned him around and pushed him to the corridor outside the operating theatre where Rebecca had been taken. 'She's still in there,' the porter said soothingly. 'She might be a while yet. I'll leave you in the chair here. I'll be back, but I've got to go and explain what I've done with you!'

'Thanks,' Simon said gratefully, and turned his attention to the double doors.

It seemed like hours since he'd come into the hospital with Rebecca. It seemed like hours before the surgeon and his staff emerged and removed their masks. By that time Andrew, Dorothy, and Arthur had all joined him. They hardly spoke, and when they did, Simon never joined in. Eventually they all lapsed into silence and just waited.

When the surgeon emerged he looked at them all. They all looked back at him, afraid to ask. 'I've done all I can,' he said gloomily, 'but she's still hanging on. God knows, she should have died long before she reached here, but she's hanging on. All I can think is that when she was shot, her metabolism sank so low that it prevented her from bleeding to death immediately.'

'But she'll be all right?' Dorothy pleaded.

The surgeon shook his head. 'We can hope,' he said and placed his hand on her arm. 'But you must realize that if she doesn't die from shock, the loss of blood may still do it. We can't tell for sure what other damage has been caused in cases where there has been extreme loss of blood. She had four bullet wounds, one in her shoulder and three in her abdomen. We've removed the bullets, but two of them have done considerable physical damage. One passed through her liver and another entered her stomach. Of the others, one passed clean through her shoulder and the other lodged in her breast bone. Somehow, I don't know how, that one only managed to crack the bone. If it had got through, it would have carried on to her heart. At the moment, she's unconscious, but we have stabilized her condition and that's the best we can do. I'm sorry we can't do more,' he said and turned away.

'Can we be with her?' Simon asked after him.

He turned and faced Simon. He sighed and shook his head. 'She'll be in an oxygen tent to begin with. There seems little anybody can do now but wait. If you feel you have to visit her, then you'll not be able communicate. The coma could possibly mean severe brain damage.' He was about to turn away but spoke again. 'But by all means, feel free to sit with her if you want. Your presence certainly can't do any harm.

CHAPTER FORTY

Simon and Dorothy took it in turns to sit with Rebecca. Only when the doctors and nurses were dressing her wounds, did they leave her side. For hours, Andrew kept Dorothy company, and Arthur did the same when Simon was with her. Simon spent much of his time reading and talking to Rebecca during the first two days. Somehow, he hoped that she could hear his voice and know that he and her family were all right. It was important that she knew he hadn't been killed as Stubbs had told her in front of Dorothy. It was important that she knew he loved her. It was important that she wanted to live, though, God knows, she'd shown that in her own struggle to survive. Now he had to help her keep that determination. If only one word got through to her it would count, it would strengthen her resolve. He wouldn't give up unless she did, and she hadn't to.

Simon ate little and slept less during those two days. With not the slightest response from her, he had maintained his own determination to do all he could to give her the will to stay alive. It was on the evening of the third day, as he was approaching the ward to take over from Dorothy that his heart sank to his feet. Dorothy sat outside the glass panelled wall sobbing as doctors and nurses crowded into the small room.

'What's the matter?' Simon asked as he watched a trolley being wheeled into the room.

'She's died,' she cried. 'My Becki, my poor Becki!'

Simon's mind began to spin. It wasn't true! Rebecca couldn't have given up her struggle. She was made of stronger stuff than that. He pushed through the door and looked at Rebecca.

'Would you please leave?' the ward sister said brusquely.

'What's going on?' Simon asked and resisted the woman's attempt to expel him from the room.

'She's had a cardiac arrest. We're doing all we can. You must leave.'

Simon ignored her and pushed his way through. Rebecca lay naked except for a square dressing covering the wound on her breast bone and a gleaming liquid that had been smeared on her skin. He watched in despair as Rebecca's body jerked uncontrollably with the shock of each stab of electricity from the big defibrillator pads held beneath her breasts. 'Rebecca,' he shouted. 'Listen to me Rebecca, I'm here, I'm alive,' The trace on the fluorescent screen of the oscilloscope was flat.

'I need you. I love you,' he screamed as he saw the elderly doctor lift the pads off her chest and shake his head. He turned from the bed and looked at Simon with sad eyes. There was no more he could do to bring life back into Rebecca's body.

'It's all over,' he said.

'It can't be over!' Simon replied and glanced anxiously past his shoulder.

'I'm afraid so,' the doctor said sadly. 'There is nothing more we can do.'

'Doctor!' a nurse screeched. 'Doctor!' He spun around. One of the nurses was pointing at the trace on the screen. 'It moved. There was a beat!' she shouted. Another nurse was injecting something into a tube that ran into Rebecca's vein.

'Quickly, give me those pads,' he said calmly and placed them back against Rebecca's ribs. Another bolt of electricity jerked her body off the bed. The scope still read nothing. 'Once more,' he ordered, and the switch was thrown again. He waited and then shook his head. It was a forlorn try.

'Yes!' the nurse shouted again, unable to contain her excitement.

'Yes, there it is.' She pointed at the small green line. 'Look!'

Everybody's eyes swung to the screen. Sure enough, it had begun to bleep and form rugged mountainous peaks as the trace waved from left to right across the screen. It only held their attention for a brief second before all eyes fell back on Rebecca's naked form. Her chest began to rise and fall as she began to breathe again, unaided.

'Now will you leave?' the Sister asked.

'Wait!' the doctor commanded. He turned back to Simon again. 'Are you related to this girl?' he asked in a voice of authority.

Simon looked down at Rebecca. The nurse had dried her body and was pulling the sheets back over her breasts.

'No,' he answered and turned away dutifully.

'Then I suggest you stay and let her know you want to be,' he said and brushed past Simon's shoulder as he walked out of the door.

Simon didn't need telling. Once again, the constant vigil began.

Two days, three days, and then four. When her physical wounds had begun to heal, the oxygen tent was removed, but still Rebecca remained comatose.

Simon was discharged from hospital but, with the help of the same senior doctor, he rented a private ward so that he could be close to Rebecca. He never wanted to be far away from her. Occasionally, as he talked to her and told her light hearted stories about himself, he would stop and become more serious. 'Rebecca,' he would say. 'You haven't told me yet.' He'd wait and see if she responded, and then, when there was no perceptible movement, he would go on. 'Rebecca, don't you remember, I've asked you to marry me. You'll have to answer me sooner or later, so why not get it over with and put me out of my misery?'

Rebecca never answered. But Simon never gave up asking. As the days turned into weeks, Simon never gave up hope. 'Some day,' he said to Arthur, 'She'll give me my answer. You'll see.'

Arthur nodded and put his hand on Simon's shoulder. He looked at Simon as he sat as near to the bed as he could, holding Rebecca's hand and squeezing it gently. His face was thin and drawn, his body was showing the affect of weeks of little sleep and sparse meals. He knew that if Rebecca didn't answer Simon soon, he would undoubtedly lose them both. 'Then you're going to have to pull yourself together and get some good food inside you, or there'll be nothing of you for her to get hold of when she finally does wake up and say yes!'

Simon grinned and looked up into the face of his old friend. 'You know, you can be quite funny without trying,' he chuckled.

Arthur smiled back. It wasn't such a bad smile if he'd practice it a bit more often, Simon thought as he squeezed Rebecca's hand.

'I suppose you will both have to go on a special diet to build yourselves up to it,' Arthur still jibed.

Again, Simon chuckled, and again he squeezed her hand as if by reflex. He sniffled and turned his head to look at Rebecca. Slowly and deliberately, he relaxed his grip. 'Once for yes,' he said. 'Then I'll start building up my strength.'

'I tell you, Simon, with a girl with a constitution like hers, you'll need to!'

Simon chuckled again, and then, his heart suddenly began to pound as he realized that he hadn't squeezed Rebecca's hand at all. It *was* a reflex. Slowly and deliberately, Rebecca's hand closed on his. 'Oh, my God,' he gasped and closed his hand on hers. 'She moved, Arthur! Her hand! She moved!' he cried as tears filled his eyes and his face crumpled as he fought to control his emotions. 'Rebecca, squeeze once for yes.' Slowly, her fingers moved again as she returned his gentle grip.

'Yes!' he sobbed as tears rolled down his cheeks. 'Oh yes!' he whispered, grinning strangely as his facial muscles insisted that he cry. 'She said yes, Arthur. See!' He held her hand up and let it squeeze his own again.

He looked up at his friend. Arthur had taken out a large white handkerchief and was blowing his nose. 'Damned colds,' he said. 'I shouldn't be in here really,' and then stuffed the handkerchief back in his pocket.

A short time later, Rebecca opened her eyes. Simon was still clasping her small hand, unable to let go lest she slipped away again. She blinked, and turning her head, she stared at him for a long time before smiling. His face was unshaven and black shadows hung round his dark eyes. She gripped his hand tightly this time and said, 'Yes, Simon.'

He touched her cheek lovingly with his fingers then kissed her gently on her lips. As Rebecca's eyes closed again he looked up anxiously at the attending nurse.

'Don't worry Mr Park,' she said assuringly, 'she's resting now.'

CHAPTER FORTY ONE

Rebecca was discharged from hospital ten days later. During that time, she had visits from all the farm workers and their families, while the presence of Simon and Dorothy was mandatory.

Simon left the hospital, and rented a room in The Windsurfer hotel where he spent only his nights. Every day he was by Rebecca's side.

Andrew spent as much time as he could at her bed side, but, already, he had undertaken to restore the running of the farm to some kind of normality. It wasn't easy. All the farm records had been destroyed, and he had to move house to Drayton Cottage, an empty dwelling at the furthest end of the estate. Earnest Henshaw was left to run the farm as over-manager, while Andrew struggled with the insurance companies to get work under way on building both a new farm house, and the replacement for his own Sunnybridge Farm.

What made things more difficult, was that the landlord of the estate, Spears Trusts, was unable to give him quick and precise answers to his questions about the design and structure of the new house. All he got was a letter from the agent saying, carry on and use his own judgement, and that the trustees would back any decision he made.

It wasn't too difficult moving, they had little or nothing to take with them. The little house had been empty for years, but it had been kept in good repair and, between them, Dorothy and Andrew had the place ship shape by the time Rebecca came home. It was a pleasant slate-roofed, single storey building with an attached barn which had never been converted into domestic accommodation. With three bedrooms a living room and a small kitchen and even smaller bathroom, it would suffice.

Simon bought some loose fitting clothes for Rebecca. She still had tender scars where the four bullets had ripped into her. He drove slowly from the hospital to Drayton Cottage. It was a bright morning and Rebecca wanted to see as much of the countryside as possible. It was good to be alive. It is a feeling that you only get when you have been near to death, seeing the clouds in the sky, breathing and smelling the cold, clean country air, hearing the sound of the rooks in the nearby woodland. Even the bare, leafless trees have a particular beauty about them.

Rebecca asked Simon to stop when they got to Thatch Cottage. She insisted on him telling her exactly what happened. As they drew into the yard, the bare and blackened stone walls of the once beautiful, chocolate-box cottage, told much of their own story. She got out of the Saab and walked around the walls, looking into what had been each room. She still had some pain from her injuries, but was determined to overcome it. 'What a mess,' she said.

'We'll soon get it sorted out,' Simon said confidently.

'I suppose Pendle Court looks the same.'

'Very much of a likeness, I'd say.'

'We're going to have to talk,' Rebecca said and walked across the paddock.

Frowning, Simon watched her as she walked away. 'What about? 'he called after her.

Rebecca limped up to a bank beneath a hedge and sat down. 'Phew! Hard work this!' she said, grimacing as Simon came over to join her.

'No rush to get back to running about is there,' Simon said with a serious face. 'Unless you've been accepted for next year's London marathon, that is.'

Rebecca laughed. She sucked in a deep breath of fresh air, looked up into the sky and exhaled slowly. 'I've got to be fit for my wedding day!' She beamed radiantly as she lowered her eyes to meet Simon's.

'Well then, when do you want to have and to hold me?' Simon asked, a mischievous smile trickling across his lips.

'Get married you mean?' Rebecca said, raising her eyebrow.

'Oh, that as well I suppose,' Simon grinned and she slapped him on the shoulder. For a long minute she stared into his eyes and then put her hands on his face and drew closer to him. She wet her lips and then gently pulled until his lips pressed hard on hers. Simon put his arms around her and pulled her body close to his.

CHAPTER FORTY TWO

Dorothy had made dinner and was just preparing to serve it out when Simon arrived with Rebecca. It was the first time they had all sat down around a table together.

'We've named the day,' Rebecca announced as the conversation took a definite turn towards Simon and herself.

'Oh that's wonderful!' Dorothy exclaimed. 'Tell me. Don't keep it a secret.'

'In five weeks,' Rebecca announced.

'Oh, that would be around...'

'Christmas day,' Rebecca stated. 'And it's going to be a Christmas to remember!'

'It certainly will,' Andrew beamed, getting up and slapping Simon on the back. 'This calls for a little extra celebration,' he said happily and disappeared into the lounge. A moment later he came back with four glasses and a bottle of wine. 'What a fantastic time to get married, he exclaimed as he eagerly uncorked the bottle.

Dorothy wasn't just as sure that they'd picked the right day, but she knew whatever day they picked for their wedding day it would be special to all of them. She smiled 'If that's the date you want then you'll have to get a move on and see that you have somewhere to live.'

'That brings me to the question of whether you'll be continuing your contract, Becki,' Andrew interrupted in business-like manner.

'Hmm,' Rebecca sighed. 'I don't know if I can answer that yet, Uncle Andrew.' She looked at him with eyes that pleaded for more time.

'The trouble is,' Andrew began, 'I don't know whether I'm going to be able to pass the lease over to you, or whether I'll have to release it back to the owner of the estate. The trust seems happy for me to do either, and they couldn't have given me more leeway with the plans for the farmhouse.' He paused and the others watched as he poured out the wine. 'But,' he continued, 'I'd have thought that your marrying a well known writer would take you out of the farming league.'

'The question is,' Simon commented, 'do you mind her living in the new farmhouse when it is rebuilt?'

'Not at all,' Andrew replied immediately. 'Originally, I had expected to stay there, but since the fire, I think I would be better taking a back seat from a distance. I was thinking of rebuilding Sunnybridge Farm to suit a smaller family.' He looked at Dorothy. 'That farm's my own, and it will be enough for me to potter about on.'

'If I may say, you don't strike me as the pottering type,' Simon stated truthfully.

'Ah, well, old age catches up to us all eventually you know.'

'Oh, I know that all too well! But how does that affect you?' asked Simon, feigning perplexion.

Andrew laughed. 'I'm twice your age!'

'Don't rub it in,' Simon said, pretending that his feelings had been severely injured.

'Anyway, seriously,' Andrew chuckled, 'the trust will no doubt be looking for a younger person to take over the farm.'

'Not necessarily. It depends whether you want to vegetate,' Simon said with a frown.

'Oh, I don't want to sit down and do nothing, but the plan was to give a younger member of my family benefit from my lifetime's work. It isn't just as simple as owning the farm and leaving it to her.'

Simon sat back and sipped his wine. 'I think it is,' Simon said bluntly.

'Oh no,' Andrew argued. 'It is altogether different.'

'May *I* say something?' Rebecca asked lightly. 'You know; the one you're discussing?'

'But of course!' Simon said with a mischievous smirk. 'If you must! Can you keep it brief?'

Rebecca stuck her tongue out at him. 'I was going to discuss it with you first,' she said, remembering how she had been distracted by other things when they lay in the paddock at Thatch cottage. 'I don't know how it fits in with your work. You haven't really told me much about yourself you know.'

'Ah, that's where you're wrong,' Simon said, waiving his finger at her triumphantly, 'I must have told you a thousand times when you were lying in that hospital. But besides that, you did have the chance to find out for yourself. The trouble is you went and got kidnapped instead!'

Rebecca scowled. 'Simon, what are you talking about?'

'The file that you left in the Merc,' he explained dramatically.

'You knew about that file! I knew you had something to do with it! Just wait till we're married! I'll divorce you. That'll make you sorry!'

'But there are mitigating circumstances,' Simon pleaded. 'Honest.'

'Such as?' Rebecca challenged. 'Name a thousand.'

'Such as that you never read the complete file, did you?'

'No.'

'You didn't happen to see some brown envelopes in it did you?'

Rebecca thought for a second. 'There were some at the back of the folder.'

'Well if you had read what was in them you would know that you, as Mrs. Simon Pears...'

'I prefer your famous name,' Rebecca butted in. 'Might as well share the glory, if nothing else!'

'Huh, well, as I was saying before you so rudely interrupted...'

'I can see your marriage working out just fine,' Andrew commented. 'Just the right amount of arguments to make it interesting!'

'Wait till you hear this then,' Simon said and smiled. 'Mrs. Park will be half owner of Spears Trusts.'

'Heh,' three voices said in unison, and three pairs of eyes locked on him.

'S. Pears, get it?'

'You! You are Spears Trusts?' Andrew exclaimed.

'More or less,' Simon replied casually.

'No bloody wonder I can't get a straight answer about anything!'

Simon chuckled and looked at Rebecca. She was smiling at the repartee, but her face still showed astonishment. 'Does it make any difference?' he asked her sincerely.

'Does it!' she gasped. 'You're blinking right it does!' Her face was serious.

There was a sudden silence as Simon's smile disappeared. 'Why?'

'I'll have to cancel my contract with Uncle Andrew for one thing!' She burst into laughter at the look on Simon's face. 'Apart from that, though, I can't wait to get married.'

'Oh good,' Simon retorted, 'because I was going to say, that if it made you change your mind about marrying me I'd stop you taking over the lease.'

'You what?' Rebecca grabbed the tea towel out of her mother's hands and hit him with it. 'You wouldn't have dared,' she said as he scrambled out of reach. 'It would have been more than your life's worth,' she shouted and limped after him in hot pursuit.

'I can quite well believe it,' he called over his shoulder as she chased him out of the tiny kitchen and into the garden where there was just a bit more room and a lot more privacy to corner him.

The wedding could hardly be described as a quiet little do. Andrew gave the bride away, and, you've guessed it, Arthur was best man. The Christmas feast cum wedding reception was held at The Windsurfer. Mary Blandford insisted on preparing everything for them down to the last serviette - for a price, which included a kiss of the groom! Her husband thought it a small sacrifice in exchange for a kiss of the bride. Rebecca's white, silk dress, with its pink embroidered flowers around the hems, made her the talk of the village for months to come. Her limp had gone, and, as promised, she had got herself fit!

Andrew and Arthur both made speeches, and after the cake was cut, Simon presented Rebecca with a special gift. It was wrapped in a silver paper with black spots. It was the only thing he'd saved out of the fire at Pendle Court.

Arthur wandered among the guests, almost unrecognizable with a glint in his eyes and a beam on his face that would have lit a football pitch. The brandy may have had more than a little to do with that. It surprised Andrew just how friendly Arthur was. Somehow, he felt they'd been friends much longer than the few months since he stopped Stubbs killing the small detective. 'Back to London after this, is it?' Andrew asked as they watched the bride and groom depart.

'Yes,' Arthur said and nodded.

'Anything unusual?' Andrew asked interestedly.

'Probably not,' Arthur replied and thought about his next assignment. Vickers was going to be a piece of cake after his last job. There were still some loose ends Arthur hadn't tied up concerning the first fire, the one at Sunnybridge farm, though he thought he knew after he'd seen the fight between Stubbs and Andrew. They weren't so important now. Dorothy never admitted to him that she found the diamonds and Rebecca knew she'd lied to Stubbs when he asked where they were. She'd had to. He'd needed a plausible answer. He should have known that the inspection pit in the garage at Cil Cwm had already had a new bottom in it before her husband died but Dorothy gambled that he didn't, and was right. He was just a lousy copper though and through.

CHAPTER FORTY THREE

Rebecca snuggled into Simon's shoulder as he drove to the airport. They'd been quiet for some time. Rebecca had been thinking about the wedding and how successful it had been. Eventually she lifted her head and looked at his face. He smiled as he realized he was being watched. 'Penny for your thoughts,' she said and cupped her hands on his shoulder.

'I was just thinking,' Simon said with a grin, 'Since my last book went up in flames, I might start a new one.'

'What about?'

Simon didn't answer straight away. 'The problem is,' he said eventually, 'did your mother find the diamonds. I'd have to know if she did, and if she did, what did she do with them?'

'Oh. That story! Well I hope you don't intend starting it on our honeymoon.'

'Oh no, nothing like that.' He thought for a moment. 'Although if I have some time to kill I might just start making a few notes.' He smiled and looked down at her radiant face.

'You won't have,' Rebecca grinned back confidently.

In the Dead of Day

- THE END -

Printed in Great Britain
by Amazon

21097477R00185